PRAISE F

PRAISE FOR *DO WHAT GODMOTHER SAYS*

One of NPR's 2024 Picks for "Books We Love"

An *Elle* "Best Mystery and Thriller of 2024"

"Stratton's thriller featuring two women facing daunting obstacles and danger is dark, twist filled, and suspenseful."

—*Booklist*

"Stratton (*Not So Perfect Strangers*) interweaves the stories of two budding artists living a century apart in this entertaining chiller."

—*Publishers Weekly*

"Stratton delivers a tightly woven dual-timeline thriller. Elements of occult horror, historical fiction, and whodunit will intrigue readers of all stripes. Give this to fans of Alyssa Cole's *When No One Is Watching*."

—*Library Journal*

"Author L. S. Stratton does a marvelous job of interweaving the stories of two women across generations and how time might not separate them as much as it seems."

—*Historical Novel Society*

"This captivating dual-timeline Gothic thriller . . . skillfully reveals the intricacies of creative ownership, particularly in the context of race and wealth."

—*NPR*

PRAISE FOR *NOT SO PERFECT STRANGERS*

A Book Riot Best Mystery & Thriller of 2023

"What Stratton does is take our assumptions and turn them upside down. *Not So Perfect Strangers* is a thrilling read with much to consider about marriage, prejudice, abuse and parenting."

—*The Book Reporter*

"In addition to being a really good read, *Not So Perfect Strangers* is a smart criticism of the intersections of race, patriarchy, and privilege."

—*Book Riot*

"*Not So Perfect Strangers* is a gripping, twisted ride! You think you know what's happening, but you don't. Chock full of surprises, this dark story unfolds perfectly right up to the last page."

—Samantha Downing, #1 international bestselling author of *For Your Own Good*

"I was delighted to be caught in the crosshairs of this deliciously devious cat-and-mouse game between two strikingly different, but equally magnetic women as they duked it out for justice, revenge, love, and power. This one keeps the reader guessing until the very end."

—Chandler Baker, *New York Times* bestselling author of *Whisper Network*

IN DEADLY COMPANY

IN DEADLY COMPANY

a novel

L.S. STRATTON

UNION
SQUARE
& CO.

NEW YORK

UNION
SQUARE
& CO.
NEW YORK

UNION SQUARE & CO. and the distinctive Union Square & Co. logo are trademarks of Hachette Book Group, Inc.

Text © 2025 L.S. Stratton
Cover illustration © 2025 Joan Wong

All rights reserved. No part of this publication may be reproduced, stored in a retrieval system, or transmitted in any form or by any means (including electronic, mechanical, photocopying, recording, or otherwise) without prior written permission from the publisher.

ISBN 978-1-4549-6073-7 (paperback)
ISBN 978-1-4549-6074-4 (e-book)

Library of Congress Control Number: 2025008931
Library of Congress Cataloging-in-Publication Data is available upon request.

Union Square & Co. books may be purchased in bulk for business, educational, or promotional use. For more information, please contact your local bookseller or the Hachette Book Group's Special Markets department at special.markets@hbgusa.com.

Printed in Canada

2 4 6 8 10 9 7 5 3 1

unionsquareandco.com

Cover design by Joan Wong
Interior design by Kevin Ullrich

For the clever gals out there who finally found their self worth—and for those still searching.

CHAPTER 1
NICOLE

NOW

"Ben!" a voice barks behind me. "Jesus Christ, can't you do anything right?"

When I hear it, I have an almost primal response, even though my name is Nicole, not Ben. Even though the person who used to snap at me like that is long dead.

Like a lactating mother who hears her infant's wails in the middle of the night, or a hungry dog who stumbles upon the most fragrant slab of Wagyu beef miraculously abandoned on a city sidewalk, I have an instant physical reaction. My muscles tense. My heart starts racing. Beads of sweat form on my upper lip.

I forget that I'm in Los Angeles, sitting on a banquette next to the concierge desk at a luxury hotel, sipping complimentary espresso while I wait for my driver to arrive to take me to a film set. Instead I'm hurled back more than a year ago when I was standing on the seventy-fifth floor of a high rise in Manhattan and my boss Xander

Chambers is asking me why I couldn't finagle him a last-minute invitation to the Met Gala.

"Well, *fuck* me!" Xander cried in exasperation. "Elon's gotten in at least twice. You're telling me I can't get *one* little invite?"

"Xander, they probably come up with the guest list a year in advance . . . and it's four days away," I replied.

"Which should be plenty of time for a good assistant," he said before popping a CBD gummy into his mouth.

But I was a good assistant. One of the best, actually.

"I'll keep trying," I insisted.

He stared at me for a long time, still chewing. "Yeah, you do that," Xander finally said.

I then watched as he swiveled around in the custom ergonomic chair made with 150-year-old trees from some remote Scandinavian forest. He faced the floor-to-ceiling windows, turned his back to me, and answered the call in his earbuds.

"John, you asshole, so you finally called me back," he said with a laugh. "What's up?"

I now look up to find a potbellied, balding man dressed in all-white linen and striding toward the hotel's sliding glass doors. He doesn't resemble Xander in looks but certainly does in attitude. There's something in his strut that conveys his sense of entitlement, like an invisible red carpet is stretched out before him. The model-type blonde walking beside him, who seems to be one-third his age and also dressed in all white (a mini slip dress and thong sandals), is the obligatory accessory for men like him. Trailing behind them both, juggling two cell phones, a leather satchel, and a Louis Vuitton suitcase, is a bespectacled, beleaguered-looking young man I quickly guess is Ben. It's evident from the way he flinches when the man in linen rants, "Never again! Never again will I let you book me a suite in this dump. Next time we're staying at the Beverly Hills Hotel. You hear me?"

"Absolutely, Mr. Ariti," Ben mumbles before his boss walks through the sliding glass doors.

As he passes the banquette where I sit, Ben and I momentarily lock gazes. Over the lip of my coffee cup, I give him a small smile of reassurance. I've been where he's been. Felt how he's probably feeling right now. And, if it hadn't been for the events of the three most tumultuous days of my life more than a year ago, I would probably *still* be in his place.

Ben doesn't acknowledge my smile, though. His eyes guiltily dart away and he picks up his pace, almost dropping his suitcase. His boss shouts, "Ben, let's go! We don't have all day!"

"Y-y-yes, sir. Sorry, Mr. Ariti," he mutters as he dashes through the parted doors.

I watch as a bellhop, pushing a loaded-down luggage cart, pulls up the rear, and the sliding glass doors close behind them.

CHAPTER 2

"You can follow me, Ms. Underwood," the production assistant or assistant director says.

"Nicole," I offer.

The young, redheaded woman frowns and yanks down the mic of her headset. "I'm sorry . . . what?" she shouts over the noise around us.

A multitude of voices and a mechanical banging sound echo around the soundstage.

"I said you can just call me Nicole." I tuck my braids behind my ears and incline my head. "You don't have to call me Ms. Underwood. It's just . . . Nicole. Or Nikki. Either will do."

"Oh." She gradually smiles and nods. "OK, cool. This way, Nicole."

She doesn't offer her name in return. I don't think she even gave me her job title earlier. She's back to barking into her headset as we hop over wires and what looks like a kiddie train track.

I've been trailing her since she came to get me at 9:00 a.m. from the small office they set up for me at the studio. It's a six-by-six-foot room with an IKEA loveseat, coffee table, small desk, chair, and on the door my name printed in bold black letters with the word CONSULTANT underneath.

I'm now being taken to the set for one of the scenes on the shooting schedule today. Some of the filming for the movie will take place here at the studio, but from what I understand most of it will be shot in a mansion on a private vineyard and estate somewhere in the San Fernando Valley. How they will make that estate resemble Xander's Colonial Revival mansion and his estate in Hudson Valley, New York, is beyond me, but I'm interested in seeing them try.

As we draw closer, I see one of the soundstage's sets. I slow my steps and my eyes widen.

It's an almost perfect replica of Xander's Midtown office. They have his glass desk and floating glass shelves. Both the Basquiat and Matisse hang on slate gray walls. They even have his Hans Wegner Swivel Chair, although this one has its original paint job; Xander had his chair's wood stained black to match his office decor—something that would've probably made Mr. Wegner himself faint. The set even has a series of ten-foot-tall LED screen panels made to look like the view of the Manhattan cityscape at sunset. I spot the Empire State Building and a few other Midtown landmarks you could see from the penthouse of our old office building on Lexington Ave.

"It's awesome, isn't it?" the young woman says, noticing my gobsmacked expression. "The set designer worked off some video footage and a few photos from a *Vanity Fair* profile they dug up."

I remember that profile: I had to convince Xander to come back and finish the interview after he pulled a bitch fit and stormed out when the reporter mentioned his mother's car crash. Bridget Chambers's untimely death had been a touchy subject with Xander.

"They did a really great job," I acknowledge with a nod, and she leads me to a line of director's chairs behind a series of video monitors.

In one of the chairs sits one of the most beautiful women I've ever seen in real life, which says a lot when you're in a town like Hollywood, which has more conventionally attractive people in a five-mile radius than are probably in the entire state of Wisconsin. Her dark curly hair is piled atop her head in a sexy messy bun held in place by two pencils, for some reason. Under the bright lights of the film set, I can see that her golden skin is flawless.

It's Asia Wilkerson, the indie actress who will portray me on-screen. The last time I saw her was her smoldering headshot in the online *Deadline* article announcing that she would be the star of *Murder in the Valley*. This is my first time meeting her in person.

When we approach, Asia raises her green eyes from a few binder-clipped pages of the script that she's been highlighting. She gazes at us quizzically.

"You'll be over here during filming today, Nicole," the young woman beside me says, gesturing to the other empty chairs.

"*Nicole?*" Asia asks. "As in *Nicole Underwood*?"

I nod. "That's me." I turn to say goodbye to the production assistant/assistant director, but she has already walked off and is back to talking into her headset.

"Oh, my God!" Asia squeals before she hops out of her chair and rises to her feet. She sets down her script pages on the seat and extends a hand to me for a shake. "I'm Asia Wilkerson. I play you in the film!"

"Yes, I know," I say, shaking her hand. "It's a pleasure to finally meet you."

"I can't believe I didn't recognize you. I had no idea you'd be on the set today. It is such an honor!" she gushes.

"Why thank you. I'm . . . I'm honored that you're honored."

She laughs and eagerly nods as we continue to awkwardly gaze at one another. The longer I stare, the more I think, *I can't see it. I can't see her as me.*

I mean I'm sure she's a great actress and a nice person, but I don't understand why the casting director chose this ambiguously raced movie siren to play me. I thought a film that was going to be about a chunk of my life story might give a few dark-skinned, Black actresses a shot at a leading role in Hollywood, but I guess I was wrong.

Asia is wearing office clothes for the scene today—a gray blazer and matching slacks—which is a lot more formal than what I would've usually worn. She's also wearing black stilettos, which is the perfect match for her sexy messy bun but would have killed my feet and ankles if I'd had to walk around in them during my twelve-to-sixteen-hour workdays.

"I'm so happy that you're here!" Asia says, oblivious to my misgivings. "I've been wondering a few things about my character. I mean, about *you*, and I'd love, love, love . . . *loooove*," she practically sings, "to pick your brain."

"Sure, of course," I say with a nod as Asia's comely face suddenly brightens. She raises her hand and waves, beckoning someone toward us. "Troy! Troy, come over here! You have to meet Nicole Underwood. The real-life inspiration for the movie that all of Hollywood fought over!"

I can't help but roll my eyes.

Let's be honest. If it hadn't been for Xander's and the other deaths . . . if it hadn't been for the investigation, news coverage, true crime podcast, and Netflix documentary, no one would care about me or my life. The studios never would've engaged in that bidding war over the script. I wouldn't be here, but back in New York at my old apartment in Brooklyn trying to convince myself not to quit every day that I woke up to the sound of my pulsing alarm clock. To see it all through to the end. To just hold on for *one . . . more . . . day*.

I'd balked at first at the idea of selling the rights to my story, of reliving the past, but the filmmakers promised me the chance to finally share the truth without the twisting I'd seen in the media.

However, judging from Asia's casting and her outfit, accuracy isn't paramount so far.

I slowly turn around to face the direction that Asia is now looking. My stomach drops. My pulse starts racing. For the second time today, beads of sweat form on my upper lip.

Xander is walking toward us.

Memories of him have been haunting me for more than a year, but those memories now take solid form as he makes his way around two crew members who are carrying heavy cords and mounted cameras.

He looks the same as he did moments after his death. A stream of dried blood is under his broken nose. He smiles maniacally with his half-missing jaw. His left ear is also mangled, thanks to the bullet fired at close range underneath his chin. Xander comes to a stop in front of us and his bloodshot eyes glower at me with unmasked hatred and fury.

I take several deep breaths, close my eyes, and open them again. When I do, all the blood and macabre imagery is gone. I also see that it isn't Xander, just a man who looks very much like him.

The casting director at least got this role right.

"Hi, Nicole! Troy Fletcher. Great to meet you," he says, holding out his hand.

I force myself to shake it, happy to find his grasp warm and firm, not the cold and stiff hand of a corpse. "Y-y-yeah, good to m-m-meet you t-t-too."

"Troy plays Xander Chambers," Asia says.

I drop Troy's hand and gradually nod. "I'd assumed as much. The resemblance is . . . uh . . . uncanny."

"Hey, Troy? Asia?" A guy wearing a baseball cap says, gesturing to the illuminated set. "We need you guys."

"Welp! Duty calls," Troy says with a chuckle.

"We'll talk later, right?" Asia asks, placing a hand on my shoulder.

"Mmm-hmm," I murmur.

I'm starting to feel lightheaded. I practically collapse into one of the empty chairs.

Later, I'm facing one of the monitors while wearing a set of headphones. On the screen, Troy sits at the glass office desk while Asia stands a few feet away with notepad in hand. The camera closes in on Troy's face as a voice booms, "Quiet on the set!"

Everyone immediately falls silent.

Meanwhile, I'm suspended in another surreal moment where the past and present overlap. I swear Troy's face morphs into Xander's. He looks up from the cell phone he's pretending to read and stares at the camera. No, he's staring directly at me, making my breath catch in my throat and the blood roar in my ears.

"Roll camera!" the director suddenly shouts.

"Rolling!" a guy behind the camera's viewfinder shouts back.

"Roll sound!"

"Rolling!" another voice answers.

Suddenly, a clapper board appears on the screen monitors, making Xander break his gaze.

The tightness in my chest finally eases as Troy the actor reappears.

"Action!" the director shouts.

NICOLE

(A YEAR AND A HALF AGO)

CHAPTER 3

NICOLE HAD JUST STEPPED INTO THE BUILDING AND WAS ABOUT TO swipe her keycard over the metal gate reader to make her way to the elevators when she heard her cell phone buzz. She stepped back to let another woman pass, dug her cell out of her pocket, and stared down at the screen.

It was Xander.

She stifled a groan.

Any text or phone call from him before 9:00 a.m. usually wasn't a good sign. He rarely got up this early, even for board meetings. After he'd skipped two of them and the board of directors at Altruist Corporation had sent Xander a sternly worded email letting him know he was in violation of their bylaws and could be voted out as president, Xander managed to drag himself out of bed and appear via Zoom bleary-eyed, unshaven, and with matted hair like he'd literally just rolled out of bed. He'd sulked the entire meeting, making it clear to everyone present that he didn't want to be there.

Needless to say, his work ethic was a far cry from that of Altruist Corporation's founder—his now-deceased mother, Bridget Chambers. With the exception of maintenance staff and security guards,

Bridget had always been the first one on their floor in the morning, often in her office before most of the lights were on.

"When you're the boss, you hold the bar and you set the example, Nicole," Bridget used to tell her back when Nicole was her assistant. "Everyone else follows. Hold it too high and you set them up for failure. Hold it too low and they won't push themselves to succeed."

In contrast, Xander either didn't care about the example he was setting or had more of a "do as I say, not as I do" philosophy when it came to managing a holistic beauty, skincare, and lifestyle brand valued at more than a billion dollars.

Nicole reluctantly pressed the button on her cell screen to answer his call.

"Hey! Good morning," she said, pasting on a smile, hoping that cheer came across in her voice.

"Is that Xander?" she heard someone ask behind her simultaneously. She turned to find Daniel Miller, the COO and second-in-command at Altruist, striding toward the entry gates. In response to his question, she nodded. "Remind him we have that one o'clock meeting today, Nicole," Daniel said, eyeing her shrewdly. "He *has* to attend this one. We're discussing the acquisition. Word is Patrick Gallagher is sniffing around again. We need to talk about this. It's important."

"Got it. Absolutely, sir," she said while holding her hand over the phone's speaker, then giving Daniel the thumbs-up as he walked through the gate. She returned her attention to her phone.

"Hi! Everything OK, Xander?"

She knew the answer was likely no and wondered what had gone wrong this time.

Last week, she'd raced from the office to his place in Tribeca to walk his two cane corsos, Optimus and Rodimus Prime, because his dog walker was sick and Xander didn't trust "his boys" with anyone else.

Two weeks before that, he'd ordered her to book him an emergency doctor's appointment.

"There's some weird sore on my dick," he'd said, making her cringe. "Wait. Let me take a picture and send it to you. You can just forward it to the doctor. Maybe they can tell you what it is and give me a shot or pill or something."

Although Nicole had deleted the image, she would never get that picture out of her mind.

Maybe this time she'd get lucky and he'd just ask her to reschedule his ten o'clock meeting.

But the voice on the other end of the phone line wasn't Xander's. It was a woman she didn't recognize.

"Hey! Hello! Are you the chick who works for this Xander guy?" the woman asked, making Nicole's false smile fade.

"Yes," she answered hesitantly. "Is . . . is Xander all right? Is he OK?"

Nicole had half-expected that one day she would get a call from a perfect stranger—some hospital ER nurse or a cop—telling her that Xander had partied too hard, done one snort of blow too many, and suffered a heart attack, or he'd let his mouth get him into a fight that his money couldn't get him out of and met his bloody end. But she'd assumed that call would come in the middle of the night or in the wee hours of the morning. Certainly not during business hours.

"He owes me eight hundred bucks and this dumbass says he doesn't have any cash on him," the woman said between gum pops. "He says you're good for it."

"I lost my wallet!" Nicole could hear Xander slur in the background. "And for some reason, she doesn't take Venmo."

"Shut up!" the woman snapped. "Look, either someone comes here and pays me, or my man is gonna come here and take it out of his ass!"

Nicole closed her eyes and sighed. "Text me the address. I'm on my way."

CHAPTER 4

THE DRIVER CAME TO A STOP IN FRONT OF A GLASS FACADE—A FOUR-star boutique hotel in Hell's Kitchen. Nicole didn't wait for the doorman to open the Lincoln Town Car's passenger door before she leaped out and rushed across the sidewalk to the hotel's revolving doors.

Nicole had already called ahead to let the front desk know that she'd be arriving. A smiling hotel staffer stood in the lobby, waiting for her.

"Hello, I'm Miss Underwood," she said, looking around the hotel lobby's understated modern decor and furniture, searching for the elevators. "I need to get to Suite 4883. It's currently being occupied by one of your VIP guests."

The older man's mouth fell open in surprise. He slowly looked her up and down. "*You're* Miss Underwood?"

She was used to that response. Even when she'd been Bridget's assistant, most hadn't expected a twenty-something Black woman with boho braids and hoop earrings to walk through the door at meetings or cocktail parties. But Bridget, who hired her while she was still in college, had accepted that Nicole could be the best assistant Bridget ever had without whitewashing herself. Nicole had learned that lesson from watching her mother bend over backward for years to meet a corporate aesthetic her white counterparts found more appealing, while still getting stepped over for promotions and having the door to the proverbial boys' club slammed in her face.

"Yes, I am Miss Underwood," Nicole now repeated with a slow nod.

Her enunciation became more pronounced. Her gaze remained steady. She had her "assistant to a major CEO" armor on.

"And like I said, I need to get to 4883. ASAP, please. Per Mr. Chambers's request."

She'd had to stop at an ATM on the way to get the eight hundred dollars, not wanting to dip into their executive office's petty cash to pay for sex work. Nicole now worried that she'd taken too long with her detour and the woman on the phone had made good on her promise to have Xander roughed up by her pimp.

No chance in hell of keeping that out of the gossip columns, Nicole thought with exasperation.

The Chambers family had finally made it out of a news cycle that they'd dominated for the past couple of months thanks to Bridget's fiery car crash back in February. The news coverage had been mostly a mix of glowing retrospectives on Bridget's life and impact on the beauty industry and details of the crash, but a few more tawdry websites and social media posts shared rumors and speculations on why Bridget had really gone off the road that night. Was it an accident, or had there been foul play?

This could put the Chamberses back on New York's front pages again.

"Yes, of course," the hotel staffer said, plastering on a tight smile. He gestured toward his left and did a slight bow. "This way, ma'am."

Two minutes later, they arrived on the forty-eighth floor. Even though she was trailing behind someone who knew the way, Nicole could've easily found the suite herself; she simply had to follow the sound of raised voices.

As they approached the suite's door, she heard the loud bang and a crash of breaking china.

"Did you just throw that at me?" Xander's muffled voice yelled.

"You're damn right I did! Where's my money, you piece of shit?" a woman screamed, then another crash.

"What the hell," Nicole whispered then grimaced, not looking forward to what awaited her inside the hotel room. "I can take it from here," she told the older man whose blue eyes were now as wide as saucers. He nodded his graying head limply, then retreated. Nicole took a deep breath, raised her hand, and knocked.

"What is it now?" Xander shouted.

"It's me, Xander," Nicole answered.

Within seconds, she heard the wrenching metal sound of a deadbolt being unlocked. The door swung open.

"Jesus Christ!" he exclaimed, throwing out his arms. "What took you so long, Nicole? I've been stuck in here, basically being held hostage by this psycho!"

The hotel's complimentary bathrobe he wore was drooping open, revealing his bare chest and Hugo Boss boxer briefs. His hazel eyes were puffy and bloodshot. He smelled vaguely of weed. Xander was definitely not in any condition to make his ten o'clock meeting. Luckily she'd anticipated as much and already canceled it.

"I came as fast as I could," Nicole explained before shutting the door, stepping around him, reaching into her purse, and pulling out an envelope filled with eight-hundred dollars in twenty-dollar bills. She strode to the annoyed-looking blonde in the sequined halter dress who was standing next to a white sofa now stained with red wine. Several feet away was a broken flower vase. Water and a pile of tulips now littered the bamboo flooring.

"Your money," she said, holding out the envelope to the woman who promptly snatched it.

Nicole watched as she took out the bills and counted them once, then twice. She squinted at Nicole. "No tip?"

"Just get out," Xander said, flicking his hand toward the front door. He grabbed a coffee cup from a nearby end table and gulped some of the black brew.

"Asshole," the woman whispered. She stomped to the suite's door, opened it, and slammed it closed behind her.

"What a way to start the day, huh?" Xander muttered with a chuckle as he roughly raked back his dark hair with his fingers. He tightened his bathrobe and strolled across the suite's living room to the floor-to-ceiling windows.

"Yeah," Nicole murmured, finding it to be the understatement of the year.

It would've been nice, but Nicole knew she'd die waiting to get a thank-you from Xander or some acknowledgment of her efforts.

Again she was reminded of how different he was from Bridget—a boss who knew when to give praise and encouragement. Again Nicole regretted agreeing to be Xander's assistant in order to help him and the company transition as he replaced his mother as Altruist Corporation's CEO and president.

Three months, Nicole silently told herself, picking up the discarded clothes Xander had tossed onto the living room floor. *I agreed to stay for three months. No more.*

And she only had two-and-a-half more weeks to go. But Nicole had noticed that Xander made excuses whenever she offered to show him résumés of possible replacements. He also refused to let her hand off duties to other employees in preparation for her departure.

For an assistant he found so lacking, he seemed reluctant to let her go.

"I'm going to have these dry-cleaned," Nicole said, gesturing to the clothes in her arms. "I canceled your ten o'clock, but you still have that meeting at one o'clock with—"

"Cancel that too," he said, closing his eyes and shaking his head. "There's no way I'm up to that today."

"Xander, that's the monthly organizational meeting with half of the C-suite. You already skipped the last one, and this time you don't have the excuse that you're traveling."

"So?" he snapped.

"Well," she began, taking a step toward him, "you're under a microscope now."

Just that morning, she'd seen a segment on CNBC where they mentioned Altruist and how Bridget's death and recent layoffs showed trouble at the company. Their acquisition of a health supplements and nutrition company was also starting to look shaky thanks to meddling by Patrick Gallagher, the CEO of their chief competitor, Wellness Way. All this would be discussed at the meeting that afternoon.

"You reflect on Altruist as an organization," Nicole went on, "and the stock has been on a downward slide these past few months. You know the board is—"

"Fuck the board," he said, opening his eyes to glare at her. "And fuck this lecture! What are you? A fuckin' . . . fuckin' company prospectus? I don't need you to explain things to me, Nicole. I've worked at Altruist longer than you have!"

Yeah, as an intern, she thought sarcastically. After Xander graduated college and tried and failed at every job from nightclub promoter to cryptocurrency founder, Bridget gave Xander a cushy position as Chief Culture Officer at Altruist—a title she created specifically for him. But the most Xander did for company culture as CCO was host the occasional office holiday party and send out staff email blasts of his favorite business podcast episodes.

"I'm the CEO and president now," he ranted. "Me. *I* make the decisions." He pointed at his bare chest. "You'd think running a company would have its perks but instead it's nothing but meetings and phone calls and stupid obligations." He kicked aside a discarded pillow on the floor.

Then step down, you petulant child, she wanted to say.

He wasn't ready to lead. Everyone knew it—even Bridget.

"Give him a decade or two and my son will grow up. I hope so, anyway," Bridget had confided to Nicole once. "By then I'll finally be ready to retire and hand over the reins of Altruist to him."

But life is full of the unexpected, and Bridget hadn't expected to have to do it this soon—fifteen to twenty years ahead of schedule.

Nicole walked to the cordless phone in the suite's eat-in kitchen. "Do I need to order you breakfast?" she asked, changing the subject. "Have you eaten anything?"

"I'm not hungry," Xander mumbled. He shoved his hands into the pockets of his robe as he continued to gaze out the window. "Haven't had much of an appetite lately. I've been so stressed out."

Well, being screamed at and having a vase thrown at you by the sex worker you refused to pay will do that, Xander, Nicole thought as she dialed the concierge desk.

"I haven't been in a good headspace. There's just . . . just a lot on my mind lately," he said, and Nicole stopped dialing.

Her ears perked up. She lowered the receiver from her ear when she saw in the window's reflection a tortured look in his eyes.

"Like what?" she asked.

Xander slowly turned to face her. When he did, his pensive expression disappeared. Whatever worry had been plaguing him was instantly forgotten. He grinned. "Nothing. I think I just need to relax. Get away from the city. Have some fun!"

Nicole couldn't fathom how Xander could have any more "fun" than he already had on a daily basis.

More than that would kill the average person.

"I've got a birthday coming up in three weeks," he continued. "I should do something big."

Nicole winced when the phone started bleating. She placed the cordless back into its cradle to hang up. "You are. Remember? I already scheduled you that yacht trip in Cyprus that you're taking with—"

"No, think *bigger*, Nicole!" he said, spreading out his hands for demonstration. "Bigger! Use some of that imagination of yours. I want a real bash. Something to liven the mood. Fireworks. Fire-eaters. Acrobats. All of it! Maybe we can even book a performer like Dua Lipa or Post Malone. Someone cool."

"*In three weeks?*" She pursed her lips to keep from screaming. Her nostrils flared as she took a slow, deep breath. "It . . . uh . . . could be a struggle to find a venue that big so soon that could accommodate a celebration that size." Not to mention all the planning and organizing it would entail on top of everything else she was doing. "How about we—"

"You don't need to find a venue. Just do it at Maple Grove."

"*Maple Grove?*" Nicole stilled. "Are you sure that's a good idea, Xander? You really want a big party there so soon?"

"Why not?" he said with a shrug. "Life goes on, right?" He nodded in agreement with himself, not giving her a chance to answer. "Yeah, Maple Grove it is."

She watched as he opened a door leading to the balcony and strolled outside. He stared at the scenic views while he finished his coffee.

Maple Grove was the Chamberses' property in the Hudson Valley—the same place almost three months ago where Bridget's car had careened off an icy road and burst into flames. And now it looked like they were going to throw Xander's thirty-second birthday party there.

CHAPTER 5

NICOLE TRUDGED UP THE STAIRS TO HER THIRD-FLOOR WILLIAMSburg walk-up. She could hear the far-off wail of police sirens and the neighbor in Apartment 3B badly playing an acoustic guitar rendition of a popular hip-hop song. When Nicole reached the alcove outside her apartment, she searched for her keys, juggling her purse and a bag of Chinese takeout.

She'd purchased the food for lunch hours ago but hadn't been able to eat more than a few bites because she was so busy finishing the myriad tasks that she would have done if she hadn't lost time babysitting Xander. She'd spent at least two hours at the hotel, settling his bill after the staff assessed the damage to Xander's hotel suite while she listened to his plans for the impromptu birthday bash.

"The guest list has to be at least a hundred . . . *minimum!*" Xander had mused as he paced in front of the floor-to-ceiling windows, sipping a mimosa while a hotel maid quietly swept up the mess from the vase and wineglasses that were thrown earlier that morning. "And it can't be just one evening. I want a whole weekend. No, make that *three* days! Friday through Sunday. And it should have a theme. Nothing cheesy, though. Maybe we should all wear masquerade masks. Or all white. What do you think?"

"Why not both?" Nicole had muttered, but he hadn't caught on to her dry tone and instead snapped his fingers and nodded eagerly.

"You're right. You're absolutely right!" He downed the rest of his mimosa. "Let's do both."

"Let's do both," she now repeated in a mocking high-pitched voice while rolling her eyes.

After a minute of struggling, Nicole managed to find her house keys and unlock her front door. She felt around the dimly lit living room that was partially illuminated by the streetlamps below her windows and turned on a light switch. When she did, she saw her ginger cat and only consistent man in her life, Nemo, rise from one of her loveseat cushions, stretch, and casually stroll toward her. She smiled.

"Hey, buddy," she whispered before shutting the apartment door behind her. She lowered her bags to the floor and leaned down to give his head a scratch. "How was your day? Hope it was better than mine."

Nemo purred in response.

Nicole grabbed the takeout bag and strolled to her walk-in kitchen. She took out the containers, setting them on the laminate countertop, hearing her stomach growl at the prospect of popping cold orange chicken and steamed wontons into the microwave.

Her phone buzzed, halting her just as she opened one of the overhead cabinets. She loudly groaned. "Jesus," Nicole murmured. "I just got home."

She reached into her sweater pocket to pull out her cell, expecting to see Xander's name or someone from the office or maybe even a text from her mother. But her screen was slate black; her cell wasn't the one that buzzed.

Nicole's shoulders went rigid as a cold tingle went down her spine. She walked across the living room, almost tripping over Nemo, who was headbutting her and snaking between her legs, begging for more attention. She ignored him, bent down, and quickly opened one of the cabinets of her small entertainment unit. On top of the plastic cover of a vintage record player was a phone she'd picked up at a Duane Reade. Her burner phone.

She'd kept it hidden as a precaution, although she didn't know who would find it. She doubted anyone would break into her apartment looking for the burner. That they even knew the phone existed. Maybe Nicole was just being paranoid, but she felt better stowing it here.

She reached inside the cabinet and read the text on-screen: **Any updates? Did he say anything?**

No. Not today, Nicole typed back before closing the cabinet door and sitting on the parquet floor.

She saw a few blinking dots on-screen, then another text.

The clock is ticking. We need to move this along.

Well, duh.

I've tried, Nicole typed. **I've been doing the same thing for months but nothing is working.**

More blinking dots, then: **We are RUNNING OUT OF TIME, Nicole!**

Nicole blew hot air through her nostrils in frustration.

We've come this far. I need to know if you can do this, they typed.

She thought for a second before typing back, **Look, Xander mentioned something today that could present an opportunity. It could change everything but things might get complicated.**

Go on, they typed. **I'm listening.**

Nicole started to type a reply but paused and pressed the button to call them instead. Her thumbs were getting tired, and a complicated plan like this one was easier to say than text.

CHAPTER 6

Two weeks later, Nicole scanned her badge over the metal gate reader and raced toward the waiting elevator. Even as she ran, she was careful not to spill the coffee and toasted croissant that she'd bought only minutes earlier and had planned to place on Xander's desk before he arrived for the workday. *If* he arrived for work today. Who knew when it came to Xander?

Less than a minute later, she stepped off the elevator on her floor.

"Good morning," she said to the front desk receptionist Deidre, whose curly head was bent over her laptop screen.

"Morning," Deidre murmured back.

Later Nicole would realize that Deidre hadn't given her usual broad smile and wave with her greeting. Later she'd also realize how Deidre's eyes had anxiously darted to her left as Nicole began to wind her way through the maze of gray cubicles that would take her to the slightly larger cubicle next to Xander's massive corner office. If she'd followed Deidre's gaze, she would have seen them before they saw her: two of New York's finest heading in her direction.

Nicole's eyes practically bulged out of their sockets when she spotted their uniforms and grim faces.

As the cops approached, she steeled herself for what would happen next.

They'd ask if they could speak with her privately, or maybe not even bother with the pretense of asking. Instead they'd tell her to come with them. Then, in a room with no windows and all-white walls in some Manhattan precinct, a lieutenant or captain would tell her they'd gotten word from the cops in Westchester County to make an arrest because detectives finally knew the truth.

And Nicole would lower her head and close her eyes with relief. She wouldn't have to carry the burden of all these secrets anymore.

But instead of doing that, the police officers walked right past Nicole. One tipped the brim of his hat to her in greeting, making her blink in surprise. She turned and watched as the NYPD officers continued to the elevators. She only tore her gaze away from them when the elevator doors closed.

"Some excitement to start the day, huh?" Nicole suddenly heard behind her, making her whip around.

This time, she didn't drop the coffee but some of it sloshed through the lid opening and burned her hand, making her wince.

She found Sara, the assistant director of marketing, standing near one of the vacant cubicles with eyebrows raised. A twinkle was in Sara's big brown eyes. An iced matcha was in her hand.

Nicole frowned and blew on her burned fingers. "What excitement?"

"What do you mean, 'What excitement'?" Sara shook her drink, took a sip, and pointed to the elevators. "Didn't you just see the cops walk out?"

Nicole nodded as she started walking again toward her cubicle. "Yeah, I did. Do you know why they were here?"

If anyone at Altruist knew the details behind the cops' presence, it was Sara; she was a notorious office gossip. She said, as assistant director of marketing, it was her job to stay abreast of everything that went on at Altruist—big and small. This included what was going on in the personal lives of those who worked there.

"I think it had to do with one of the accountants. Her crazy stalker ex-boyfriend," Sara said in a breathy whisper, leaning toward Nicole as they walked. "I heard she has a restraining order against him, but he cornered her in the parking garage this morning. She was filing a police report."

"Whoa, that's scary," Nicole muttered, the knot in her shoulders loosening now that she was reasonably sure she wasn't the reason the cops were here. "Hope they catch the guy before he gets . . ."

Nicole's words faded when she rounded the corner and saw a spray of yellow Asiatic lilies and fat white roses in a glass vase sitting on her desk. Next to it was a gift-wrapped box of chocolates.

"Speaking of boyfriends," Sara said with a wry smile. "I guess you've got one of the good ones. He certainly has good taste in flowers. What's the occasion?"

"I don't have a boyfriend," Nicole mumbled before setting down the coffee cup and bagged croissant on her desk.

"Does *he* know that?" Sara asked with a laugh as Nicole picked up the envelope that was tucked inside the bouquet. She pulled it out and opened it, reading the handwritten note inside.

> *Happy five-year anniversary to a stellar assistant! (Just in case no one at Altruist remembered.) —Patrick*
>
> *P.S. My invitation still stands.*

Nicole gritted her teeth, wanting to hide them or dump the flowers into the trash can. She probably would have if they weren't so beautiful and if Sara wasn't standing next to her.

"Who's it from?" Sara asked, taking a sip of her drink, leaning over Nicole's shoulder.

Nicole folded the note closed before Sara could read it. She forced a smile as she tucked the note into her pants pocket. "My mom," she lied. "She knows I've been stressed out and moody lately so she decided to cheer me up."

"Well, that's nice of her. Why have you been stressed out lately?"

"Just juggling lots of stuff. When I'm not doing things at the office, I've been at Maple Grove, Xander's place in Westchester, getting the property and mansion ready for the birthday party next week."

"Ah, yes," Sara said with a slow nod. "I've heard about the grand birthday weekend. It's *the* coveted invitation. Not everyone in the company was invited—including me."

"Sorry. It was a limited guest list, Sara," she said as she pulled out her chair. "Xander decided who to invite."

That wasn't completely true. Xander decided on all the guests, but Nicole had made certain a few choice names were on his lists— the few that would be important for what she needed to accomplish next weekend.

"Well, don't get too stressed out. And try to have fun for me while you're there," Sara said before glancing down at her Apple Watch. "I should get going. I've got a 9:30 Zoom with the graphics team. See you later."

"Bye," Nicole replied.

She watched Sara walk away, waiting until she was out of sight before taking the note out of her pocket. She read it again then shook her head.

Why would he send this here? *To her office?* Anyone could have read his note. And this wasn't the first time he'd done something like this. Did Gallagher want someone to suspect her? To find out what she'd been up to? It was a dumb move for a man who was supposedly so savvy.

Nicole ripped the note into tiny little pieces and tossed them into the waste bin by her desk. She then stood, grabbed the cup of coffee and Xander's breakfast, and took them to his office.

CHAPTER 7

DC's Union Station was always busy on Saturdays, but it seemed even more crowded today. Nicole zigzagged her way through the travelers and tourists, listening to the train announcements echo their way to the plaster ceilings of the main hall as she dashed through the automatic doors. She then ran past a line of people on the sidewalk all staring down at their phones, either waiting for Ubers or searching for the names of their hotels.

"It started with a *w*, I think," she heard one man mutter to a woman in a wide-brimmed hat.

Behind the row of taxis parked along the curb, Nicole spotted a lone BMW.

The luxury vehicle was so old that its silver varnish had started to fade to a dull gray, but the car was one of her mom's most prized possessions—the first she'd ever paid off.

"Is that what you're wearing?" her mom asked, furrowing her brows as Nicole swung open the door while juggling a gilded box and the glass vase brimming over with one-day-old roses and Asiatic lilies. "And what's with the flowers?"

"It's my gift," Nicole said as she climbed onto the passenger seat and shut the door behind her.

They were headed to Cousin Makayla's baby shower. It was only a twenty-five-minute drive to the suburbs of Maryland, but it meant Nicole's mom had to battle Saturday DC traffic to get there, which wasn't quite as bad as New York City traffic but still made the older woman keep a white-knuckled grip on the steering wheel as she merged onto First Street.

"I bought flowers and Godiva chocolate," Nicole explained while buckling her seatbelt. "I figured that . . . well, people always bring gifts for the baby at these things. No one ever thinks about the mom so why not—"

Nicole stopped short and tightened her grip to keep the vase from flying out of her hands when her mother slammed on the brake and blared the horn.

"Stay in your damn lane! Can't you see the line?" her mom shouted at the driver of a tan Lexus who'd almost sideswiped them. She then turned her ire on Nicole. "Nikki, they bring gifts for the baby because it's called a 'baby shower.'"

"Yes, Mom, I know that," she answered tightly.

"Then why would you bring flowers and chocolate? This isn't Valentine's Day! A gift like that will look out of place or like an afterthought."

Probably because it *was* an afterthought.

The truth was with her crazy work schedule and Xander's even more constant demands now that his party in the Hudson Valley was less than a week away, Nicole barely had time to eat and sleep.

That morning she'd woken up at two o'clock in a panic when she realized that, in all her manic flurry of tasks, she'd forgotten completely about agreeing to go to Makayla's baby shower. She hadn't bought anything off the baby registry either. So she grabbed the bouquet of flowers and chocolate she'd gotten as a gift at work and brought them instead. It was either that or a gift card purchased at the train station.

Besides, it wasn't like she wanted to go to this shower anyway; her mother had practically bullied her into attending. She had too much on her plate as it was.

"Forget it," her mother murmured, gazing out the windshield again. "I'll just add your name to my gift. We'll say it came from the both of us."

Nicole frowned. "What did you get her?"

Knowing her mom, it probably wasn't something she would have chosen in a million years; their styles were so vastly different. Even for the baby shower, Nicole had chosen to dress casually in Vans sneakers, a tank dress, and an oversized sweater, while her mom donned a mauve business suit and snakeskin pumps. The older woman looked like she'd just come from interviewing candidates for a job opening at the lobbying firm in DC where she'd been working in HR for the past fifteen years, whereas Nicole resembled the college grad her mother would most undoubtedly reject for the position.

"Does it really matter?" her mother asked as she drove. "At least it's better than flowers and a box of chocolates."

"Fine. Whatever. Just add my name to the gift," Nicole said before slumping back into her seat.

"This is so cute, y'all! Isn't it cute?"

Nicole barely looked up from the email on her phone screen, catching in the corner of her eye the yellow baby gown with matching lace booties that her cousin Makayla was holding aloft for all the women assembled at the baby shower to *ooh* and *aah* over.

The living room was jam-packed with bodies and awash in a sea of white, pink, and pastel blue. Balloons and ribbons festooned the staircase banister, framing Makayla, who was surrounded by baby gifts and discarded boxes. A pile of tissue paper littered her feet. Makayla's Scottish terrier, Dior, sniffed at the mound suspiciously.

As Makayla resumed ripping at wrapping paper, Nicole returned her attention to the email, rereading an overview of the contract terms for the aerial bartenders that would be at Xander's birthday bash. She'd already booked the fire performers and dancers, but Xander had decided to add another act after attending a party in Las Vegas last week. The party had featured alluring women in tasseled bras and G-strings who dangled from gilded hoops suspended from the ceiling as they served Jell-O shots and cocktails to guests.

She wasn't fond of these last-minute additions, but she'd at least managed to talk Xander out of the sexy burlesque act after reminding him that his three-year-old goddaughter, Harper, and a few other kids were among the many party guests who'd already RSVP'd. Their parents probably wouldn't appreciate that kind of entertainment.

Now Nicole was double-checking that Xander's luscious bartenders were going to be fully clothed or, at minimum, in more than only bras and G-strings while serving drinks at the bash.

"The one in the green gift bag is from Nicole and me," Nicole heard her mother say before taking a sip of fire engine–red fruit punch.

They were sitting next to each other on Makayla's leather sectional, sandwiched between Makayla's mother-in-law, who was wearing so much perfume that Nicole's eyes were starting to water, and a woman whose name Nicole couldn't remember but who kept shifting around beside her and constantly bumping her shoulder. Nicole was now being nudged again—this time by her mother, who whispered through a tight smile, "Get . . . off . . . your . . . phone."

"Oh, wow!" Makayla now cried while removing the tissue paper and pulling out a mini-sized leopard-print jumper with matching faux fur beret. Both were adorned with cubic zirconia embellishments.

The outfit was hideous. Nicole wouldn't have chosen it as a gift even at gunpoint.

"How nice," Makayla said, before lowering it back into the bag. "Thanks so much, Nikki. Thanks, Aunt Juanita!"

"Don't mention it, baby," Nicole's mother assured with a wave of her manicured hand.

Nicole watched as Makayla's bestie, Tiffany, rose to her feet and stood beside the mother-to-be. She clapped her hands gleefully. "OK, y'all! Now that we're done with gifts, we're gonna do one final game before we cut the cake." She held up a jar of Gerber baby food. "Whoever can finish a jar of baby peas first . . . *wins!*"

Nicole winced at the squeals and cackling laughter that ensued from Tiffany's announcement. She even heard a few groans.

"Would you look at that? Someone at the office is calling," Nicole lied, staring down at her phone again. "Sorry, Mom. I'll be right back."

She didn't wait for her mother's response before she rose to her feet and fled to Makayla's kitchen, considering it better to hide among the dirty dishes and pans with her dignity and stomach intact.

CHAPTER 8

"That was a long phone call," Nicole heard her mother say behind her.

Nicole turned away from the kitchen bay window where she'd been staring at the squirrels scurrying around Makayla's backyard to find her mom strolling toward her, carrying a paper plate and plastic cup.

Nicole shrugged. "I had to take it. But everything is all good now."

"Uh-huh. I'm surprised you haven't glued that thing to your hand. You're always on it," her mom murmured. "It seems even more lately."

"Well, a lot more has been going on—at . . . at work, I mean," she added quickly.

Nicole hated lying to her mother. She used to do it all the time when she was younger, lying about everything from whether she'd brushed her teeth the night before or put away her laundry. Lying had come easily, and she'd been so believable that it frightened her mother.

Nicole only stopped when her mother made her sit for three minutes with a bar of Dove soap in her mouth.

She swore she could still taste its chalky, medicinal residue to this day.

Nicole watched as her mother tossed her paper plate into a nearby trash can in disgust.

"I don't know who made the potato salad, but they should be shot. Thank God we're getting dinner later."

"Sorry, Mom." Nicole grimaced. "I can't do dinner tonight. I forgot to tell you . . . I'm catching an earlier train back to the city."

"*What?* Why?" The older woman's finely arched brows knitted together. "We had plans. I made reservations and everything, Nikki."

"I know, but like I told you, I'm just super busy at work. I have to get back."

The truth was, she loved and respected her mother, but the less time they spent in each other's company, the better. Every conversation they had inevitably turned into an argument. It had been that way since her childhood. The two women always clashed, like polka dots and plaid.

Her mother sighed and slowly crossed her arms over her chest. "Well, it's real nice of you to go above and beyond like this, especially since your last day is next week." On the other side of the kitchen door, there came another chorus of laughs and squeals. Then applause. "You were counting down the days. You've gotta be counting down the hours now, huh? Have you gotten any callbacks so far from the jobs you applied for?"

"I'm in talks with a few companies, but nothing definite yet." Nicole picked up her phone again, pretending to be engrossed by something on-screen.

She hadn't told her mother that she'd postponed her resignation as Xander's assistant because of the celebration. Nicole figured she'd lasted this long. What was a few more days?

Besides, she had a greater goal to accomplish, and it finally seemed within reach.

"So, he hired your replacement?" Her mother twisted her mouth into a wry smile. "Let me guess. Some pretty young thing with blond hair and big tatas? Is she at least an actual personal assistant this time?"

Nicole had tried once to explain to Xander that her job title was *executive* assistant, not personal assistant, and the unique requests he asked of her weren't traditionally under her purview.

He responded with, "executive . . . personal. What the fuck is the difference?" Before telling her to pick up his dry cleaning.

"No, he hasn't hired anyone yet, unfortunately," Nicole muttered.

"But you aren't planning to stick around to help train his assistant when he finally does pick one, are you, Nikki?" Her mother narrowed her eyes at her as she walked around the granite island. "Come Friday, you're done with that job, right?"

Again, Nicole continued to tap on her screen. She didn't answer.

"*Nicole?*" her mother repeated tightly.

"I don't know, Mom! I haven't thought about it. I haven't had the chance to."

Her mother loudly groused. "It was bad enough that you slaved after that woman for four damn years."

"Ugh, Mom, don't say it like that." Nicole cringed as she lowered her phone. "It's so offensive. To me *and* to Bridget."

"But it's true."

"No, it is not. I didn't 'slave' after her. I was Bridget's assistant. When you work for the CEO of a major corporation, it's normal to—"

"And now that she's dead and gone—God rest her soul and all that," her mother said before making the sign of the cross, "you're doing the same damn thing for her son."

Nicole had known for years that her mother hated her job.

"I can't believe she graduated valedictorian from her high school class and summa cum laude with a dual degree from Cornell just to become *a secretary*," her mom would lament on occasion to no one in particular, like it was an echoing thought she felt compelled to voice out loud.

Her mother also hated her close relationship with Bridget.

"*'Bridget said this. Bridget said that,'*" her mother said in a singsong voice more than a year ago. "Do you have to quote her so much, honey? It's weird."

But her mother didn't realize one of the reasons Nicole had identified with Bridget so quickly and easily was that Bridget had reminded Nicole of her mother. Both were plainspoken, driven, and resourceful. Both were self-made women who had pulled themselves up the socioeconomic ladder.

Unfortunately, Nicole's mom was unwilling to see those similarities; she had only seen Bridget as someone trying to dominate her daughter's life—a position her mother felt only she should occupy.

"When is it gonna end, Nikki?" her mom now asked. "If you're gonna hustle *this* hard, shouldn't it be for yourself? For your own dreams? Your own life?"

"Trust me—I am, Mom. When I'm done what I need to do here, there are so many things I can do with my career and—"

"I'm not just talking about that," her mom interrupted. "I'm talking about how you never go anywhere. You never do anything. When was the last time you've gone on vacation, Nikki? Dipped your toes in the sand of some beach and had a fruity drink with an umbrella in it? When's the last time you've even been on a date?"

Nicole's cheeks warmed at the memory of the last "date" she'd been on. It left her with a bad hangover as she did the walk of shame to the subway the next morning. It was yet another example of what happened when she took her eye off the ball. When she veered off the plan.

She cleared her throat and pushed the memory to the back of her mind.

"So, that's what this is about? *Me dating? Settling down?* You know my life's purpose has never been to get married and have babies, Mom."

"You think that's what I want for you, Nikki?" her mother asked, screwing up her face. "For you to just get married? For me to end up at another stupid baby shower in a cramped living room with thirty grown women gorging themselves on baby food? Be for real! I want *more* for you."

Someone loudly cleared their throat. They turned to find Tiffany, Makayla's bestie, standing awkwardly in the entryway, holding a tray covered with plastic spoons and half-empty baby food jars. Nicole could tell from Tiffany's facial expression that she'd caught the tail end of their argument.

"We're . . . uh . . . we're done with the game and we're about to cut the cake if y'all . . . umm . . . want some," Tiffany said limply.

Nicole gave a forced smile. "That's OK. We were just leaving."

Less than half an hour later, Nicole sat silently in the passenger seat while her mother drove them back to Union Station so she could catch the 3:46 p.m. Acela to Penn Station. She stared out the window the entire time, ignoring her mother as the older woman drummed her fingernails on the steering wheel, kept changing radio stations every five minutes, and muttered to herself about the traffic.

When they reached Columbus Circle and Nicole spotted the water fountain, marble statues, and state flags, she had to fight the urge to unlock her seatbelt and fling open the passenger door to escape the tension inside the sedan. Instead she waited until her mother pulled up to the curb and came to a full stop while other travelers rushed past them on the sidewalk, dragging suitcases.

"Thanks, Mom," she said as she unbuckled her seatbelt and unlocked her car door. "I'll call you later after I get home, OK? Or maybe tomorrow."

"Nikki," her mom called out, making Nicole pause midway as she opened the door.

"Yeah?" she asked, turning around to face her mom. Her hand was still on the door handle. Her body was still tilted at an angle, ready to bolt.

"I hope you give some thought to what I said back at the baby shower. About how you should stop sacrificing yourself . . . your needs . . . for this job. And this is speaking from the perspective of a woman who did it most of her life."

Nicole loudly sighed. "Mom, I'm not—"

"Look, honey, if you're not gonna listen to me, then think about what she would've wanted for you."

Nicole squinted in confusion. "*She?* Who is *she*, Ma?"

"Bridget," her mother said, making Nicole go still. "If she was as good a person as you said she was . . . if she didn't just think of you as some assistant, what would *she* have wanted for you, Nikki? It couldn't be this. To have to keep playing the thankless servant to that . . . that feckless idiot—even if he was her son. Would she?"

Nicole hesitated, considering her mom's question. She nodded.

"Yes, if you really wanna know the truth, she'd tell me to stay. She'd tell me to focus on the big picture and suck it up." She then shook her head with impatience. "Besides, what does it matter? Bridget is dead. She's gone, Mom. What she would think . . . what she would say right now doesn't matter anymore."

But what I'm doing . . . what I have been doing all these months does matter, she thought, but she couldn't say aloud. *I've got to focus on the objective.*

Her mother's shoulders slumped.

"Look, I really have to go, or I'll miss my train. I love you and will talk to you soon," Nicole whispered before giving her a quick kiss on the cheek and stepping onto the sidewalk.

"Nikki," her mother called after her, but Nicole didn't look back as she slammed the car door behind her. She walked toward the sliding glass doors, disappearing into the crowd.

CHAPTER 9
NICOLE

NOW

I CLOMP DOWN THE STEEL GRATE STAIRS ON THE STUDIO LOT TO THE asphalt below, juggling the *Murder in the Valley* script, my purse, and my cell phone. It's the second week of filming and I already got new pages this afternoon. They were waiting for me on my desk after I returned from the set to my little corner office on the second floor. Their blue tint stood out like a neon sign against the stark white of the old pages.

I know it's not unusual to make changes to the script during filming, but when I found the binder-clipped pages on my desk, my heart lurched a little.

I thought the filmmakers had settled on a narrative of what happened. The basic sequence of events. The characters and the tone. I know the other survivors had given their sign-offs on the film treatment. I'd given my input on the script.

What have the writers changed since then?

I walk toward the studio gates where a black SUV waits to take me back to my hotel. I flip through pages, trying my best to read while I walk across the lot and talk to Mom.

"Yes, I asked, but I don't think she's going to play you, Mom," I say, balancing my cell between my cheek and my shoulder. "I think they cast someone else."

"But Angela Bassett would've been perfect," Mom laments.

"I know, I know, but maybe there were scheduling issues. She does have that TV show. And, I'll be honest, Mom. Your part is pretty small. Most of the focus is on the people that were there at Maple Grove that weekend. I bet a lot of our scenes might end up on the cutting-room floor, anyway."

I hear a horn beep behind me and I hop aside, nearly dropping my phone and the script, barely averting being clipped by a golf cart. It's driving at full speed past one of the studio hangars. The passenger, who's in a World War II army uniform, has his feet up on the dashboard. They're heading in the direction of the actors' trailers. I do a double take when I recognize the passenger's face.

Wait. Did I almost get run over by a multi–Academy Award winner?

"*Are you serious?*" Mom squawks, yanking back my attention. "After all that drama you put me through. Do you remember what happened *after* the murders? How are they not going to put that . . . put *me* in the movie, Nikki? Or are they just going to make stuff up?"

"I didn't say they wouldn't put you in, Mom." I start walking toward the gate again. "I said you might not make the final cut. The operative word here is 'might.'"

I return to scanning pages, reading the new lines among the text, trying to figure out if it changes the story substantially.

"Fine. *Fine!*" Mom loudly exhales on the other end of the line, not masking her disappointment. "But I still want to know who they cast. I hope it's not someone too old. I'm a mature woman, but I don't want to look elderly on-screen. If not Angela Bassett, then

Tracee Ellis Ross could work. She's sexy *and* funny. Or maybe Sheryl Lee Ralph. I just love her, and you know she'd be good, too."

"Nicole! Hey, girlie!" I hear someone shout. "There you are. I've been looking all over for you!"

I raise my eyes from the script, glance over my shoulder, and find Asia, the actress who's playing me in the film, jogging toward me. She's wearing a midriff-baring tank top and low-cut jeans. Her dark curls bounce jauntily around her shoulders. She's been on set all day, since her 5:00 a.m. call time, but she doesn't look remotely tired. Her natural bombshell glow hasn't faded. Meanwhile I'm pretty sure I have bags under my eyes from the little sleep I've been getting since arriving in LA.

Mom's worried about looking too old on film, while I must come to terms with the fact that the Nicole everyone sees on-screen will look *nothing* like me.

"Tracee Ellis Ross or Sheryl Lee Ralph. Got it. I'll let them know," I mutter into the phone. "Let me call you back, Mom."

I quickly hang up, tuck my cell into my back pocket, and turn to face Asia. I try to match her eager smile but I'm not the same caliber actress that she is.

"Hey, Asia! Did you need something?"

"Weeeeell," she says slowly, "I was just wondering if maybe we could grab dinner tonight and talk. Bill decided not to reshoot one of my scenes, so I'm finished for the day. They don't need me again until we go on location tomorrow. That means I have the whole evening free, girlie! I know this awesome new sushi place in WeHo where we can chow down and vibe. What do you say?"

I purse my lips. Over the past couple of weeks, Asia has asked me to lunch or for a quick meetup in her trailer a few times, but each time I've begged off.

"I want to know more about you, Nicole," she said to me a few days ago. "I *need* to know more."

But I can't see how telling Asia what I like to eat for breakfast every morning or the name of the guy who took me to prom will help her "get into character." It sounds like one of those self-indulgent actor exercises that is ridiculous if you aren't Daniel Day-Lewis or Joaquin Phoenix.

"Uh, actually," I begin, "I am just so exhausted, Asia. I'm still struggling with jet lag and didn't fall asleep until like . . . two o'clock this morning."

"But you've been on the West Coast for a while now, and you're still having sleep issues?" She frowns. "Have you tried melatonin gummies?" She snaps her fingers. Her green eyes widen. "You know, my Pilates instructor swears by these magnesium infusion shots she gets once a week. It totally made her insomnia disappear."

"Those all sound like good ideas. I'll look into them. In the meantime, I should get back to the hotel and start reading these pages," I say, gesturing to the script in my hand. "Then I'll . . ."

My words taper off when Asia reaches out and places a hand on my forearm. She takes a step closer so that we're eye to eye.

"Nicole, can I be frank with you?"

I hesitate. "Uh, sure."

"We're going to start shooting scenes tomorrow showing what happened at Maple Grove, and they are just so . . . so . . ." She clenches her free hand into a fist. "They are just so intense! There's so much happening, and you're going through all these emotions and making all these really complicated choices. I still feel like I'm struggling to get a handle on who you are. Who my character is. I know my lines, but that's not enough. One line can be read about a dozen different ways."

"Asia, I've seen you on set. You're a great actress. Whatever decisions you make creatively, I'm sure will be fine."

"But fine isn't good enough," she insists. "I can't get a handle on the character because I haven't connected with your psyche. Who you are. What motivates you. I want to get to know you as much as I can, Nicole. I'm serious!" she says, when I start to look doubtful again. "I want to know how you really felt when all this happened.

I can make it up, but it wouldn't be authentic. I'd much rather make it as true to life as possible, which is what you want, right?"

Gradually, I nod. "Of course."

"So, have dinner and drinks with me tonight. *Please?*"

She looks so desperate. And she's trying to give me what I asked for: showing the truth of what really happened, for once. How could I possibly say no?

"Sure," I say. "Let's meet up for dinner."

CHAPTER 10

I ARRIVE AT THE RESTAURANT IN WEST HOLLYWOOD A LITTLE AFTER eight. I changed the clothes I wore to the studio today to a fitted blazer, jeans, and heels that are pinching my feet and will likely give me blisters later. I even refreshed my makeup because I googled the sushi restaurant and discovered that it's *the* new hotspot in town. But when I step out of the car and see the building in front of me, I wonder if someone, maybe Asia, is playing a practical joke on me.

"Are you sure this is the place?" I ask my Uber driver as I pivot on the sidewalk and look down at him warily through the car window.

He nods from the front seat. "It's the address you gave me, lady."

The sun is starting to set, and streetlights flicker on. I gaze at the white industrial building stained gray with smog and its plain black steel door. It looks like it could house storage units or maybe some sketchy clothing factory where young women sew fast fashion for less than minimum wage.

The only thing that gives any hint that it's a sushi restaurant is the two-foot-tall sign in Japanese script over the door. Is that the name of the restaurant? Or maybe I'm wrong and the sign says, "Woe to All Those Who Enter!" Unfortunately, it's not like I can tell the difference.

I scan around me to see if maybe there's another building nearby that could be the restaurant instead, but there isn't. There's a nail salon across the street and a cupcake place next door. This must be it.

I hear the Uber driver gun the engine and watch his Volkswagen drive away. Left with no other option, I take cautious steps over the cracked sidewalk to the door, reach out, and tug the handle to open it.

It's like a scene in a fantasy novel when the character opens a door, steps into a closet, and enters a magical realm. But unlike the kids in *The Lion, the Witch and the Wardrobe* who suddenly find themselves in Narnia, I find myself in a chic bistro filled with long teak tables, low lighting, bamboo slats along the high walls, and several well-dressed diners. An abstract sculpture that vaguely resembles a flying octopus hangs from the ceiling.

I stroll toward the maître d' desk, where a beautiful East Asian woman stands.

"Welcome to O-ku," she says. "Do you have a reservation, ma'am?"

I begin to answer but pause when I see a man striding toward me. My stomach drops when I recognize him.

It's Xander.

No, it's not him, I remind myself, despite my rapidly beating heart. *Xander is dead.*

Thanks to the actor Troy Fletcher and the movie production, I've been seeing Xander more and more lately. In my dreams at night, making me lurch awake, and now, during the day. He's gone from a disembodied voice inside my head that I had to take several months of therapy and antidepressants to quell, to a ghost that I run into at random.

Xander pulls out a cigarette and gives me a brief smile, with all his bloody and broken teeth. I suck in an audible breath as he passes me. When I turn around completely to stare at him, to watch him open the steel door and step outside into the warm, lavender-sky night, he glances back at me. His face has changed. The lips are different. So is the nose. His eyes are blue, not hazel. He's a guy I don't recognize.

"Ma'am," the woman at the desk says again, making me turn back to face her. "Do you have a reservation?"

I shake my head. "Umm n-n-no," I stutter. "I mean . . . I'm meeting someone who does, I think. She should already be here. Asia Wilkerson."

A minute later, the hostess escorts me to the table where Asia is sitting. I find the actress talking on her cell.

"So, did they like my audition?" Asia asks the person on the other end of the phone line. She looks up at me and waves as we approach. "*What?* . . . Why do they want to do a second round? What do you mean it's between me and her? Isn't she like . . . some chick on YouTube? Does she even have any film credits? . . . Five million subscribers, huh?" Her megawatt smile starts to fade. She gnaws her glossy bottom lip. "No. *No*, Eve! I did that for Soderbergh last year, and I didn't even get a callback. Why would this be any different?" Asia wrinkles her cute, pert nose and sighs as I pull out a chair and take the seat facing her. "Look, Eve, I have to call you back. I'm in a very important meeting with a VIP." She gives me a wink. "Yeah . . . yeah, we can talk about it tomorrow. OK. Bye."

Asia presses a button on-screen, lowers her cell to the table, and rubs my arm. "Hey, girlie! I'm so glad you came," she gushes.

"Of course," I say, though that's a lie.

I almost talked myself out of coming a half dozen times. I'd start to text her an excuse but then delete it when I realized how lame and fake each of the excuses sounded.

The truth is I'm not eager to tell Asia what I figure she wants to know, what she *needs* to know to do her job: *What were those last days like at the mansion? What had gone through my mind as I watched everything unfold?*

I don't want to excavate those emotional depths again. Lucky for her, the fact that I keep seeing Xander tells me that my memories are getting more vivid; they're not fading. I'm digging them up despite my best efforts to suppress them.

"Good evening, ladies," says the waiter who sidles up to our table. "Have you had a chance to read the menu?"

"No, she hasn't yet. We're going to need a little more time for the food, but maybe drinks in the meantime." Asia gives me an eyebrow wiggle while holding up a martini glass. "I wanted to wait but I got started without you. You can order something and catch up."

"I'll have a negroni," I say to the waiter. "Thanks."

"No problem, ladies. I'll get your drink while you have the chance to look over the menu."

"I highly recommend the lobster sashimi. It's the absolute best," Asia says after he walks away. I flip open the leatherbound menu as she pops the olive from her martini into her mouth.

"*Soooo*," she says as she chews, "how was your day? I don't get to talk to you on set most days because I'm either on camera, getting ready in my trailer, or studying lines. Are you enjoying the whole experience so far?"

"Uh, sure," I say as a busboy pours sparkling water into my glass. "It's . . . good. Interesting. I'm learning something new every day. It's a great movie."

They're boilerplate answers but she nods like I've just said something brilliant. Truly profound.

"Nicole, I am just so, *so* glad to hear that, because I think this movie is going to be phenomenal. I mean when I first read this script, I was riveted. It's a mystery with complex relationships between the characters. There's sex. Social commentary. And it has all this intrigue. And I was just so moved by your character. Your life! Everything that you went through." She leans across the table toward me. "I mean, all this drama swirling around you, and you were like this secret spy. And you did it just because you were trying to be a good assistant. You were just doing what you had to do."

Did I have to do it?

No one forced me to participate in the drama and intrigue at Maple Grove during that birthday celebration and the days leading up to it. No one made me lie and keep secrets from everyone, including my own mother, but I did it willingly.

I just didn't know what all those lies and secrets would eventually lead to.

That day at Makayla's baby shower, my mom had asked, "When is it gonna end, Nikki?"

In death. That's how it ended. With people dying, including my own boss.

"Here you go," the waiter says. He sets my negroni in front of me and a bowl of wasabi peas at the center of the table. We give him our orders. I go with the lobster sashimi like Asia suggested.

"I want you to tell me *everything*," Asia says as I take a sip of my drink. Her green eyes are bright and eager. Her bleached white smile is almost carnal. "I want to embody Nicole Underwood when I'm on that screen. I want to be who you were those three days. Don't hold back!"

"Of course."

I'll try my best even though each time I end up inevitably holding back some pieces. I can't tell if it's a form of self-protection or if I'm wary of overembellishing . . . of exaggerating what happened for my benefit. It rarely matters, though.

To the media, I was a suspect at first, painted as a diabolical ringleader of an elaborate murder plot, until the evidence from that night and the weeks leading up to it exonerated me.

In the documentary, they painted me as a saint. A victim of circumstances beyond my control. A symbol of the oppressed who are manipulated and made to suffer at the hands of callous one-percenters like Xander and his friends. But I was able to rise above it all with cunning, wit, and determination. I was one of the few who survived in the end.

Roll credits and play triumphant rock music.

I know the movie will be more nuanced, and the director and Asia want to portray me as a sympathetic character to make the movie more marketable. That's probably what those new blue pages are, which I still haven't finished reading. No one wants an unlikeable lead. Especially an unlikeable woman lead, not to mention a *Black* woman lead. But the truth . . . the pesky truth is a lot more complicated.

"Start from the beginning," Asia urges me, motioning to the waiter to get his attention so he'll bring her another martini. "I'm listening."

So I gulp down the rest of my negroni, work up my courage, take a deep breath, and begin my tale, starting my story on that Friday morning—the first day of that fateful three-day birthday weekend.

NICOLE

(FRIDAY, THE DAY BEFORE THE BIRTHDAY BASH)

CHAPTER 11

"What in the hell?" Nicole muttered as she paused at the entrance of the outdoor tent that seemed a better fit for Ringling Bros. and Barnum & Bailey Circus than for the lush, undulating grounds of Maple Grove.

The event planner they'd hired had told her that the tent would have to be big to accommodate everything Xander wanted for the birthday bash tomorrow, but Nicole hadn't expected it to be quite this massive. Now, as she stepped inside, she expected to find marching elephants, pirouetting Clydesdales, or maybe even tightrope walkers scaling across the roof of the tent, rather than the bar, round tables, and highboys she'd ordered. Thankfully, there were no animals in here, but there weren't any tables or seating either, making her frown. Under closer inspection, all the chairs and tables still sat under plastic and tarp and were pushed against one of the tent walls, waiting to be assembled. Nicole searched for the event planner, Gustaf, to get some answers.

"Can we raise that up higher? *Higher*, please!" Gustaf ordered.

The rail-thin man dressed in all black was standing near the center of the tent on the parquet dance floor. He pointed at the ceiling while three workers on scaffolding raised an oversized crystal chandelier. More than a half dozen other chandeliers also dangled from the canopy above. A woman stood beside Gustaf, also dressed in black, holding an iPad, scanning through images on-screen.

"Just two more meters," Gustaf said, puckering his lips beneath his pencil-thin mustache. "Yes! Yes! Perfect."

"Gustaf," Nicole called out, making him and the woman turn and notice her for the first time. "Why isn't anything set up? Where are all the flowers and all the other decor?" She threw out her hands and looked around the mostly empty tent. "It's almost noon and I'm not seeing any progress."

They still had some time, but not much. Today—Friday—was the birthday weekend kickoff that would begin with Xander greeting the guests who were staying on-site at the mansion and hosting an eight-course welcome dinner that night. Tomorrow would mark the official birthday blowout celebration. On Sunday, Xander planned to offer the remaining guests brunch and a tour of the nearby winery in the valley that the Chamberses owned before thanking them with a lovely dinner and sending them on their way.

There was a lot Nicole had to do in the next few days, and she didn't want to waste time worrying that Gustaf and his team were falling behind.

Gustaf gave a patronizing smile and inclined his head. "Miss Underwood, I have done many, *many* events on this scale with tighter deadlines. Rest assured; everything will be done by tomorrow evening when the festivities will take place. Now if you'll let me get back to my work," he said before clasping his hands together. He whispered something in Norwegian to the woman beside him who nodded and snickered. He then returned his attention to the ceiling.

"On second thought, can we lower it a bit?" he asked one of the men on the scaffolding. "After that, it will be perfect, gentlemen."

"Sure, I'll let you get back to your work, but . . ." Nicole took another step toward him. Her assistant armor—breastplate, chain mail, *and* shield—were back on. "Just know that if everything isn't done by tomorrow *before* 6:00 p.m. Eastern time, Mr. Chambers won't be happy. And when Mr. Chambers isn't happy, things get *ugly*. Generally my job is to make sure that doesn't happen, but as far as I'm concerned, I gave you fair warning. So, if there are any issues, I will point him to you. OK?"

She watched as Gustaf's self-assured smile faded. He gave an audible swallow.

Good, she thought. *I got my point across.*

Xander's tantrums were legendary. Although many wanted access to the Chamberses' money and prestige, few wanted to deal with him directly.

Only Nicole could handle Xander on her best days when his Mr. Hyde took over.

Nicole now turned on her heel and stepped around a worker pushing a dolly loaded with crates. She walked out of the tent back into the warm May sunshine, held her hands over her eyes, and looked up. There wasn't a single cloud in the sky. The temps were already in the low 80s back in the city and probably felt even hotter thanks to the smog, asphalt, and congestion. But it was a balmy day on the Chamberses' property. And according to the forecast, it would stay that way for the party tomorrow as well.

That's a relief, Nicole thought. She didn't want the weather to delay guests' flights or impede her plans. There couldn't be any hiccups.

For this to work . . . for all the elements to fall into place, everything had to go smoothly.

She lowered her gaze to see several cars and vans making their way toward the mansion. Most had decals on the side, denoting the branded names of the caterer, lighting company, and even the pyrotechnics they would use on-site at the end of the celebration. She searched for Xander's silver Porsche roadster among the many vehicles parked along the circular driveway or driving uphill, but she didn't see it.

Nicole gritted her teeth, pulled out her cell phone, and fired off a text.

Hey, Xander! Just checking on your ETA, she typed, then pressed send.

She'd asked Xander to get here before his guests started arriving so he could personally greet them and host the grand welcome dinner, but she should've known, despite the alert she put in his calendar and text messages she'd sent last night and this morning, that he wouldn't show up on time. Now the task of greeting the guests would fall squarely on her shoulders.

"Speaking of guests," she muttered when she saw a familiar black Audi convertible sail into view. She tucked her cell back into her pocket.

She knew the driver. It was the COO Daniel Miller. He'd been invited to stay at Maple Grove this weekend.

Nicole watched as he pulled into the driveway. By the time she'd reached the bottom of the hill, Daniel had already popped open the trunk and taken out his luggage.

"Hello, Mr. Miller," she said.

"Hey," Daniel answered distractedly, pushing his Ray-Bans to the crown of his salt-and-pepper head and throwing his laptop bag over his shoulder as one of the house staffers removed his luggage from the trunk and carried them inside.

"I see you brought some work with you," she said, eyeing his laptop bag and briefcase. "I did too. Hard to leave it behind."

He glanced down at both. "Yeah, I figured if I have to be here for three days, I should at least be productive."

Have to . . .

He could've declined Xander's invitation to the three-day celebration or made up an excuse not to come, but Daniel was too much of a brownnoser to do that. It was one of the reasons he'd moved up the company ladder, after all.

"So, are you sure you guys have enough room for me in there? I mean, I can still get a hotel room," he said, looking up at the mansion's imposing exterior, tilting back his head to take it all in. "You're probably already swarmed with party guests."

The Chamberses' mansion was a cross between a church and a granite castle with its spires, tall-arched windows, and vaulted forty-foot ceilings. In fact, it used to be a church. The previous owners who were the descendants of one of the founding fathers donated the home to a Lutheran parish back in the late 1800s, from what Nicole understood.

Bridget had purchased the home and the surrounding 120-acre property at a steal for almost $17 million more than a decade ago. She'd ditched all the crosses and religious paraphernalia and gutted the whole thing, keeping only the hardwood and the staircases. The mansion now boasted nearly two dozen bedrooms, an indoor basketball court, Olympic-sized pool, ballroom, and ten-car garage.

Of course they had room for Daniel. They had enough room to house a small village.

She nodded. "Yes, sir. We reserved one of the guest rooms just for you."

"Great! I'll need this taken to my room as well," he said, shrugging off the strap of his laptop bag. He held out the bag to her, as if expecting her to carry it inside like she was one of the mansion staffers or some bellhop. He then handed his car keys to a waiting valet.

Nicole glanced down at the bag.

"Wonderful! I'd be happy to show you the way so you can get set up, Mr. Miller. Come with me," she said with a smile, turning around and heading toward the mansion's grand oak doors, not taking the bag.

Daniel hesitated a second or two before trailing behind her. She saw the disgruntled look on his wrinkled face in the reflection of one of the windowpanes near the entrance and she stifled a laugh.

She got paid to play babysitter and servant to Xander Chambers and Xander Chambers only—and even that was only for a bit longer.

"Interesting choice of venue for this shindig," he commented as they walked over the Italian marble tiles of the great hall toward the staircase that would take them to the east wing.

"What do you mean?" she asked, glancing over her shoulder.

"Well," he braced a hand on one of the cherrywood newel posts, "Bridge died here just a few months ago, didn't she?"

It was a rhetorical question. Everyone in the company and probably the entire borough of Manhattan knew that.

"On the property . . . yes," Nicole said as they began to climb to the second floor. The sound of their ascent was muffled by the plush carpet, although Daniel huffed slightly with each step upstairs.

"And I guess Xander doesn't care about the rumors," he said, making her pause. She turned around to face him. "That having the party here might start the whispers again."

"What rumors?"

Daniel raised his gray brows. He let out a startled laugh then eyed her. "Oh, come now. You mean you really haven't heard them?"

Where was he going with this? "Unfortunately, there are lots of rumors about Xander and his family, Mr. Miller. You're going to have to be more specific."

"The rumors are that . . . well, that poor Bridge's accident wasn't an accident. That some foul play was involved. Maybe someone tampered with her car or drove her off the road," he said, his words echoing to the coffered ceiling.

Nicole took a measured breath. She waited a beat to be careful of her response. "No, Xander hasn't mentioned anything about it." She then resumed climbing until they reached the second floor.

They soon arrived at a long corridor leading to some of the guest rooms. "This way," she said, pointing down the hall.

Xander had redecorated most of the first floor in a modern, minimalist style that made the spaces look like some edgy art gallery. He'd done it soon after his mother's death, raising quite a few eyebrows. Your mother dies tragically and you immediately start buying furniture and knocking down walls in her vacation home? But others . . . those of a more sympathetic bent speculated that it was Xander's way of dealing with the loss. He was obviously trying to distract himself from his mother's absence with a new project.

Xander and his designer hadn't managed to get to the guest rooms on the second floor yet. They still retained the soft French country decor that Bridget had painstakingly chosen with her designer when she purchased the mansion years ago.

Daniel and Nicole finally reached Daniel's room. Nicole pushed open the door, revealing a large bedroom with a four-poster, king-sized bed.

"Here we are." Nicole turned back around to face him. "You can text me if you—"

"And how do you feel about the rumors?" Daniel interrupted. "The rumors about Bridget, I mean. About foul play. I'm sure you have your own theories. You two were so close."

His blue eyes scoured her. He was paying attention to more than her words now.

Daniel wasn't just a brownnoser; he was also shrewd.

Even when she was Bridget's assistant, Nicole always felt like Daniel had some ulterior motive when they interacted. Whenever he stopped by her desk or caught her in the hallway, he'd start with pleasantries but then shift to asking questions. They'd seem simple enough, but she knew intrinsically that they weren't. Daniel was trying to coerce her into either doing something—or revealing something. Anything that could help him gain the upper hand. She felt the same way now. Fortunately she couldn't be so easily manipulated.

"I think if there were any signs of foul play, the police would have said so. I also think we should respect Bridget's memory and not spread those kinds of rumors—unless you know something about her death that I don't, Mr. Miller."

She saw something change in Daniel's eyes. The keenness disappeared and was replaced with irritation. He eased back from her and nodded. "You're right. You're absolutely right. That was in poor taste, wasn't it? Thank you for pointing that out, Nicole." He stepped past her, carrying his bags through the door. "Bridget was right to choose you as her assistant. Even in death, you've remained so steadfast and loyal."

There was something in his tone that sounded almost snide. It made Nicole's hand tighten around the door handle.

"I have to get back to the party prep. I'll let you unpack, sir. Let me know if you need anything," she said, keeping her voice even.

He set the laptop bag and briefcase on his bed. "Oh, don't worry. I'll find you if I need you. I know you'll be lingering around here somewhere."

She kept her polite smile in place until she closed the door behind her.

What was with that line of questioning about Bridget's death and it being a possible murder? Did he suspect something? Did he know what she was up to? Maybe it was a bad idea to invite Daniel here this weekend. He could ruin everything.

Nicole gradually exhaled. *It's fine. Nothing changes*, she told herself. *Stick to the plan and focus on the objective.*

She pushed back her shoulders and walked down the corridor, returning her focus to the tasks at hand.

CHAPTER 12

Nicole had just reached the end of the hallway, trying her best to push Daniel Miller out of her mind, when she heard it: a high-pitched scream that made her halt in her steps. Then came another scream—this one truly bloodcurdling.

It sounded like someone was being stabbed, like they were enduring the worst torture imaginable.

"What the hell?" she murmured.

Nicole rushed toward the stairs and leaned over the banister to peer at the floor below, expecting to find some horrific murder scene. Instead, she discovered a downy-haired toddler lying on the imported marble tiles, kicking her legs and flailing her arms like she was convulsing. The little girl's cherubic face was beet red. Her eyes were squeezed tightly shut and her mouth was formed into such a wide O that Nicole worried she was choking on her own wails.

It's Harper, she realized. *Xander's goddaughter.*

As Nicole ran down the stairs to aid the little girl, a young woman who seemed to be no older than twenty rushed toward Harper and knelt down at her side.

"*Jesucristo*, kid! They said you can have another yogurt pop later!" the young woman shouted, trying to be heard over all the yelling. "I swear to you, it's not worth this!"

"Is she OK? She's not having a seizure, is she?" Nicole called down. "Do I need to call 9-1-1?"

The young woman looked up, seeming surprised to see Nicole standing there. The two locked eyes for a few seconds before the younger woman forced a smile and gradually shook her head.

"No need! She's cool," she assured, despite wincing as Harper let out another horrifying scream. She pushed back a curtain of jet-black hair. It had fallen into her face, which was just as plump and cherubic as Harper's although several shades darker.

It was an innocent face. Sweet. Trustful.

"It's just a tantrum," she explained and shrugged her shoulders in a "What can you do?" gesture. "Harper has them sometimes. I think she's had too much sugar. You know how it is."

Nicole resumed walking down the stairs just as a man strode through the opened doors into the great hall, pushing the sleeves of his shirt up his tan forearms like a bouncer prepared to expel an unruly patron from a bar. A blond woman with a chic pageboy haircut in a royal blue sundress came click-clacking in high heels behind him.

Nicole recognized them as Harper's parents, Charlotte and Mark Danfrey.

Mark was one of Xander's college fraternity bros and oldest friends.

"Dammit, Elena, we heard her all the way from the car," Mark said, jabbing his thumb over his shoulder. "We pay you to handle her and keep her under control," he said to the young woman, like he was talking about a pet, not his daughter.

Mark then stood over the toddler and glared down at her. "Harper, we're not doing this. Get *up*!"

"Nooooooooooooo!" Harper growled back.

Nicole didn't know a voice like that could come out of such a little person. What was Harper going to do next? Spin her head a full three-sixty and projectile-vomit pea soup?

"Mark, don't yell at her," Charlotte insisted. "Remember what the therapist said? Gentle parenting gets better results."

"Yeah, well, gentle parenting wears thin after twenty solid minutes of listening to her yelling inside an SUV."

Charlotte sucked her teeth before returning her attention to their toddler. "Harper, honey," she cooed while bracing her hands on her knees and bending down slightly, "I know you're upset. But do Mommy and Daddy a favor and just take a deep, *deep* breath. OK?"

Harper whimpered in response and kicked off one of her canvas shoes, hitting her mother in the shin and making her shrink back and cry out in pain.

"That's it! *That is it!* I've had enough of this," Mark said. He reached down to grab the little girl and drag her to her feet, but before he could, Elena got in his way. She grasped the little girl by the shoulders and grinned down at her.

"Eh, I know what'll get you off the floor," she said, reaching down and tickling Harper's arms and then her belly.

Harper's screams and cries abruptly ended and she started giggling. "Stop!" she squealed. "Stop, Elly!"

"Come on," Elena said, motioning for Harper to stand. "Show's over. That's enough drama for one day, kid, or at least for the next few hours. Huh?"

Harper nodded before hopping to her feet like nothing had happened, like she hadn't been screaming her head off a minute ago. Harper shoved a thumb in her mouth as Elena retrieved her shoe and eased it back onto her extended foot. She then wiped dust off Harper's pink polo shirt and matching skirt.

"Umm, hello," Nicole said with a wave, making everyone whip around to face her.

Mark still looked pissed. Charlotte absently rubbed the sore spot on her leg. Harper continued sucking her thumb as Elena picked her up and propped her on her hip.

"I'm Nicole, Xander's assistant. We've met before. I hope your drive here went smoothly."

"Traffic was tolerable. The ride was torture," Mark said as their driver carried in their bags. "Could you just take us to our rooms? We'll need two. My wife and I would like one for ourselves. The other, for our daughter and her au pair."

"Sure. Absolutely," Nicole said. "We have the perfect spot for you: two adjoining rooms that you could—"

"We don't want adjoining. We want separate rooms," he said.

"Mark's a light sleeper," Charlotte explained, inclining her head toward her husband.

He rolled his eyes. "I'm not a light sleeper, Charlotte. I just prefer not to be woken up by cries or someone screaming for a cup of water or that they have to pee in the middle of the night."

"Yes, I see." Nicole nodded. This family was going to be a handful. "We can do that. Separate rooms, it is." Nicole turned and gestured to the stairs. "Please follow me."

CHAPTER 13

Nicole showed Mark and Charlotte to their room first. The entire time, Mark typed on his cell, barely looking up from the device as they walked and Harper danced down the corridor, swinging hands with Elena, and singing some Disney tune.

"And this is your room," Nicole said, opening the door, revealing a light-filled bedroom. "I hope the size and accommodations work for you. If it does, we'll have someone bring your bags upstairs to the r-..."

Her words drifted off when Mark squeezed through the doorway past her and inside the guest room. He beelined to the en-suite bathroom and slammed the door shut behind him, making his wife wince. They could hear his muffled voice on the other side of the door, mostly laments about a bad investment and shouts to sell another stock short.

"Uh, the room is fine," Charlotte said, looking a little embarrassed by her husband's behavior. "Thank you so much, Nicole."

"I wanna sleep with you, Mommy," Harper whined, tugging at her mother's skirt.

"Aww, sweetheart." Charlotte bent down and ran her fingers through her daughter's platinum blond curls. "I want you in here with us, too, but Daddy and I think it's best for you to sleep in your own room."

"But why?" she cried, her face going red again.

"Well, because . . ." Charlotte seemed to think for a bit. "Because Mommy and Daddy stay up very late. We don't want to interrupt your beauty sleep."

"Don't worry about it, kid," Elena said, rubbing Harper's shoulders, "we'll have a good time. Drink milk, eat cookies, and watch *Toy Story* for the five hundredth time."

"And it's a *really* nice room," Nicole assured the little girl, leaning down to her eye level. "It has big bay windows that face the garden and two double beds with fluffy sheets and lots of pillows."

"Perfect for a pillow fight, huh?" Elena interjected.

Harper gave an exaggerated pout but, to Nicole's surprise, didn't have another tantrum. She lowered her head and nodded.

"Awesomesauce! So, give your mommy a quick hug so we can go see our new digs, *niña*," Elena said, nudging her.

Harper dragged her feet as she walked toward her mother, but she wrapped her arms around Charlotte's waist and hugged her nevertheless.

"Let's go!" Harper shouted a few seconds later, before turning away from her mother and charging out of the bedroom.

"Wait! You don't even know where we're going, kid!" Elena called as she ran out the door after the toddler, muttering to herself in Spanish.

Nicole marveled at how quickly the toddler's emotions could shift.

I'm glad I'm an assistant and not an au pair, she thought. *It looks exhausting.*

She couldn't imagine Xander having children; working for him was mentally and emotionally taxing enough.

Nicole turned to follow Harper and Elena but stopped short when she felt a hand clamp tightly around her arm. She looked down to see that it was Charlotte's hand.

"Is Xander here?" Charlotte whispered. "We've been trying to reach him, and he hasn't answered any of our phone calls or texts."

He hasn't responded to mine, either, Nicole thought.

"He's not here yet, but—"

"Shhhh!" Charlotte urged, bringing a finger to her lips. Her grip tightened. The nails were almost digging into Nicole's skin. Charlotte glanced at the closed bathroom door where her husband was still on the other side, then returned her attention to Nicole. "Softer. Speak softer."

Nicole's frown deepened. What was with all the subterfuge?

"No, he isn't here," she whispered back. "Not yet, anyway, but he should be here shortly." She hoped she was right.

Charlotte loosened her hold. She bit down on her bottom lip. "Well, please tell him that I . . . I mean, *we* need to speak with him right away."

Nicole nodded though she wondered why Charlotte was so desperate to speak with Xander. What had he done now?

"Of course, Mrs. Danfrey."

The bathroom door suddenly swung open, filling the bedroom with the sound of a flushing toilet. Charlotte let go of her. The other woman's ditzy smile was back as Mark raised his zipper and looked around the bedroom.

"Where's Harper?" he asked before tossing his cell onto the bed.

"She's headed to her room with Elena. Nicole here was just about to show them the way there," she said. "Weren't you, Nicole?"

"Uh, yes. Yes, I was," Nicole said as she backed toward the door. "Again, let me know if you need anything."

She then turned and left.

When she found Harper and Elena, Elena was sitting cross-legged on the floor while Harper twirled in circles.

"Sorry. Didn't mean to keep you guys waiting," Nicole said.

Elena casually waved her hand before climbing to her feet. "It's fine. She was entertaining herself anyway." She tugged her purse strap onto her shoulder. "Harper, time to head to our room."

"Yay!" Harper cried mid-spin. She then grabbed Elena's hand.

The young woman laughed and gestured to Nicole. "Lead the way."

Their bedroom was three rooms down from Mark and Charlotte, which Nicole assumed was Mark's preference. Nicole opened the door and Harper immediately galloped inside, all while whinnying like a pony. She climbed onto one of the double beds and started to bounce up and down.

"Jump with me, Elly!" she yelled. "It's fun!"

"Maybe later, kid," Elena said.

"It seems like she likes the room. Does it work for the both of you guys, though?" Nicole asked.

"Come on. Does it really matter what I think?" Elena replied with raised brows. She shrugged. "It's fine. The two beds are nice but, to be honest, she'll probably end up climbing in bed beside me. Harper hates sleeping by herself," Elena confessed as they observed Harper giggling and bouncing on the mattress, reaching her tiny fingers for the crystal chandelier overhead. "She can be super clingy during the day. It only gets worse at night."

"Man," Nicole grimaced, "I do not envy you. All this . . . can't be easy."

"Eh, no harder than what you have to do, I bet."

They locked eyes again.

Oh, she is good at this, Nicole thought with awe. *Unnervingly good.*

Not only was Elena an amazing au pair, but she was also a believable one, which is exactly why Nicole had hired her. You'd think Elena was some trained actress or CIA agent rather than a part-time college student looking for an easy way to pay for her tuition by taking on an "unconventional" nannying job—a position that had come open after yet another one of the Danfreys' au pairs had quit. Nicole's instincts about Elena had been correct.

"Yeah, we all have our parts to play, I guess," Nicole murmured, ignoring that pesky knot forming in the pit of her stomach.

What if Xander pulls a no-show? Then none of this works.

No, a voice in her head replied. *He's going to show. He has to show. It's his party.*

"You're right." Elena tilted her head and crossed her arms over her chest. "And this is my part. It could be worse, you know. I could be working behind a fast-food counter right now or at some gas station on the night shift in my old neighborhood. Instead, I'm staying in a place like this," she said looking around the room. "And I'm getting paid *a lot* of money to babysit one kid, and when I'm not doing that," she leaned toward Nicole and dropped her voice to a whisper, "to disappear into the background like furniture and keep my eyes and ears open." She stepped back and winked. "Seems like a good deal to me."

"Well, let me know if you need anything. This party weekend is going to be hectic, but I'm not far. Just two doors down from her parents' room."

"Don't worry. I'll reach out if I need you," Elena said, returning her attention to Harper.

Nicole lingered a few seconds longer, then left the room, hearing the echoing trail of Harper's giggles.

CHAPTER 14

"Umm, Ms. Underwood?"

Nicole looked up. "Yes?"

She'd been sitting on the sofa, trying to untangle a giant ball of charging cords for the past fifteen minutes. She'd asked one of the waitstaff to do it since a few guests had requested spare chargers. Later she found said ball abandoned in one of the sitting rooms. She supposed if you wanted things done right, you had to do it yourself. But now Nicole was being interrupted by yet another of the mansion staffers. The young woman stared down at her, looking very pale and very panicked.

"We have a problem, ma'am."

Nicole set down the bundle of cords. "OK," she uttered slowly, "what's the problem?"

The more operative question was: *What's the problem* this *time?*

She'd put out quite a few fires today, including a literal fire in the downstairs kitchen that required one of the fire extinguishers. The fire destroyed a day's worth of catering prep work for the party and filled the first floor with smoke. They'd been trying to get rid of the smell for hours.

"Anna Quinton," the young woman now said. "She's here, and she's not happy."

Anna Quinton. Bridget's big sister and one of the founders of Altruist, although she'd stepped down from her position of COO and accepted a buyout of most of her stock five years ago—right before Nicole joined the company. Bridget would stay on at Altruist and end up on the cover of *Forbes* magazine and be named one of *TIME*'s Most Influential Women of that year. She earned being on a first-name basis with Oprah Winfrey, Hillary Clinton, and Jeff Bezos and got a dinner invite from Ivanka Trump that she politely declined.

Meanwhile Anna had gracefully accepted early retirement and chose to spend her days split between her apartment on the Upper East Side and on the sunny beaches of Florida, living off her millions from her sale of her stocks and accumulating a series of boy toys.

So, she's arrived too, Nicole thought. Yet another guest had made it to Maple Grove for the birthday bash before the birthday boy.

Nicole nodded at the staffer and quickly climbed to her feet. "I've got it. Where is she?"

A few minutes later, Nicole jogged into the great hall and then into one of the sitting rooms to find Anna pacing and spinning in circles, talking furiously into her cell phone while shoving her fingers into her hair.

It was auburn now. At Bridget's memorial service, she'd been brunette. Six months before that she'd been sun-kissed blond.

"Xander, pick up! Pick up, dammit! I don't know what's going on," she lamented before pressing a button on-screen and glowering down at her cell. She turned to look at someone else. "Xander isn't answering my phone calls, and everyone here is completely useless."

Nicole walked farther into the room and saw who Anna was complaining to. When she did, she paused. She should've known he'd be here, but her pulse quickened nevertheless.

On the other side of the sitting room, in a pair of blue jeans and a powder blue dress shirt open at the collar, was Anna's new boyfriend, Jeremiah. He was nearly half Anna's age and had the face of an Adonis. A face Nicole had been trying to forget for the past few months.

He sat in one of the lounge chairs, staring into the distance with an air of disinterest while drumming his fingers on one of the many luggage cases stacked next to him as Anna continued to freak out.

Anna had started dating Jeremiah only recently, around six months after she'd dumped the last boy toy when she'd discovered he'd been stealing her jewelry and buying gifts for other women with her AmEx card. At least according to what Bridget had told Nicole. The previous one was long-limbed, dark-haired, olive-toned, athletic, and unnervingly attractive—a lot like Jeremiah. Which is why Nicole had chosen him.

When Jeremiah spotted Nicole, his dark eyes brightened with surprise then recognition. She had expected him to be here, but he obviously hadn't expected her to be.

He sat upright in his chair and stopped drumming his fingers. A small flirtatious smile crept to his lips, making her cheeks warm and her eyes dart away.

"Nicole! Ah, there you are!" Anna cried after looking up from her phone. Anna's green silk caftan billowed around her like a bedsheet as she strode toward the young woman. "I heard Xander isn't here yet. You'll have to help me then."

Nicole tried her best to look solemn and pretend as if whatever Anna was about to say was of the utmost importance. She nodded. "I'll try my best, Ms. Quinton."

"Good! Because we have a minor catastrophe on our hands."

As if to demonstrate the sentiment, she grabbed Nicole's hands and held them tightly within her own. Anna's hazel eyes were wide. Her tan face was trying to do its best expression of earnestness, but it struggled against her frequent Botox treatments.

"I went to my room . . . the very room where I've stayed every time I've visited Maple Grove since my dearly departed sister purchased this home and I . . . and I . . ." She paused dramatically as if struggling to find the right words. "I saw that someone else is staying in my room, Nicole. *My room.* Their things were everywhere. How could this happen? I mean, where am I supposed to stay? In the butler's pantry? In the greenhouse?"

Nicole had braced herself for this reaction from Anna.

She'd put the Danfreys in Anna's usual guest room—and not the room she'd originally planned—because Mark wanted to be nowhere near his own daughter. And because it was one of the few bedrooms in the mansion that were bugged with audio surveillance devices. Now she would have to do some fast-talking to explain the change in accommodations without upsetting Xander's aunt any further than the drama queen already was.

"I know, and I am so, *so* sorry, Ms. Quinton, for the unexpected change. Yes, we do have another room prepared for you."

"But why can't I have *that* room? I *always* stay there; it is *my room*," Anna insisted.

"I know, but we had to think fast and put Mark Danfrey and his wife there."

"Mark Danfrey? You mean Xander's frat buddy?"

"Yes, exactly. They wanted the room for medical reasons. His wife, Charlotte, needed a room closer to the main stairs."

"*Near the main stairs?*" Anna repeated vaguely. She let go of Nicole's hands. This time, despite the Botox, she did manage a frown. "Well, what medical reason would require her to—"

"Unfortunately, I cannot share that highly personal information, and frankly, it's complicated. But I knew of all the guests I could ask to change rooms to accommodate a guest in need, *you* would be the most reasonable and sympathetic, Ms. Quinton," Nicole whispered, leaning toward Anna.

"That . . . that makes sense," Anna said, her frown softening.

"We have another room . . . the family *suite*, waiting for you to use however you wish. Double the square footage."

"The family suite? Well, it does have better views," Anna said. "I suppose if the move was for a good reason and it's been aired out, too? It isn't stale, I hope. I absolutely hate stale air, Nicole. It dries out my skin."

"Yes, Ms. Quinton, it's been aired out, and cleaned from top to bottom."

Anna sighed, making her thin shoulders slump beneath her caftan. "Fine. Show us to the suite." She turned toward her companion. "Jerry, honey, we're heading upstairs now."

"Everything's fixed?" he asked, rising to his feet.

"Yes, it looks like they have a room for us. We don't have to set up a tent on the front lawn after all."

"Cool." He grabbed one of the bags and threw the strap over his shoulder. He strolled toward them.

"I suppose I should do introductions since Jerry will be staying here as well," Anna said. "Jeremiah, this is Nicole Underwood, my nephew Xander's assistant. If you need anything, just ask her. Nicole practically runs this place."

"At least for the next few days until the festivities are done," Nicole said.

"Your name's Nicole?" he asked.

"Yes, Nicole," she repeated.

"Right." He nodded slowly. "Well, pleased to meet you, Nicole." He held out his hand for her to shake.

"Pleased to meet you, too," she murmured, and their gazes locked as they shook hands.

When they touched, Nicole instantly felt an achingly familiar charge shoot up her arm and her cheeks flame with heat. Her breath caught in her throat, and she quickly let go of Jeremiah's hand.

"Uh, you can leave your bags here, and we'll have someone take them upstairs. Let me show you to your room," she said.

CHAPTER 15

"You were right, Nicole. There is lots of light." Anna nodded appreciatively less than a minute later as she wandered through the bedrooms. "And more than enough space." She tapped her index finger on her chin. "I think . . . I think this will work."

The young man had been slumped against one of the bedroom walls, observing Anna as she inspected the rooms. Nicole had been keenly aware of his presence the whole time—could practically smell his cologne—and had been trying to ignore him. She watched now as he pushed himself away from the wall and walked toward Anna.

"See? Problem solved, babe," he said. "I'll be back in a sec. I've got to grab something I left in the car. Do you need me to get you anything?"

Anna rose to the balls of her feet. "No, darling, but thank you for always being so helpful." She toyed with one of the buttons on his shirt, then gave him a kiss.

"Of course," he whispered, kissing her back.

Nicole turned and quietly stepped out the door. She began to walk down the corridor to return to detangling cords, but she stopped short when she heard, "Hey, Nicole, wait up!"

Her heart jumped into her throat at the sound of his voice. She gazed over her shoulder to find Jeremiah jogging toward her. She took a deep breath. "Yes, how may I help you, sir?"

"*Sir?*" he repeated and chuckled. "Really? We're gonna be that formal?"

The smell of his cologne was overwhelming. It was a spicy musk. Warm and tantalizing. She could feel his body heat, too. She instinctively took a step back.

"How may I help you, Jeremiah?" She raised her brows. "There. Is that better?"

"It's a start," he said, dropping his voice to a whisper that sent her heartbeat into overdrive. "So, this is where you work?" He looked around him. "I didn't know you were her nephew's assistant. I didn't know your name was Nicole, either. You told me it was Lisa."

What the hell was he doing? Why was he talking about this now? *Don't break character, Jeremiah.*

"I'm sorry but I don't know what you're talking about." Her robotic smile didn't budge. "I think you've confused me with someone else."

He shook his head. "No, I don't think so."

"Jerry!" Anna called, interrupting their conversation. "Jerry, darling!"

Nicole peered over his shoulder to see Anna poking her head out the doorway.

"What's up, babe?" he asked as he turned around with a lazy grin.

Nicole almost sighed with relief. He was back to being the boy toy.

"While you're downstairs, can you grab my La Mer hand cream? I may have left it in the glove compartment," Anna said while twisting her hair into a bun at the nape of her neck. She then snapped her fingers.

"Oh, and Nicole, I'd like a sparkling water with a slice of lemon, please. Can you have it waiting for me when I get out of the shower?"

He faced Nicole again. "Did you catch that?"

She nodded. "Yes, I did. And I'll have it brought to your room right away, ma'am," she said, turning and fleeing before Jeremiah could ask her anything else.

CHAPTER 16

Nicole blew air through her inflated cheeks and flexed her sore shoulders when she reached the top of the staircase. It was almost midnight. All the guests were either asleep or in their rooms for the night. It had been yet another long and exhausting day, as mentally and emotionally challenging as it was physically.

"You were counting down the days. You've gotta be counting down the hours now, huh?" her mom had asked just last week.

You have no idea, Mom. Nicole just wanted to collapse into bed.

But she paused and frowned when she saw what looked like a dim light shining beneath the double doors near the center of the hall. The light was coming from Xander's bedroom.

She walked swiftly toward it, feeling her first wave of relief all day.

Xander had finally arrived for the birthday weekend. Not in enough time to host the big welcome dinner that she'd been forced to downgrade when most of the guests decided to skip it, but in enough time for the actual birthday party tomorrow.

Thank God. Better late than never, Nicole thought as she neared the double doors. She could go over tomorrow's schedule with him and flesh out a few details if he wasn't too exhausted and willing to humor her.

"Xander," she called out before knocking. "Xander!"

No one answered but Nicole could hear shuffling on the other side of the door. Someone was clearly walking around in there.

Nicole tried the handle and eased the door open, holding her hand in front of her eyes just in case he was in the shower or in some state of undress.

She'd already seen his penis in digital format; Nicole was not eager to see it live.

"Xander," Nicole said as she stepped inside his bedroom, "sorry to barge in. I knocked but you didn't answer."

She peeked between her fingers and saw Charlotte—not Xander—standing in the center of the bedroom, catching Nicole off guard. Nicole quickly lowered her hand.

The other woman was in her robe and silk PJs and holding a coffee mug.

"Charlotte . . . I mean, Mrs. Danfrey, I-I didn't know that . . . I thought it was . . ." Her words drifted off.

"No," Charlotte said, holding up her hand and stepping away from the bed, "my apologies. I was thirsty, so I got some tea downstairs. I was heading back to my room and saw a light on and the door open. I thought I heard Xander in his bedroom and came by to . . . to say hi." She smiled awkwardly. Her cheeks went pink. "And to . . . well, to speak with him."

"I'm sorry but he's still not here yet. Is there anything I can do to help you?" Nicole asked.

Charlotte loudly cleared her throat, then shook her head. "No. No, I . . . uh, I should get back to my room. Mark is probably wondering what's taking me so long," she whispered then rushed past Nicole. "Good night," she called over her shoulder before walking into the hall.

Nicole listened to Charlotte's receding footsteps. She then gazed around the room.

It was the second-largest bedroom in the mansion—nearly two hundred square feet smaller than Bridget's old room, which has been untouched since the crash. Xander's room was decorated in simple Japanese-style furniture with a fireplace and massive wall panels that when pressed revealed hidden drawers and cubbies.

Nothing looked out of place in his room. No drawers were open. The door to his walk-in closet and the bathroom door were still closed. The only thing different was an indentation on the comforter of Xander's low-profile bed. It looked as if Charlotte had been sitting there.

"Made herself comfortable, huh?" Nicole murmured.

Had the door been left open and a light on, like Charlotte said? Nicole found that hard to believe.

Xander always kept his bedroom door locked when he wasn't at Maple Grove. Only Nicole, Xander, and the housekeeper had a copy of the key to his room. But maybe that wasn't true. Had Xander also given Charlotte a key?

Nicole had heard that while Xander, Charlotte, and Mark were all attending the University of Pennsylvania, Xander had been the first one to ask out the cute Charlotte Kaminski. They had briefly dated before she moved on to his fraternity brother Mark. Nicole had also heard a few whispers that Charlotte and Xander had carried on an affair after she and Mark got married, but Nicole had dismissed it as malicious gossip.

Xander and Charlotte always acted cordial around each other, and Nicole had never seen signs of anything more than that. No stolen kisses. No lingering looks. And Mark seemed like the territorial, domineering type. Surely, there was no way they could carry on an affair under his nose without him knowing.

But now Nicole wondered if maybe they had done it. Maybe all those naughty rumors were true.

Through the opened curtains, Nicole could see the windows of the other bedrooms and wrought iron balconies on the other side of the courtyard and garden. The lights inside some of the bedrooms still burned bright. In one, she spotted Mark Danfrey. Despite the late hour, he was talking on his cell phone, pacing in front of a desk where a laptop sat open. He stopped pacing and glanced over his shoulder. Within seconds, Nicole could see Charlotte stroll toward him with her coffee mug in hand. His wife smiled and kissed his cheek.

They looked like a contented couple, but Nicole suspected it was a false image and Charlotte Danfrey was no longer doing a good job of hiding it.

Nicole turned off the overhead lights, stepped back into the hall, and closed the double doors behind her.

CHAPTER 17

A minute later, Nicole shoved open her own bedroom door.

She couldn't believe the party was mere hours away. She'd thought the event would give her a chance to pull off her grand plan, to cross the finish line she'd been running toward since Bridget's car careened off that road back in February.

All the right players were supposed to be at the bash. The circumstances had seemed right on paper, but in real life, things were getting unwieldy. She could sense the odds beginning to stack against her.

She wasn't sure if it was paranoia, but she was starting to suspect that Daniel wasn't as clueless as she thought. Did he know what she was doing? Had he figured out her plans? What had clued him in? Had the housekeeper she hired to monitor him at his home tripped up and revealed something? Add to that the fact that Xander still had not arrived yet, although he was supposed to be here today. Nicole had texted him no less than a dozen times and he hadn't responded to any of them.

As Nicole pushed open the door, she looked down to find a folded note waiting for her on the hardwood floor. She frowned, bent down, and flipped it open.

> I've still got questions. I said I would only do this if we were both on the up and up. What else haven't you told me, Lisa/Nicole?

"Jeremiah," she whispered before shutting her door, ripping the note into little pieces, and tossing them into a nearby trash can.

Her mind replayed a series of images from their drunken one-night stand at a hotel in SoHo a few months back. Her skin tingled at the memory, but she pushed those images and sensations aside, shuttering them into a mental closet and latching the door closed so she could return to the bigger issue at hand.

Jeremiah was another factor... another person who wasn't behaving how she'd thought he would. She didn't know why he was so irritated with her. She guessed that con artists didn't mind lying, but they hated it when you did it to them.

Should she pull him aside? Maybe she could explain to him why she lied and gave him a fake name.

No, Nicole thought, shaking her head, remembering how her heart raced by simply being around him.

It was better to keep her distance this weekend. That way she could focus on her job, while he focused on his.

Nicole kicked off her shoes and padded barefoot to her bed. Just then, she heard a buzz. It sounded muffled, which meant it was the phone she had hidden under her underwear in one of her dresser drawers. They were only supposed to call her in case of emergencies. What could have possibly happened now?

She stomped across the room and yanked the drawer open. She then stared down at the screen.

Day 1. The stage should be set, the text said. **Can we proceed as planned?**

Nicole hesitated.

She should tell them what was happening, that things were starting to look shaky. She'd tried her best. It wasn't her fault if this didn't work out.

But then Nicole remembered two weeks before the accident in February, how Bridget had called her to her brownstone on Central Park South for a late-night, impromptu meeting.

"I've discovered something, Nicole," Bridget had confessed while sitting down on the sofa facing her. "Something I hadn't expected. That I still can't believe."

Bridget was usually so refined and composed. Like a magazine cover. But that night she'd been wearing her silk robe, and her hair was pulled back into a messy bun. She had on not an ounce of makeup. Her feet were bare, and her face was grim.

"What is it, Bridge?" Nicole had asked, distraught by the older woman's bleak tone and look in her eyes. It had scared Nicole to see her idol that way.

"It's something very important," Bridget had explained. "Something that I'm . . . I'm going to need your help."

She'd listened to Bridget's story and, at the end, made a promise.

But Bridget was gone now. Should Nicole still feel obligated to keep that promise?

Yes, we can proceed, Nicole typed.

She then tossed the phone back into her drawer and slammed it shut. She walked back to her bed, spread her arms, and landed face down on the duvet. She closed her eyes and waited for the wave of sleep to wash over her.

Better to conserve her strength because she would have to put on yet another performance tomorrow.

CHAPTER 18

NICOLE RUSHED DOWN THE CORRIDOR AFTER CHECKING OFF YET another to-do item on her party prep list.

She'd barely slept a wink, tossing and turning in bed most of the night. She had way too much coffee that morning, and eaten only half a croissant. She was wired and filled with so much nervous energy that she could probably break a four-by-four in half with one chop.

As she turned the corner and neared the stairs, she swore she could feel the minutes ticking by, drawing closer and closer to the party. She'd stopped by Xander's room that morning, hopeful that he'd arrived in the middle of the night or the wee hours of dawn. But she'd found the suite empty.

She now paused at the top of the stairs when she felt a buzz on her hip. It was her cell. She frantically dug it out of her shorts pocket to check to see if Xander had left a voicemail or replied to one of her texts. Something to explain why he was so delayed. Instead she saw an alert that she'd sent to herself last night.

Check in with Elena.

Her shoulders fell. She'd completely forgotten that she'd decided to stop by Elena and Harper's suite to ask Elena if she knew what was going on with Charlotte Danfrey. Especially after that episode in Xander's bedroom last night. But then again, that was the point of the reminder.

Nicole sighed, turned around, and headed back where she came. She knocked on the au pair's bedroom door.

"*Elena?* Are you there?" she asked before trying the knob then pushing the door open. All the lights were out. Elena and Harper were nowhere in sight.

She started to ease the door closed just when she heard someone ask behind her, "What are you doing?"

Nicole whipped around to find Mark Danfrey frowning down at her.

"I was . . . umm . . . looking for Elena."

His frown deepened. "Why do you need to talk to my au pair? What's wrong?"

"Nothing, Mr. Danfrey! Nothing at all," she said, regaining her bearings. "Elena mentioned yesterday that sometimes Harper likes a midmorning snack, but I realized that she hadn't mentioned what snacks Harper prefers so that I can let our chef know. *Does* Harper have a preference, sir?"

He shook his head and tightened the belt of his terry-cloth robe. "I don't think she needs a snack today. Besides, if she gets hungry, Elena will just give her a banana, some grapes, or whatever is by the pool. That's where they are now. I heard you guys have a whole buffet down there."

"Indeed, we do. And will you be joining them?" Nicole asked, gesturing to the bathrobe and flip-flops he was wearing.

If that was the case, she'd talk to Elena later.

"No, I'm headed to the sauna. I . . . uh . . . don't swim."

"Really? I'm not much of a swimmer either. I barely know how to dog paddle." She laughed.

"Being able to swim isn't some great feat. It's pointless cardio. A waste of time."

Pointless cardio? What an odd way to describe the act of swimming, Nicole thought, making her wonder if the real reason a guy like

Mark didn't swim was because he refused to admit he couldn't swim.

"Well, enjoy the sauna," she said. "I guess . . . I guess I'll be on my way downstairs to the pool then."

"All right," he said, cocking an eyebrow at her as she stepped around him and walked back to the stairs.

A couple of minutes later, Nicole stepped through the sliding glass doors leading to their pool area. More than a dozen guests were lounging around the pale blue water in chairs or seeking refuge from the sun in blue and white cabanas. A few were swimming in the water.

Some of the waitstaff handed out drinks while others manned a small bar area where they served fresh fruit and party-themed hors d'oeuvres.

She spotted Harper and Elena near the shallow end of the infinity pool. Harper was wearing pink floaties and goggles, lying on her back in the water while Elena held her up, keeping the little girl's head above water.

Nicole started to walk toward them when Anna raised her hand in greeting and called out to her. "Nicole! Hey! Over here."

Nicole pursed her lips in frustration. She stopped mid-stride, turned, and walked back to Anna. "Good morning, Ms. Quinton. Enjoying the sun, I see. Planning to hop into the pool?"

The older woman tilted back her wide-brimmed hat. She was wearing another one of her caftans. This one was jade green. Nicole supposed she had a bathing suit underneath.

"Oh, I'm not planning to swim today. Just enjoying the view," she said with a smile before lowering her Chanel sunglasses down the bridge of her nose and staring in front of her.

Nicole followed her gaze to find Jeremiah doing laps up and down the pool.

"Lovely, isn't it?" Anna said with a chuckle, making Nicole clear her throat.

"Can I help you with anything, Ms. Quinton?" she asked.

The woman could admire Jeremiah all day for all Nicole cared, because Nicole had other things she needed to accomplish.

"Actually, I was wondering where my nephew is," she said. "I've been looking around for him but haven't been able to track him down all morning. I had something I wanted to talk to him about before the party."

"I'm sorry. I don't think he's here yet," Nicole said.

"*What?*" Anna cried, ripping off her sunglasses and sitting upright. "But his party is tonight. How could he not be here? He has to come."

"He'll be here. He's still on his way," Nicole assured feebly. *Or at least I hope he is.*

In the corner of her eye, she saw Jeremiah had finished his laps. She tried her best to ignore him even as what he did next seemed to happen in slow motion.

Jeremiah grabbed the pool ledge, pushed himself out of the water, and climbed to his feet. He shook out his dark hair and he pinched the bridge of his nose. Water glistened off his tanned skin in the sunlight and dripped from sinewy muscle and long limbs, which were on full display thanks to his tight, square-cut swim shorts, as he strolled back to where Anna was lounging.

Anna had been right; it was quite the view. One worth salivating over. Nicole noticed several women and one or two guys eyeing or outright gawking at Jeremiah as he walked by.

He paused when he drew near them, and Nicole gave him the most nonchalant expression she could muster.

"Hey," he said, gesturing to Nicole, "could you toss me that towel there?" He pointed down to one neatly folded on the pool chair beside Anna.

The towel that's sitting literally right in front of you?

Nicole hesitated then nodded. "Uh, sure. Of course." She forced a smile and leaned down to retrieve the striped beach towel. She handed it to him.

"Awesome," he said before wiping off his face and chest. "Thanks, Lisa."

Nicole's smile withered. She went stock-still while Anna put on her sunglasses again and laughed.

"Her name is *Nicole*, Jerry," Anna said. "Remember, honey?"

"Oh, right!" he said with a sly grin, still wiping himself down. "My mistake. Thanks, Nicole."

Nicole gritted her teeth. "It's fine. Please excuse me," she said, beelining to the other side of the pool where Elena was wrapping a towel around Harper. She excused her way through a few people before finally catching up with the au pair and her charge just as they stepped back inside through the sliding glass door.

"Elena, hey! Wait up!"

The young woman paused on the marble tile and turned around to face her. "Hi, Nicole."

"I was wondering," Nicole said, dropping her voice to a whisper, "if I could talk to you. I wanted to ask you something."

Elena gradually nodded. "Sure. What do you need?"

Nicole noticed Harper standing between them. She was holding Elena's hand and gazing up at Nicole curiously.

She didn't know a lot about children, but she knew they heard and understood more than you would think. Maybe it wasn't a good idea to have this conversation in front of Harper, but she couldn't very well ask the three-year-old to leave the room.

"Hey, Harper," she said, leaning down to gaze at her, "would you like a strawberry-flavored slushie?"

"What's that?" Harper asked. She tugged her thumb out of her mouth, looking wary.

"You've never heard of a slushie? Well, it's a flavored drink made with ice. It's very yummy and refreshing, especially on a warm day like today. Would you like one?"

Harper seemed to consider her question for a few seconds then nodded. "OK," she chirped.

Ten minutes later, Harper knelt on a stool in the deserted bar prep area behind the pool, enraptured as she watched the red ice churn around and around.

"Look, Elly!" she squealed over the loud humming sound, pointing at the machine.

"Yeah, I see!" Elena shouted back from the other side of the enclosed area, before facing Nicole again. "Umm, isn't that a daiquiri maker?"

"Don't worry," Nicole said with a wave of the hand. "There's no alcohol in there." She eased closer to Elena and dropped her voice back to a whisper. "So, I wanted to ask you if you'd noticed anything unusual with Charlotte."

Elena adjusted the towel around her waist. "What do you mean by 'unusual'?"

"She said yesterday that she really needed to talk to my boss, Xander. And then I found her hanging out in his bedroom around midnight. She said she was looking for him. Whatever she had to say to him, it seemed really important. Do you know what it is?"

Elena shook her head. "No idea, but . . ." She paused.

"But what?"

"I noticed that she and Mr. D have been fighting more than usual lately."

"Fighting about what?"

"If it's not about Harper or the money Mrs. D spends, then it's about work. They had this big blowup just last week about how he's never home and always working. How she feels lonely. I heard it through the bedroom walls. He said he had to work so hard to pay for her expensive clothes, her trainer, and the new house they're building in Connecticut. It got really intense."

Nicole remembered how Mark had constantly been on the phone yesterday. He'd even taken a phone call in the bathroom. But Mark Danfrey was in investments. Men like him were always working deals, even on supposed vacations.

"But you haven't noticed anything else? Neither of them mentioned anything about Xander?" Nicole asked.

Like her having an affair with Xander or conspiring with him to commit a murder.

"Outside of talking about the party tonight?" Elena shook her head again. "Not as far as I can tell."

The loud humming sound stopped. Harper hopped off the stool and ran toward them.

"It's ready, Elena! It's ready! Can I have my slushie now?" she asked, shoving between the two women and hopping up and down on her bare feet.

"Sure, *niña*. Maybe I'll even have one, too." She placed her hands over Harper's ears and leaned toward Nicole. "But put a splash of tequila in mine, please. This is gonna be a long day, and I think I might need it."

Nicole nodded. "Me too."

CHAPTER 19

"Nicole!"

"Nicole, there you are!"

Nicole stopped in the middle of the foyer and whipped her head from left to right, unsure where to look.

It had been like that all day, feeling as if she was being pulled in a million different directions as the hour of the birthday party drew closer.

She saw Daniel strolling down the staircase and Anna sauntering toward her down the corridor. Both were trying to get her attention, but when they spotted each other, they paused simultaneously.

"Good morning, Anna," Daniel said, dipping his head slightly in greeting.

"Daniel," Anna replied with a pinched smile.

Nicole glanced between the two.

She'd always noticed a palpable tension between Daniel and Anna whenever they were in each other's company. Nicole wondered if it was because Anna found Daniel as annoying as she did. Or maybe it was because he'd been promoted into Anna's position as COO at Altruist after she left the company. Except Anna had resigned from Altruist voluntarily, from what Nicole had been told. The company had booked a posh restaurant in New York for Anna's retirement party. Several who were in attendance—including Daniel—gave heartfelt speeches about how much of a joy it had been to work with her.

And Anna had been eager to step down as COO and move on to the next stage in her life—at least that's what Bridget had told Nicole.

"If I wasn't such a workaholic, I would've retired like my sister," Bridget remarked once. "Spending my days sunning on a beach with white sands and turquoise blue water and sipping margaritas would be amazing."

"I see you were looking for Nicole as well," Daniel now said as he stepped off the last stair onto the Italian marble of the foyer. "Was it to ask about our host? I thought maybe Xander had finally arrived. I have a few questions for him."

"No, actually, I was going to ask what the dining arrangements are for tonight," Anna said. "Will we be provided dinner prior to the party? If not, then do we have to fend for ourselves if the party tonight is canceled because the darling birthday boy doesn't show up again?"

Nicole opened her mouth to answer, but Daniel spoke instead. "I wouldn't worry. I'm sure Xander will be here soon, Anna."

"*Wouldn't worry?* Are we talking about the same Xander Chambers?" Anna barked out a laugh. "Why do you assume he'll be here in time?"

"Well . . . it is his birthday celebration," Daniel answered limply.

"Yes, it is. And he is nowhere in sight. Is he responding to your calls? Your texts? Because he hasn't responded to any of mine."

"No," Daniel said with a slow shake of the head and a patronizing smile, "but—"

"So, although you mean well," Anna interrupted, tossing her long auburn hair over her shoulders, "your assurances regarding Xander mean nothing."

Daniel's smile evaporated. His face reddened.

"We will provide dinner no matter what, upon request," Nicole interjected, hoping to head off any further disagreement or growing hostility between the two. "I can even have dinner sent up to your room, if you wish, Ms. Quinton. Say at 6:30?" She turned to Daniel. "I can do the same for you, Mr. Miller, if you'd like."

Daniel shook his head. "No need. I have plans at 6:30. I'm meeting someone for drinks before the party."

"Oh, will they also be coming as a guest tonight?" Nicole asked. "I'd be happy to add them to the list."

"No, he won't be coming to the party. Edward would find it too awkward," he said looking pointedly at Anna. "See you tonight, ladies."

Awkward? Why, Nicole thought, eyeing him as he walked back upstairs.

"Edward, as in my ex-husband Edward. That must be who he's meeting for drinks tonight," Anna said as Daniel reached the top of the staircase and disappeared into the upstairs hallway.

"Oh," Nicole replied, unsure of what else to say.

"They remained golf buddies after our divorce, which almost bankrupted me until I got my stock parachute. Daniel got the COO position thanks to my sister *and* he has my husband's friendship. Now I have neither. Hmph," Anna grunted before turning on her heels and striding back down the corridor.

Nicole stared after Anna, wondering if maybe Anna's departure from Altruist truly was as amicable as she thought.

CHAPTER 20

"Ms. Underwood?" a voice called faintly through the closed bedroom door.

"Yes?" Nicole called back as she rushed across the room, grabbed her earrings, and adjusted the spaghetti straps of her silk gown. She paused and grimaced at her reflection.

The dress looked different now in her bedroom mirror than it had on the rack at Saks. She looked like she was wearing a floor-length negligee rather than the casual, chic dress she had been shooting for tonight. Nicole hooked her teardrop earrings into her earlobes, sighed, and shrugged in defeat.

Nothing I can do about it now.

This was the dress she'd bought for the party. The only entirely white outfit she had in her wardrobe.

The show must go on, Nicole thought before she turned away from her mirror. She walked toward her bed and sat down. She raised the dress's hem so that she could step into her high heels.

"Yes? You can come in," she repeated while lacing the straps around her ankles.

The door opened, revealing a young woman dressed in black vest and knee-length skirt. "The party guests are starting to arrive, Ms. Underwood. You told me to let you know."

Nicole had figured as much. Through her window, she could see the headlights of the many cars coming up the driveway. She could hear the music now blasting in the tent several yards away from the mansion.

"Yes, thank you. I'm about to head down there," she said, rising to her feet.

The young woman nodded and began to close the door but stopped when Nicole shouted, "Wait! Is Mr. Chambers here yet? Do you know?"

The young woman shook her head, making her ponytail swing like a pom-pom behind her. "I don't think so."

Nicole grimaced again. "OK. Thanks."

When the young woman closed the door, Nicole walked to her dresser on the other side of the bedroom. On top of it was her purse, phone, and the masquerade mask she planned to wear tonight: black and bejeweled with a shock of bright peacock feathers. She stared down at her phone screen to see if she'd gotten a text message or call back from Xander, but there still was none.

He was cutting it down to the wire.

Nicole had even called the housekeeper who cleaned his place in Tribeca and asked if she'd seen Xander. Did she know where he was? The woman said she last saw him yesterday morning at around 9:00 a.m. when he was passed out, still fully dressed, in his bed. She had shut his door so she wouldn't wake him while she cleaned and vacuumed. The door was still closed when she'd left his home.

Nicole spoke to Xander's driver, too. He last saw Xander a few hours before that, at around 4:30 a.m. yesterday, after he dropped off Xander who had partied most of the night at The Box. The driver returned Friday afternoon to take Xander to Maple Grove, but Xander never showed up. When the driver called him to tell him he was waiting downstairs, Xander never answered, so after circling the block for almost an hour, the driver left. He assumed maybe there was a change of plans and Xander made the journey to the Chamberses' estate on his own.

Had Xander driven from the city to Maple Grove in his Porsche, been high or drunk, and gone off the road? Was he bleeding in a ravine somewhere?

Or he's just being an ass—per usual—and doing what he wants, when he wants. No consideration for anyone else.

After all this planning and money, was he really not going to show up to his own party? She couldn't believe he would do that. Even someone as irresponsible and selfish as Xander wouldn't ghost three hundred people, including his own friends and family. She silently assured herself that he was still coming, that for once he wouldn't disappoint her.

Nicole donned her mask, grabbed her purse, and headed downstairs.

"Nice dress," Nicole heard a familiar voice say behind her as she reached the end of the corridor and neared the great hall.

She whipped around to find Jeremiah standing a few feet away, holding a jester's mask.

Where the hell did he come from? She hadn't heard his footsteps.

He was wearing a suit of the palest blue seersucker. He'd paired it with a white shirt and tie. Jeremiah hadn't adhered to tonight's dress code exactly, but he still looked damn good in it. *Debonair. Timeless.* Like one of the characters in *The Great Gatsby* had stepped off the page and into the Chamberses' mansion.

"You too," she replied. "Nice suit."

"So were the masks your idea?" He gestured to the one in his hand.

"What do you think?" she asked him sarcastically, pushing her own mask to her crown.

Jeremiah strolled toward her and shrugged. "I don't know. You seem to like hiding identities. Maybe a mask is on brand."

She rolled her eyes in exasperation. "Are we really doing this again? Will you let it go?"

"No, I won't let it go. You told me your name was Lisa."

"Yeah, and you called me that at the pool this morning, which was petty and unprofessional. Why would you do that in front of Anna?"

"Oh, please," he said, curling his lip. "You're lucky that's all I did. You got off easy, sweetheart. We established ground rules in the beginning, and you've already broken one of them."

Sweetheart? Oh hell no.

Nicole took a quick glance around her to make sure no one else was in the corridor, that no one could see or hear them. She then stepped into one of the vacant sitting rooms and waved for him to follow her. When he walked inside, Nicole quietly shut the door behind them.

"Jeremiah, seriously, I have *so* much on my plate right now, dealing with your misplaced anger is at the very bottom of my list. You didn't know my real name, and I don't know yours, either."

"Yes, you do. It's Jeremiah."

She inclined her head. "You use your *real* name? You expect me to believe that? And considering who you are and why you're here," she dropped her voice to a whisper, "please don't get sanctimonious with me. You're here to do a job, or did you forget?"

She watched as the muscles in his cheek rippled when he clenched his jaw. His eyes narrowed.

She was pissing him off, which was something Nicole wanted to avoid because she needed his help for all this to work. But she had to establish some boundaries, and that *she* was the boss.

She'd seen Bridget do it with managers who spoke over her during meetings or when policy changes or contracts were signed off without her final approval. She'd once brought their director of public relations to tears when he issued a press release she hadn't reviewed.

"As a woman in charge, you're constantly vulnerable to being undermined. Be steady and firm. Let them know who is wearing the crown and that your rule should never be questioned," as Bridget would say.

Nicole always suspected this advice may not work for her as a Black woman, but she figured it was worth a try, anyway.

"It's a job you've done several times before, which is why I hired you," Nicole went on. "And you're getting paid handsomely for it, I might add. Let's not make this personal, OK? Let's keep it professional. Please, don't complicate things."

He laughed. "Nicole, I hate to break it to you, but things got complicated back in March when we 'got personal' three times in that hotel room at the Arlo. Four, if you count what we did in the shower. Or did *you* forget?"

Nicole felt a hot flush wash down her cheeks, neck, and chest. She swallowed. "That . . . that was a mistake."

One she was still kicking herself for.

Before she'd hired him, Nicole had interviewed Jeremiah, trying to decide if he was right for the job. He'd come highly recommended by a private detective who'd used him to gather intel.

Jeremiah had flirted with her the entire interview, but she hadn't taken it seriously. She'd assumed it was part of his con, that he was showing her how he could charm a woman and convince her to do just about anything he wanted. Jeremiah was extremely handsome. Funny. Magnetic. He had fit what she needed, and at the end of the interview she was about to tell him as much, then he'd offered her a free "demo" to show her what he was truly capable of.

"Meet me here at the bar downstairs tomorrow night at 9:30," he told her before writing the address on a napkin and sliding it across the bistro table at the coffee shop where they'd met. Curious, she decided to take him up on his offer.

Nicole had arrived at the low-lit speakeasy at the appointed time to find him completely in character. They drank, ate oysters and spicy ceviche, and talked late into the night. After a while the flirting wasn't just one-sided. Maybe her mom was right; it had been *way* too long since she'd been on a real date. Or maybe the alcohol and atmosphere had clouded her judgment because, after a while, Nicole forgot that it was just a "demo." That Jeremiah was just putting on an act for her. It felt real, and the attraction between them felt real, too.

She couldn't remember who had kissed whom first, but when it got heated, he was the one who suggested they head to one of the hotel rooms upstairs. She should have told him no, but she didn't. Nicole had enjoyed herself that night—thoroughly.

The next morning, she told Jeremiah he was hired. She then got dressed and got out of there, outright rejecting his offer to see each other again. It was too dangerous. *He* was too dangerous. Who in their right mind would agree to start a relationship . . . a situationship . . . *whatever* it was with a grifter they barely knew? How could she ever be sure he wasn't conning her, too? She had a clear objective of what she needed to accomplish, and being around Jeremiah just made things fuzzy.

"Right. A mistake. Got it," he now muttered. "Regardless, I told you when I agreed to do this that I had to know what I was doing and who I was working for. No lies. No surprises. I choose my marks carefully based on specific criteria. I don't walk into jobs where I don't know the scope and the risk, and this is starting to feel like a job I usually avoid. You lied to me, and I wanna know why."

She opened her mouth then closed it and opened it again, unsure of how to answer the question. Of how much to reveal.

He cocked an eyebrow. "Clock's ticking, Nicole. Don't give me an answer and our deal is off."

"*What?* Are you serious?"

"Pretty much."

"I already paid you!"

"And I've given you more than two months' worth of work. I'm packing my bags and walking away tonight, unless you give me an answer."

"I was hiring a con man," she finally blurted out. "I didn't know if . . . if I could trust you. If I could be blackmailed or manipulated.

You might go running to Anna and tell her what was going on, so . . . so I gave you a fake name."

But she hadn't given a fake name to Elena or any of the others she'd hired or consulted in the past few months. He didn't need to know that though.

Jeremiah continued to eye her. "That's it? That's the only reason. Nothing else?"

She threw out her hands. "What other reason could there be?"

"I don't know. Maybe you've got something to hide. You could be the one doing all the manipulating. Maybe the reason I'm here isn't the reason that you told me."

"Jeremiah, I swear to you that the reason I asked for your help is still the same reason I gave you at that coffee shop: I need to solve a murder. My boss, Bridget, is dead. I know someone who is here tonight on this property," she said, pointing to the floor, "conspired to kill her. She suspected it when she was alive. That someone close to her wanted her dead. I need to know exactly who that person is, why they did it, and if they acted alone. That's why you're here."

Jeremiah went silent for several seconds. He continued to squint down at her and shook his head. "You're a good liar, but you're not that good. That's not all of it."

"That's not all of what?"

"That's not the whole story. You're still hiding something. I can tell. You're holding something back."

She was still holding something back, and it annoyed her that he knew. That he could read her that easily, especially when she'd managed to convince everyone else. Should she just tell him the whole truth?

Of course not, she thought with disgust. What if it jeopardized her whole plan? *No, I have to stay focused on the objective.*

But he wasn't going to let this go. She had to say something.

"Shit, I don't know! Maybe . . . maybe because you're picking up on . . . on other things I'm trying to hold back," Nicole confessed. "Complicated feelings. They don't make sense, and I don't have time for them right now, so I'm trying my best to . . . to ignore them."

He smirked. "What complicated feelings?"

Need, she thought without hesitation. *You make me ache with need, and it scares the hell out of me.*

Most of the time, especially at the office, she felt like some sexless robot that existed strictly to serve and troubleshoot. But Jeremiah reminded her that she wasn't a robot. The way he looked at her made her remember that she was a living, breathing woman.

"Don't be an asshole," she snapped instead. "I told you, I don't have time for this."

He laughed and took another step toward her, closing the space between them. She could feel her heart rate picking up.

"No, I wanna hear it," he insisted, lowering his voice. "And don't lie, because I'll know."

She shook her head with impatience. "I'm not doing this. I've gotta go." She picked up the hem of her gown and started to walk around him toward the door. "The party is about to start and I'm hoping to sweet baby Jesus that Xander finally sh—"

She stopped when Jeremiah grabbed her arm and pulled her against him. He lowered his mouth to hers, catching her off guard.

He's a con artist, a panicked voice in her head reminded her. *You don't need this distraction. You've got too much to do!*

Regardless, within seconds, she wrapped her arms around his neck and kissed him back. She did it almost as a reflex.

He raised her slightly and backed her up against the sitting room wall. She could feel the fabric of the grasscloth wallpaper against her bare shoulder and the wainscoting digging into her back. The kiss deepened and things got fuzzy like they always did whenever she was around Jeremiah.

God, this feels good.

She let go of him and wrenched her mouth away only when she heard laughter and voices in the hallway. The couple leaped apart and turned toward the door. She adjusted the front of her dress. With the back of his hand he wiped the lipstick now smeared on his mouth.

Lucky for them, the door didn't open. Whoever was on the other side kept walking. The voices and footsteps receded and faded away.

"Shit," she muttered breathlessly, placing a hand to her chest where her heart was racing. "That was close."

He nodded, looking a little flushed himself.

"Jeremiah, this isn't going to work if that . . . if that keeps happening. We can't—"

"I know," he whispered back, wiping roughly at the last of the lipstick still smeared on his bottom lip. "Stick to the job. Got it."

She headed to the door again but paused to look at a wall mirror. Her lipstick was smeared, too. She reached into her purse, took out a lipstick tube, and began to try to reapply it when Jeremiah said, "Anna was acting weird when I last saw her."

Nicole frowned, turned away from the mirror, and faced him. "*Weird?* Weird how?"

"She was talkative all morning. Wouldn't shut up. But she's been quiet most of the evening. Distracted."

"Do you know why?"

He shook his head. "She took a bath at around three o'clock. She went in there with a big stack of magazines and some mail. She wanted to relax and freshen up a little before the party, but when she came out of the bathroom, her mood had changed. She said she felt sick to her stomach. She said she didn't want to go to the party but we had to because she wanted to talk to Xander. I heard her trying to call him a few times later today. She's been asking around for him out there, too."

Nicole's frown deepened. "That's strange."

"Yeah, that's why I told you."

It was a reminder of why she'd hired Jeremiah. He was more than good looks and charm.

"Thanks for . . . well, for being so observant. Let me know if you notice anything else." She took a final look at her reflection and shrugged. Her attempt at her makeup fix wasn't perfect but at least she no longer looked like she'd decided to sneak off and snog a guy in one of the sitting rooms. She dropped her lipstick back into her purse. "I'll see you outside."

He nodded.

"Wait a minute or two before stepping out after I leave. OK? I don't want to risk anyone seeing—"

"I've got it, Nicole," he said tersely. "I'm gonna need a minute, anyway."

He was still breathing hard. His face was still ruddy.

"Nikki," she corrected.

"What?"

"You said to be honest and give you my real name. My friends call me Nikki." She then donned her mask again, opened the door, and stepped back into the hall.

CHAPTER 21

"Oh my God!" one of the partygoers cried as she stepped past the bare-chested fire-eater near the entrance. A twelve-inch flame burst from his mouth, sending her into nervous giggles. She and her companion walked hand in hand through the tent's parted curtains. "Are you seeing this, Hailey? This is absolutely insane!"

Nicole walked in after the two women and followed the path of where one of them was pointing.

In addition to the fourteen crystal chandeliers hanging from the ceiling, there were three bartenders dangling from silver hoops over the Lucite bar toward the right. On the other side of the tent was the stage where a DJ who had performed at Coachella two years ago now fist-pumped to the club mix he was spinning. Above him, on two platforms, were dancers in masquerade masks gyrating to the music. Toward the center was the dance floor now crowded with partygoers, and around the dance floor were tables covered with abstract flower displays that looked almost like sculptures. Three attendees sampled the hors d'oeuvres and champagne the waitstaff were serving throughout the room. And under a spotlight was the seven-tiered, spiral birthday cake that stood at a whopping seven feet.

Nicole had to give Gustaf credit; he'd pulled it all together by deadline. The tent was a riot of colors and sounds. Even with all the tables and nearly three hundred guests milling about, it looked like some elaborate theatrical production, not a party.

She walked further into the tent and noticed the large portrait of Bridget Chambers sitting on a gold easel under a bright spotlight near the entrance. A sign beneath the photograph of her standing in front of her desk in her old office said, "In Loving Memory," surrounded by white roses, hydrangeas, and gardenias. It had been Gustaf's idea to give a solemn nod to Xander's mother, the woman who had made tonight's extravagant celebration possible in more ways than one. Nicole walked toward it and frowned as she drew closer. She noticed that toward the bottom of the picture, just above the desk in the background, were the words scrawled in black ink: **BEST PARTAY EVA!!!!**

"You've gotta be kidding me," Nicole muttered before rolling her eyes.

But she guessed a note like that fit the tone of the night.

Nicole stepped back from the portrait and scanned the room in search of Xander, although she knew she'd never spot him in a crowd this big.

They had planned a whole entrance for him, but he hadn't shown up for the scheduled dress rehearsal. She now had no idea how they were going to cue Xander for his speech welcoming guests to the soiree.

She cracked her first smile of the night when she spotted Elena on the dance floor, spinning Harper in a circle. The little girl was wearing a white lace party dress and butterfly wings. She and Elena looked like they were having fun. But Nicole's smile faded when she spotted a group of men standing near the dance floor. Among them was a face that looked very familiar. In fact, she'd spotted him on CNBC just a few days ago when they announced his company was acquiring Sweet Botanicals, the health supplements and nutrition company that Altruist Corporation had unsuccessfully tried to acquire.

"What is Gallagher doing here?" she whispered.

Patrick Gallagher was the CEO of Wellness Way, one of Altruist's biggest competitors. He'd tried more than once to acquire Altruist, too, including extending a tender offer for a public merger because Bridget had refused to sell it when the company was still private. Now that Bridget was gone and the company seemed to be ailing, he was circling again, waiting to pounce on his prey.

Gallagher must have felt Nicole watching because he turned slightly and paused while talking. The older man grinned, said something to his companions, and strolled toward her.

"Nicole Underwood, is that you? I barely recognized you in that mask. Don't you look fetching tonight," he said, leaning down to lightly kiss her cheek. He gazed down at her again. "Simply stunning."

"Thank you so much, Mr. Gallagher. Are you enjoying yourself tonight, sir?"

He nodded, holding a champagne flute aloft and gazing around him. "Absolutely! This is quite the show. I have to admit, I haven't seen anything like it."

"Well, I have to admit, I'm surprised to see you here, sir."

He took a sip of champagne. "Why is that?"

"It's just, well . . . I made the guest list."

He tilted his head and laughed. "Are you insinuating I crashed the party, Nicole?"

She joined him in his laughter. "Did you, sir?"

He stopped laughing. "Nicole, men like myself never crash parties. I only go where I'm invited."

Nicole squinted. *Then who invited you?*

"Don't look so confused. I told you I get things done, Nicole." He winked and took a drink from his glass. "Everything is finally falling into place."

Just then, in the corner of her eye, Nicole noticed that the crowd near the tent's entrance started to part. The music on the overhead speakers abruptly changed to the welcome song Xander had selected: 50 Cent's "In da Club." Nicole soon spotted her boss in the center of the crowd, raising his hands to the roof as the DJ played the words "It's your birthday" in a remixed loop.

So he finally showed up, she thought with relief. It was a nail biter, but he made it.

The top buttons of Xander's shirt were open and his tie hung loosely around his neck. He was flanked on both sides by two beautiful young women in short dresses and high heels. One danced to the music with her arm around his waist. Despite Xander wearing a white *Phantom of the Opera* mask, Nicole could see Xander's glassy eyes and goofy, lopsided smile.

Xander seemed to stagger slightly as he walked through the crowd, giving high fives along the way. He threw his arms around his dates' shoulders, leaning his weight against each girl. They guided him and practically kept him upright.

Nicole guessed it was too much to ask him to arrive at his own bash on time and not stinking drunk.

"He is *so* shitfaced!" someone yelled behind her before bursting into laughter.

"Where's a mic? Give me a fuckin' mic?" Xander slurred.

"No! No!" Nicole said, prying off her mask and trying her best to be heard as she shoved her way through the throng. "Don't give him a mic!"

Having him give his welcome speech now would lead to disaster.

But she wasn't fast enough and no one could hear her over all the music and noise. She watched in dismay as one of the staffers leaped off the stage and ran across the dance floor with a cordless mic in hand. The guy promptly handed the mic to Xander.

"Hey! Heeeeey!" Xander said before slapping his hand on the mic, filing the speakers with a grating thumping sound. He wrenched off his mask and tossed it aside. "Hey, everybody! Cut the music! Cut the goddamn music!"

The DJ turned off the music as requested and gave the thumbs-up sign from the stage.

"Hey, guys! It's your birthday boy, Xander. How are we feelin' tonight?" he asked the crowd as he staggered toward the dance floor.

He got several cheers and hoots in response. A few people stepped back when someone shined a spotlight on him, making him hold up his hands and squint against the glare.

"Thanks . . . uh . . . thanks for coming tonight and helping me celebrate. This place looks awesome. They even got the hanging bartenders. Would you look at that shit? We're gonna have a blast tonight, guys! It's gonna be a night to remember," he said, drawing more cheers. "The last time I had a blowout like this here at Maple Grove was when I . . . umm . . . I graduated college. Two-hundred twentysomethings and a beach-themed party. We really trashed this place, didn't we, Mark?" he said, pointing at his long-time friend.

Mark held up his champagne glass. "Yeah, we did, bro!"

"Yeah, the fuck we did! Mom said it took a week to clean the pool. To get the house decent again. And she chewed me out for it," Xander said with a laugh. A few joined him in his laughter. "I guess I deserved it. But I was always doing stuff like that. Wasn't I? Pissing her off. Disappointing her."

The few in the crowd who had been laughing and clapping went silent. Nicole started walking again. She eased her way to the crowd and finally reached the edge of the dance floor.

"Mom used to say . . . she used to say, I reminded her a lot of my dad. Another disappointment. He died of a heroin overdose when I was . . . when I was ten years old. I bet most of you already knew that, though." Xander grimaced. "No matter what I did, I'd disappoint her. Even when I was a kid. She'd make me feel like such a fuckin' loser," he said, closing his eyes.

What was he doing? What was this stuff about his mother? He wasn't about to give the grand confession she was hoping for in the middle of the dance floor at his own party, was he?

"After a while," he continued, "I stopped trying. You know? I just couldn't be what she wanted. Live up to what she expected of me though I wanted to so damn badly. 'You hold the bar and you set the example, Xander,' she used to say."

Nicole stilled at those familiar words.

"'Everyone else follows.'" His voice echoed. "'Hold it too high and you set them up for failure. Hold it too low and they won't push themselves to succeed.' Sorry, Mom. Guess the bar was too . . . too high."

Xander turned, slowly opened his eyes, and did a double take when he saw Nicole. Their gazes locked and, for the first time since she'd known him, Nicole saw pain in his eyes. Along with a solitary tear. Was he really about to cry?

"Xander," she said, taking a step toward him, seeing him differently for the first time. Nicole felt pity for him—a boss who made her days a living hell and kept her up at night.

She had no idea that he hadn't felt like he could ever be good enough for Bridget. That he was a disappointment.

Nicole reached out to him to take the mic away and usher him off the dance floor.

This was a pain he should be experiencing privately, not with an audience of three hundred people, not under crystal chandeliers and strobe lights. Nicole pitied him too much for that.

Before she could reach him, Xander's expression changed. His face hardened.

"But Mom's not here anymore, is she?" he asked with a sniff. He then whipped in a circle. "This is my party! My house! So let's get crazy! Bring back the music! Crank it up!"

The room filled again with heavy bass, and Nicole swore she could feel the dance floor vibrate beneath her feet. The crowd started dancing again.

Nicole watched as the mic fell from Xander's hand and he staggered to the edge of the dance floor. Under the spotlight, his skin looked pale and slick with sweat. He looked sick.

"Xander!" she yelled, drawing near him, grabbing his arm. "Xander, why don't you sit down? I'll get you some water." She motioned to two of the staffers standing nearby. "Can you help me get him to a chair? Help Mr. Chambers sit down."

One of the young men nodded and wrapped an arm around Xander's waist.

"I don't need to sit down," Xander slurred. "I'm fine. I wanna dance."

"Can you help too, please? We can take him over there," she said, ignoring him and pointing a few feet away as another staffer with dreads looped Xander's arm around his neck. "Thank you. I appreciate it, guys."

"You're not my fucking mother, Nicole, and I said, I don't wanna sit down!" Xander shouted, roughly shoving them all away.

Nicole watched in horror as one of the young men went careening toward a waiter, knocking over a tray of champagne flutes and sending them all crashing to the floor and to one of the nearby tables. The other young man was shoved toward the birthday cake, causing the seven-foot, twenty-thousand-dollar tower to topple onto some of the partygoers who screamed and shouted in outrage.

It started a chain reaction. Shoving to get out of the way of the toppled cake led to more shoving, then to cussing and punching. Security rushed the dance floor. In the corner of her eye, Nicole spotted Elena. She'd grabbed Harper and was now clutching the little girl to her side, trying frantically to dodge the flying fists and elbows. Like many other partiers, Elena and Harper fled the dance floor, but their panicked exodus seemed to add to the frenzy rather than dissipate it as they bumped and tripped over one another to get back to their tables or leave the tent. A few even stumbled and fell to the ground as they did it, screaming as they were shoved and stepped on by other partygoers.

The performers on the platforms stopped dancing as their platforms began to vibrate then wobble when people slammed into them. One of the dancers yelled in alarm as her platform teetered then fell like a domino. She landed in the crowd, taking down several people with her.

The DJ yelled for everyone to "just chill! Just chill! Everyone calm down, all right?"

But partygoers ignored his calls for order. They fled their tables to escape the ensuing melee, knocking more silverware, glasses, and the expensive table centerpieces to the tent floor in their wake. Someone knocked over several taper candles, too, setting one of the tablecloths aflame. The guests at the table and nearby tried futilely to put out the fire with water pitchers and champagne. Nicole watched as a waiter carrying a fire extinguisher tried to push his way against the tide of fleeing attendees and reach the burning table.

"It's a Stella McCartney, Chuck!" one woman blubbered onto the shoulder of a man beside her as they hobbled past Nicole. The woman pointed down at her gown that was now splattered with red wine and a cream sauce. She sobbed like someone had just died. "It's ruined!"

"Don't worry. We'll get it dry cleaned, sweetheart," her companion assured.

Seeing all the chaos—the broken glasses, the faces and expensive tuxedos and gowns covered in icing, the security guards trying desperately to break up four brawling partygoers, the burning dining table, the falling dancers, the guests rushing from the tent, and a mountain of cake now littering a sizable portion of the dance floor—Xander burst into laughter and abruptly leaned forward and vomited. Nicole leaped back in just enough time to save the hem of her dress and her shoes.

CHAPTER 22

"NOW *THAT* WAS A PARTY," XANDER CROAKED TWO HOURS LATER after he emerged from his bathroom. He'd taken two showers, an aspirin, and three glasses of water. He was drying his hair with a towel as he staggered to his bedroom sofa. "God, my head is fucking killing me," he groaned. "And my stomach."

Xander upchucking and ruining the cake in such a dramatic way closed the party three hours early. His big welcome speech may as well have been the closing speech, given how fast people got out of there.

Thank God she hadn't managed to book Dua Lipa. Imagine having to tell the pop star and her entourage that her performance was canceled because the birthday boy had caused an epic scene that led to pandemonium.

Nicole's eyes drifted to the bedroom's floor-to-ceiling windows. She could see the last of the partygoers meandering out of the tent, the flashing beams of a fire truck and a few police cruisers, and the taillights of all the retreating cars as they drove away. She suspected that line included cars driven by guests who had planned to stay at the mansion. She'd already seen some of the social media posts with video footage and captions like "Xander strikes again. I'm heading home," and "Why come all the way to the Hudson Valley for a club brawl that I could've gotten back in Brooklyn?"

With the exodus of so many guests, all Nicole's hopes for what could be accomplished during the birthday weekend were now dashed.

"Oh, don't give me that look," Xander said, seeing her disgruntled facial expression. "All right. Fine. Maybe . . . maybe tonight didn't go smoothly, but shit happens. That's life."

Nicole watched as Xander looped the wet towel around his shoulders, stretched, and eased back onto the sofa. He propped his feet up on the coffee table, slapped a warm washcloth on his brow, and grabbed a nearby remote. He pointed it at the framed image of a Roy Lichtenstein hanging over the fireplace that turned into a sixty-inch flat-screen TV with the press of a button. An action flick appeared on-screen.

"I had a rough few days, and I blew off some steam. Besides, people know how I can get. I'll sleep this off and just make my round of apologies, starting tomorrow. You can send them all flowers and fruit baskets next week when we get back to—"

"No," she said.

"What?" He actually paused.

"I said no, Xander. I'm not sending any flowers or fruit baskets or any other gifts to the three hundred and some odd people you made travel here just to see you get shitfaced and hurl *cake* at them. You incited a small riot!"

"Oh, come on! Give me a break. Don't you think you're being a little melodramatic?"

"Someone else can do it, Xander. Not me. Hell, do it *yourself* for once!"

He turned off the television and slowly lowered his feet from the coffee table. The washcloth slid from his forehead to his lap as he eyed her. "Look, I get that you're upset, Nicole, but watch the tone, OK? Don't forget I'm the boss and you're the assistant, and—"

"No, I'm not your assistant. Not anymore. I told you in the beginning I was willing to work for you for three months until you found my replacement." She crossed her arms over her chest. "That time is up, Xander! I agreed to help with the birthday bash and now it's over. I'm done."

She'd tried her best and had given all that she had. It was time to throw in the towel.

"So, you're just gonna abandon me now, too? Like Mom did?"

Nicole frowned, caught off guard by his question. "Xander, your mother didn't abandon you. She died. That's very different."

He gave a hollow chuckle. "She abandoned me long before that night in February. *Years . . . decades* before. I needed her and she deserted me to nannies, then shipped me off to boarding school so I would be out of her hair, and she could build her fucking business. I'm used to being deserted. I'm a pro at it. I'm just asking you not to do it now. There's too much happening. Give me another month to find your replacement. A month and a half."

She shook her head. "No, Xander."

"Goddammit! I have a pounding headache. I still feel nauseous. I just want to watch *Die Hard*, turn off all the lights, and crash. I don't need you giving me shit! I mean . . . are you trying to fuck me over? Why do you have to quit now?" He continued to eye her. "Wait. Wait one goddamn minute. It . . . it was you, wasn't it?"

"What was me?" she asked, bemused at the direction their argument was going. "What are you talking about?"

"You sent that fucking letter!" He pointed at her and unsteadily rose to his feet. His eyes were narrowed into slits. His face was red, and the veins stood out along his brow. "You thought it was . . . it was funny? *Huh?* To fuck with my head like that! You think you can threaten me, and I'll just let it slide?"

"*What letter?* I don't know what you're talking about!"

She knew he was drunk. Was he high, too?

"Xander, what the hell did you take? Are you OK? Do we need to call a doctor?"

Whatever he was on, it was making him unhinged.

He glowered at her a few seconds longer before gradually lowering his finger. The veins in his brow disappeared. "I'm fine," he said, swallowing hard as he dragged his unsteady limbs back toward the sofa. "I told you, I'm just not in the mood for this shit tonight. There's too much going on. Too much . . ." His voice drifted off. He shook his head. "I've gotta figure this out. We'll talk about it in the morning or . . . or at the office next week," he said, waving her off.

Her nostrils flared as she took another deep breath. "We cannot talk about this at the office next week, Xander. Didn't you hear me? I resigned."

"Well I don't fucking accept your resignation, Nicole!" he bellowed, throwing his towel to the bedroom floor. He then winced and grabbed for his temple.

"That's . . . that's not how this works! You have to accept it, because I quit. You can't force me to work for you!"

"If you quit, you're done! Do you understand me? I'll make sure that no reputable company in New York . . . in the fuckin' *tri-state area* ever hires you. Now go do whatever assistants do. Start ordering the goddamn flowers and fruit baskets and get out of my room!"

She gazed at him dumbfounded and watched as he flopped down on the sofa and turned the flat screen back on.

Nicole walked out soon after, slamming the door behind her.

"Tonight was quite the evening, wasn't it?"

Nicole heard the disembodied voice in the dark and halted her angry strides. Her heart was still pounding. She was still shaking. She took several deep breaths before she turned around to find Daniel Miller leaning against the wall near the entrance to the study with his hands in his pockets. He was smiling.

"So where is the birthday boy? Still wreaking havoc or sleeping it off?"

"I don't know, and I don't care," she said, making Daniel bark out a laugh.

"Well, on that note . . ." He tilted his head toward the opened doorway. "Have a drink with me. You look like you could use one."

"Thank you, Mr. Miller, but no. I'm exhausted and just want to go to bed."

"Oh, come on. It shouldn't take long," he insisted, stepping away from the wall. He strolled toward her. "After that little display at the party, I thought it better to head home early. This is my last night at Maple Grove, and I'd like to end it with a drink and good conversation. Have a whiskey with me. I won't take no for an answer."

Good God, she thought with exasperation.

Here was another rich white man demanding her time and attention like he owned her. Nicole wasn't in the mood to put on her polite assistant facade after what she'd just been through. "Well, unfortunately, you're gonna have to. Good night." She then began to walk away.

But she stopped in her tracks when he called out, "I know what you're up to, Nicole."

The blood drained from her head. Her heart started racing again. Her hands, which were already clenched and holding up the hem of her gown, squeezed even tighter, leaving little sweaty imprints on the silk. She whipped back around to face him. He was still smiling, but there was a gleam in his eyes this time.

He laughed as he shook his head ruefully. "Don't worry. I haven't told anyone else—if that's your concern." He gestured to the study's open door. "Let's have that drink, shall we? We should talk."

She knew then that it would be foolhardy to say no.

CHAPTER 23

AFTER THEY STEPPED INSIDE, DANIEL CLOSED THE STUDY DOOR behind her.

"So, what are we having?" he asked before clapping his hands and rubbing them together eagerly. "Whiskey? Brandy? Vodka tonic?" He walked to the multitiered, rolling beverage cart in the corner of the study near one of the floor-to-ceiling windows. "It looks like Xander has a pretty nice setup over here." He picked up one of the bottles and nodded in appreciation. "Not surprising with his drinking habits," he muttered.

"A brandy is fine," she replied, looking around the space.

The room used to be full of books when Bridget was alive, but Xander had tossed out most of them and torn out the grand oak shelves. He'd replaced them with expensive artwork and glass display shelving. It now looked like a smaller version of his office back in Midtown except this one also had a bizarre wall of weapons, from a bow and arrow to medieval mace to handguns that included a remake of the 44 Remington Magnum from the *Dirty Harry* films.

The shelves were also covered with other things Xander had collected over the years, from signed baseballs to action hero Funko

Pops. The only books in the study were the occasional biographies of people like Steve Jobs and Michael Jordan, motivational self-help books like *The Subtle Art of Not Giving a F*ck*, and coffee table retrospectives on the history of *Penthouse* and the Arsenals, his favorite soccer team.

The study looked like it had been designed by a fourteen-year-old boy with sophisticated taste and a hefty budget, which fit Xander.

Because he is a child. A useless, thoughtless, selfish idiot. I can't believe I actually started to feel bad for him. Nicole recalled the pity she'd experienced while listening to his rant back on the dance floor.

She glared out the window at the lit-up tent in the distance where crews were probably breaking down equipment and tables. She should be packing her things as well.

She didn't care if Xander threatened that she'd never work in New York again. She'd move to another state. Maybe even back home to Maryland. Either way, in the morning, she was heading home and washing her hands of this whole ordeal. What disappointed her the most is that she couldn't do what she came here for, now that everyone was leaving.

But dammit, I tried.

"Here you go," Daniel said, making her turn around. He was holding out a glass to her.

She whispered, "Thanks," as a reflex, and immediately regretted it.

Why should she thank him for a drink he was forcing her to have? She didn't want to be here.

It was just that Daniel's words had caught her off guard. *I know what you're up to, Nicole.*

Did he really? Or was he bluffing? If he was trying to get her to reveal something, he'd have to drag it out of her before she'd tell him a damn thing.

Daniel took a sip from his glass first and she immediately followed, shuddering a little as the alcohol burned its way down her throat. A gentler warmth spread across her chest. She watched as he sat in one of the Bauhaus chairs facing Xander's desk.

"Have a seat." He pointed to the chair across from it. "Like I said, we need to talk."

She reluctantly sat down, adjusting her gown as she did it.

"Xander made a big mistake tonight," Daniel began, reclining with one ankle slung over his knee, revealing the much paler skin above his hemline. "A *very* big mistake. Not only did he make a complete ass of himself, but he also did it in front of several Altruist board members. Board members who have not been . . . hmm, shall we say . . . impressed with him as the company president and CEO since he took on the job after Bridget's death. Something like this only solidifies their worries about him. He's unpredictable. Irrational. He's obviously in over his head. And when the events of tonight get out to the press and then to the shareholders, it'll only get worse. It might reflect poorly on the entire company."

Nicole agreed with everything he was saying but didn't comment. She took another gulp from her glass instead.

"Then there's Patrick Gallagher. That bastard was sniffing around the company when Bridget was alive. I saw that he was here tonight, too. Got a front row seat to all the carnage. Xander gave Gallagher all the ammunition he needs to start a rebellion among the shareholders so he can swoop in and pull off a hostile takeover. So, was it Xander's bright idea to add him to the guest list—or yours?"

She frowned. "Why would I invite him?"

"I noticed at the party how he walked right up to you and started talking. You two seemed rather chummy. But it makes sense," Daniel said, slowly smiling again, "since you've been in cahoots with him for quite some time."

"*Cahoots?*" she repeated, not because the word sounded so antiquated it was almost comical. "What?"

"Don't deny it! Now, I'll admit, you had me fooled for a while there. I thought you were a true Bridget convert, that you bought into the cult of personality of Bridget Chambers that so many have.

But I guess that all ended when she died and you realized she wasn't going to rise from the dead like Jesus Christ."

He was wrong; she'd never thought Bridget was perfect. She'd seen Bridget as CEO approve of or do questionable things to competitors and even her own employees over the years, but Nicole had accepted it as the price of being a successful businesswoman . . . of maintaining a flourishing company in a competitive industry. Stealing proprietary formulas. Violating noncompetes. Playing so fast and loose with advertising and marketing that it bordered on outright lying about the efficacy of some of Altruist Corporation's products. Even a hush-hush affair with one of their VPs who ended up divorcing his wife of twenty-seven years only for Bridget to end it a month later.

No one's perfect, Nicole now thought.

It wasn't fair to expect Bridget to be a saint when so many male CEOs and presidents weren't.

"Someone's been feeding Patrick info about the company," Daniel prattled on. "He's the one who sunk that acquisition. He bought Sweet Botanicals right from under us. I heard he's called the office, asking for you."

"And? That doesn't mean I'm the one feeding him company info."

"He's even sent you a gift, Nicole. A beautiful spray of flowers more than a week ago."

Nicole blanched, remembering the bouquet of flowers and Godiva chocolates she'd attempted to give to her cousin Makayla for the baby shower—the same bouquet and chocolates that Patrick had sent her one day earlier in honor of her work anniversary.

"Just in case no one at Altruist remembered," the note said.

Patrick was right; no one at Altruist had remembered.

But how did Daniel know he'd sent them? Had nosy office gossip Sara read the note over her shoulder and relayed it to Daniel? Or had Daniel opened the envelope before she got to the office that day? Did he know about the other gifts she'd received from Gallagher?

Patrick's offer to hire her? She wouldn't be surprised; clearly he was spying on her just like she had been on him.

"Look," Daniel continued, "I know you've aligned yourself with Gallagher, and it makes sense, I suppose. We all knew Xander would be catastrophic at the head of Altruist, even if Bridget couldn't accept the truth about her son. Even with supervision, everyone knows he's a complete disaster. I'm sure Gallagher has made you big promises about what will happen once he takes over the company."

He thinks he's so damn smart. That he has it all figured out. So close, yet so far away, Daniel, Nicole thought.

She shook her head. "I'm sorry to disappoint you and ruin your big conspiracy theory, but I'm not—"

Nicole stopped short when he held up his hand.

"I can offer you *more*, Nicole," he went on, like he hadn't heard her. "I know you aspire to be more than an assistant. I've already spoken to at least three board members. They'll support me if I make a play for the top spot, and I will. *Soon*. I can take this company to places it's never been, but I want you on my team when I do it. I want to make you one of my VPs."

"Executive assistant to VP? Won't that raise a few eyebrows from the staff? The other VPs and directors?"

"You're an Ivy grad who worked directly under Bridget for almost five years. That comes with a lot of institutional knowledge that we'd rather keep in-house. It'll be an easier sell than you think."

Nicole finished the last of her drink and grabbed the metal arms of her chair. She felt lightheaded. She'd barely eaten anything since breakfast. Probably shouldn't have guzzled her brandy in one sitting. Or maybe it was also fatigue. After what had happened today, she wasn't equipped for this kind of conversation. She felt like a stage actor who'd been performing back-to-back shows and just wanted to peel off her costume and makeup and return to being her true self.

"Mr. Miller, I can promise you that whatever you think is happening—isn't. I'm not colluding with Patrick Gallagher to take over the company. I work for Xander. At least up until tonight. I was *his* assistant, and frankly, this whole conversation is making me very uncomfortable."

Maybe Daniel wasn't just offering her a backdoor deal, but also trying to entrap her. Xander was already acting paranoid, hurling accusations at her. He'd threatened to basically destroy her. How the hell would he respond if he found out that she was having drinks and a midnight convo in his study with Marcus Brutus himself?

"Thanks for the drink, but I've gotta go," she said.

"All right. Fine," Daniel said. His wrinkled lips tightened so that they were no longer visible. "Cajoling you didn't work. You have your lies and you're sticking to them. I tried to play nice but let me try another tactic. I know you were the last one to see Bridget alive, Nicole. I also know that you were brought in to speak privately with police after her death."

So, he *was* spying on her.

"And? The police spoke to several people, Daniel. That doesn't prove any—"

"And now you've also been receiving gifts and messages from the same man who tried to undermine Bridget at every turn," he said, speaking over Nicole, "who wanted to buy her company out from under her. Someone else must know, too, because they've encouraged me not to keep any more secrets."

"*Someone?*" She squinted at him, now incredulous. "By someone, you mean *you?*"

"I don't know who they are but they want me to tell the truth, and by God, I will! I will go to the police and tell them all that I know, and I'm sure they can put the pieces together just like I can. They'll know you were involved in what happened to Bridget."

She burst into laughter, catching him off guard.

"What the hell is so funny?" he asked.

"You think . . . you think *I* killed Bridget? *Me?*" she said between giggles, pointing at her chest. "Be serious, Daniel. If anyone wanted her dead, it wasn't me! There's a half dozen people higher on the list, including you, Mr. 'I can take this company to places it's never been.'"

After all, it made sense. Daniel knew Bridget's succession plan and that Xander was slated to replace her as CEO upon her death or retirement. Daniel also knew the human Hindenburg that Xander was and how Daniel would inevitably be asked to swoop in to fix all the messes Xander created while leading Altruist. Finally, a calculating mind like Daniel's would know that most of the suspicion would be directed at Xander for Bridget's untimely death since her son seemed to benefit the most from it. It would be the perfect plan for a cunning climber like Daniel.

Daniel now looked outraged—or at least feigned outrage. "How dare you . . . how dare you accuse me of . . . I would never!"

"Yeah, right. You'd steal candy from a baby even if it was covered with spit and carpet lint," she muttered as she began to walk to the study door.

"I'm not kidding, Nicole," he called out to her. "I'm being very serious. I highly doubt that Bridget's death was an accident, especially after all that's happened since, and I'll tell the police as much. I'll tell them everything I know!"

"Be my guest," she said before opening the door and walking out.

Maybe he'd have better luck than she had, because the cops were of little help. She wouldn't have had to take things into her own hands if they'd done their jobs in the first place.

"I mean it! I'll do it!" Daniel shouted after her.

"Good night, Daniel," she called back.

CHAPTER 24
NICOLE

NOW

I GRIMACE AS I WALK TOWARD THE CATERING TABLE SET UP IN THE massive kitchen of the mansion where we're shooting the film on location. The eight-thousand-square-foot home is a hybrid design, a mix of old English manor with its turrets and stained-glass windows and a Spanish-style villa with its arched doorway and a courtyard. Out front, lavender and hibiscus spill onto sandstone pavers.

It doesn't look quite like Xander's mansion back in the Hudson Valley. It doesn't have the same vibe . . . that East Coast, old-money gravitas that you just can't find in Southern California. But from the scenes they've been shooting all week, I'll acknowledge that they're trying their best to replicate as much of the look of Maple Grove as they can.

I'm hungry but I'm put off from the idea of eating after watching Troy, the lead actor, reenact over and over again the moment when Xander upchucked in front of hundreds of party guests.

How many times does someone have to pretend to vomit before you get the perfect take? It turns out eight times.

I also had to watch the special effects team muddle over the perfect viscosity and color of his puke for more than an hour after Bill, the director, argued that it didn't look "believable" on camera. It left me wondering how much of the movie budget was being dedicated to this, considering how many man hours were involved.

I push my sunglasses to the top of my head as I step into the line of crew members in front of the series of chafing dishes filled with today's lunch. I now tuck the sunglasses into the collar of my T-shirt.

I'm a little self-conscious because taking off the glasses reveals the dark circles under my eyes. I rarely if ever get more than four hours of sleep a night even though I've been taking melatonin gummies daily, like Asia suggested more than a week ago. I picked up some over-the-counter sleep aids from Walgreens, too, but they aren't working, either. I'm getting so desperate that I'm considering those magnesium injections that Asia's Pilates instructor takes. Short of street drugs, I'd try anything at this point to get the full night's sleep that eludes me.

And when I do sleep, it's usually nightmares. They're either flashbacks to that weekend, replaying some gruesome scene that I either witnessed firsthand or heard about later. Or I'm imagining scenarios differently, like my brain is engaged in a game of "what if?" In my dreams, my subconscious mulls over what I could have said or done to prevent it all from spiraling out of control.

What if I'd asked Xander to explain more about the letter he'd received at his home?

What if I'd spoken to Charlotte Danfrey directly and just asked her what was wrong instead of leaving it up to Elena to figure things out? Would Charlotte have confided in me?

What if I had told all the guests to follow their instincts and leave Maple Grove early? Because it turned out that the birthday party was just a warning shot. Things would get much, *much* worse.

If I had done any of these things, would it all have been avoided?

I'm hoping when the shoot is over the nightmares will start to fade again. That my subconscious will take a badly needed break.

I look at the food sampling for today as I grab a plate and utensils wrapped in a paper napkin. Caesar salad. Grilled chicken. Rib eye steak and baked potatoes. I spot a few Impossible Burgers at the other end of the buffet for the vegans. I wait for the woman in front of me to put down the tongs so that I can scoop some salad onto my plate when I notice the script she's juggling in her other hand. I can see pink pages among the white and blue.

Are those new pages? *More new pages?*

I almost drop my plate, but catch myself before I do. I sit it down and tap the woman on the shoulder in front of me. She turns around and I see that she's one of the actors on set. I think she plays Gustaf's assistant.

"Hi," I say, "I'm so sorry, but—"

"Oh, you don't have to apologize, Ms. Underwood. It's a pleasure to meet you," she says with an anxious smile. "I mean, to speak with you. I know the movie is based on your life, and I am just so honored to play just a small part in—"

"Is that an updated script?" I say, stopping her mid-sentence. I point to the pages. She follows the path of my finger, looks at me again, then nods. Her smile widens.

"Do you mind if I look at it? I haven't gotten a copy yet, and I'd love to see what changes were made."

"Oh." She glances down at the pages again and nods. "Oh, sure! Umm, I'm finished for the day." She holds the pages out to me. "Are you . . . are you going to give the pages back when you're done, Ms. Underwood?"

"Of course," I say as I take the script. I turn away and step out of the line.

"Could you sign it, too?" she calls after me as I walk outside the kitchen and wander into one of the mansion's corridors.

"Camera points on the move!" someone shouts behind me.

I step aside to let two men lugging heavy cameras pass. I can hear the static of their radios. A voice calls them back to set for them to set up the next scene. I flip straight to the pink pages. There are more than thirty of them sprinkled throughout. I lean against the corridor wall. As I start to read, my eyes gradually grow bigger and bigger. My heartbeat picks up its pace. When I'm done reading, I lower the pages.

I need to talk to the screenwriter. Director. Producers. To *someone*, because this won't do. This won't do at all.

I find the director and some of the crew setting up cameras in one of the upstairs bedrooms that has been converted to look like a study. I think they're about to shoot the scene that reenacts my confrontation with Daniel back at Maple Grove. The set designer must not have had any source material for this one because the room's design is way off. There are too many books in there. They're all leather-bound with gold embossed titles. There's also too much leather furniture, and no chrome. The only thing they got right is the wall of weapons. A series of canned lights now shines on it, making the hilts of the swords and gold pistols glint in the light.

As soon as I approach the doorway, I'm stopped by the redhead from my first day at the movie studio who escorted me to the set. I now know that her name is Lacey; she's the second assistant director.

"Hey, Nicole," Lacey says, adjusting the bill of her baseball cap. "What's up?"

"I need to speak with Bill," I say, standing on the balls of my feet so I can peer over her shoulder at the director, who is speaking with one of the cameramen. Bill is wildly gesticulating as he does it.

Lacey follows my gaze then looks back at me. "Well, Bill's a little busy right now. We're trying to set up for the next scene. We've got a pretty busy shooting schedule today. Is there any way I can help you instead?"

I flip to the first set of pink pages. "I saw that some changes were made to the script that I wasn't consulted on."

"OK?" Lacey says slowly, cocking an eyebrow.

"They're pretty big changes that I'm not OK with. I want to talk to someone about it. If not Bill then . . . then somebody. These scenes can't be shot the way that they're written here."

Lacey nods. "Got it," she says, then abruptly walks away. I watch as she strolls farther down the hall. She whispers something into her headset.

Ten minutes later, two of the producers arrive. Clive and Gail. I can't remember their last names. I've been pacing in their absence, growing more and more irritated with each passing minute.

They've been hanging on the periphery of the set for the past week. I guess they're here to make sure the studio's money is being invested well. Maybe to make sure the production's puke budget doesn't get too out of hand. I remember meeting them via Zoom when they first pitched the project and then after contract negotiations to give me and my film agent an overview of the production timeline.

Gail is wearing her graying hair in a bun today, along with a yellow sundress and sandals. Clive is wearing faded jeans and a white dress shirt open at the collar. They look like a retired couple who decided to take a lovely trip to the vineyard for the weekend, not high-powered Hollywood executives.

"Hi, Nicole, so great to see you again!" Gail gushes, rushing toward me like we're old friends. She envelops me in a hug. Clive does the same. "We heard you wanted to have a quick convo about changes to the script."

"Yes," I say, gesturing to the pink pages yet again. "I . . . uh . . . I have some concerns. They've made changes to my scenes with Jeremiah, and I'm confused as to why."

"We get it. You're not a happy camper, huh?" Clive says with a frown. I can't tell if he's legitimately empathizing or just patronizing me. I'm leaning toward the latter. "Well, I'm sure the changes were made for good reasons. They don't substantially change the plot of the movie, do they?"

"No, they don't change the plot itself, but that's not the point," I insist. "The rewrites fudge details about Jeremiah and my relationship that—"

"What's this about my rewrites?" I hear someone say behind me.

I turn to find Bill striding toward us. He's a tall man. Lanky with craggy features. His shirt is wrinkled. His long hair is held back with a leather tie. He looks like a longshoreman or maybe a carpenter who'd be building shelves right now if he hadn't decided to direct movies instead.

"They're *your* rewrites?" I ask as the producers rush toward Bill and say, "Saw the dailies yesterday, and they look phenomenal, Bill!" and "Love what we're seeing so far. You're doing such a good job."

"Yes, they are my rewrites," Bill says with a nod, speaking over the producers. "I guess you have issues with them, Ms. Underwood."

Gail and Clive fall silent. All their eyes are now focused on me, along with the stares of a few crew members.

I lick my lips nervously then take a deep breath. I remind myself that this may be their movie, but this is my story they're adapting. I'm not being nitpicky. I've ignored other things like odd casting, set pieces that didn't look quite right, and even how the guy playing Jeremiah keeps using this weird Southern drawl. But this isn't something I can ignore; I have to speak up.

"I do," I begin. "Look, I know this is your production and I know absolutely nothing about movies, but this film is based on my life, so I'd feel weird if I didn't point out this . . . this issue. No offense."

"None taken," he says, crossing his arms over his chest.

"The rewrites," I continue, and this time he doesn't even pretend like I'm not annoying him. He loudly sighs as I point down at a page in the script. "There's a lot that was changed, but this line right here in particular was added. The part where Jeremiah says he . . .

he loves me. I mean that he loves the character Nicole . . . the one in the movie. That never happened. Jeremiah never told me that he loved me. He and I barely knew each other."

"*Barely knew each other?*" Bill repeats with disbelief. "That's strange. I got the impression from the script and all your interviews that you and Jeremiah had gotten pretty close during those few days together."

"We . . . we did." I loudly clear my throat. "But that's not what this movie is about. It's about what led to the murders and now there's this whole romantic arc that wasn't there before. This completely misrepresents our relationship. Who . . . who we were to each other."

"Right." Bill nods. "Well, there's an easy explanation for that. When our screenwriter was going through drafts of the script, there was a recurring issue of perspective and motivation for the other characters. When we told the story strictly from Nicole's perspective, we could clearly establish motivation for everything *she* did during the course of the film. We decided that she was desperate to prove her worthiness, motivated by a need for outside validation. A need probably rooted in childhood trauma."

My mouth falls open.

"No offense," he says.

"Some taken," I murmur.

"It was just our theory for the character. Not you, of course. But we couldn't establish Jeremiah's motivations. What did he get out of all of this? Why did a shrewd, seasoned con man put himself through this ordeal and ultimately suffer the fate that he did by the end of the film? It couldn't have been just for money. So we reworked it a few times. Fired the writer and brought in a new one who suggested we change part of the script to Jeremiah's perspective. Good suggestion, but the studio fired that writer, too."

"Now, now, Bill. The studio didn't fire him," Clive says, then turns to me and smiles. "The writer parted ways amicably. Just different visions for the project."

"Sure," Bill says. "Anyway, I finally had to tweak the script myself. I changed the storytelling perspective and established his motivation in the dialogue."

I stare at him blankly. "And his motivation was?"

"Love. I decided that Jeremiah was falling in love with Nicole. That's why we made the changes. Make sense?"

"Uh, yeah, I . . . I guess," I whisper.

Although I wonder why he couldn't come up with something else. *Anything* else like . . . like . . .

I draw a blank. Even I can't think of another believable motivation for Jeremiah. To be honest, I hadn't considered why he'd done everything he did that weekend. Why had he stayed, especially after he'd already threatened to leave? He'd even tried to leave toward the end, but when the final moment came for him to flee, he didn't.

"Good. Glad we're all on the same page," Bill says, cutting into my thoughts and turning away again to face the crew. He steps back into the study and claps his hands. "All right! Are we all set?"

"Hey, guys," Lacey whispers, suddenly appearing at my side. "We love having you here, but could you head downstairs for this one? We don't want any noise interference and there's wood floors so—"

"Of course!" Clive says. "We'll come back later."

Gail wraps an arm around my shoulder as we walk down the stairs to the floor below. "So happy that it was taken care of," she says. "Love it when things run smoothly. And I think adding a little more of Jeremiah's perspective to the story will tug at those moviegoer heartstrings. It certainly can't hurt!"

But can it? Now part of the movie will be told from the perspective of the man who was supposedly in love with me.

The man I would lie to repeatedly and ultimately betray.

JEREMIAH

(SUNDAY, THE MORNING AFTER THE BIRTHDAY BASH)

CHAPTER 25

Jeremiah took a bite of his bagel, trying his best to ignore the little girl across the dining room table who was tossing blueberries from her fruit bowl into the air and attempting to catch them in her mouth. One bounced off the tip of her nose and rolled onto the hardwood floor, making her break into hysterical giggles.

"Harper," said the pretty blond woman sitting beside her. "Harper, please stop."

But the little girl ignored her and tossed another blueberry.

"Harper, your mother asked you to stop," a man said, snapping his fingers and lowering the phone from his ear that he'd been barking into for the past twenty minutes.

Anna had introduced him a half hour ago as one of her nephew's friends. Jeremiah couldn't remember his name. He thought it began with an M. *Mike? Mark? Max?* No, Mark. He was reasonably certain it was Mark, along with the fact that Mark was a total prick. The little girl ignored Mark and threw another blueberry, making him snap his fingers again—this time toward the end of the table where a young Latina woman was sitting and also eating breakfast.

"Elena, handle it," he ordered. Mark then brought the phone back to his ear, returning to his conversation.

"Yes, Mr. D," she mumbled while biting into a wheat muffin. She leaned toward Harper's ear and whispered something. Harper let out a loud grumble, put down the blueberry she was holding, and resumed eating her pancakes.

"Thank you, Elena," the blond woman whispered, returning her attention to her omelet, looking relieved.

"So, you're headed on a run after this?" a voice asked.

Jeremiah shifted his gaze to see that the man beside him was staring at him intently, gesturing to Jeremiah's T-shirt and basketball shorts.

This one's name was Daniel. He was a middle-aged guy. Anna said he worked at her dead sister's company. She'd looked away and given a barely discernible flinch when she'd introduced them. Jeremiah had noted from the body language that there was some history between Anna and Daniel.

He now nodded in response to Daniel's question before drinking some of his orange juice. "Yeah, I'm gonna try to get some miles in while the weather's good."

"Some? How much is some?"

"I don't know. Five . . . maybe seven if I'm feeling up to it."

"Ran any marathons?" Daniel asked. "I did the Chicago marathon back in October."

"And Jeremiah did the New York City marathon last year. Didn't you, dearest?" Anna asked, nibbling at her quiche.

Jeremiah opened his mouth to answer, but Daniel interjected, "That one's easier to qualify for than Chicago. Less competitive. And I've done New York. *Twice*. Do you weight train?" Daniel fired next. "How much can you bench press?"

Jeremiah stifled a groan. He was growing tired of this guy and his dick-measuring contest. "I don't know. Three hundred. Three ten."

"Three *twenty-five*," Daniel said proudly with a broad smile.

"You don't say," Jeremiah murmured before he took another bite of his bagel.

In the corner of his eye, Jeremiah saw a young Black woman with braids walk through the doorway. He perked up, relieved that he wouldn't have to endure this torture alone any longer. But he quickly realized it wasn't Nicole but a staffer with similar hair carrying a coffee carafe.

Where the hell was Nicole?

Probably running an errand or doing some other menial tasks for these assholes. She was an assistant, after all.

But Jeremiah remembered the woman she'd been the day they'd met for his interview: assertive and self-possessed. He remembered the playful, sexy version of the same woman he'd spent the night with back in their hotel room. A woman with layers and secrets.

It was painful to watch her be so obsequious here, catering to every whim of these awful people. She was like all the other staffers . . . the other servants around Maple Grove who floated in the background, cleaning rooms and trimming hedges, cooking food and carrying luggage.

Did Anna, Daniel, or Mark realize who these people really were or the side of herself that Nicole was constantly holding back in their presence? Did they even care?

Of course they didn't, he thought, looking around the dining room table. Most of these bastards just cared about themselves.

Which is why he particularly loved and exclusively worked cons on the rich, although they required the most effort; he swore wealthy people needed as much coddling and attention as infants. But Jeremiah had decided when he learned the art of the con that he didn't want to steal an Average Joe's identity or wipe out some poor grandma's retirement savings to make a living. What fun was there in that? Instead he'd target those who, for the most part, could stand to take a hit. Who suffered a bruised ego and inconvenience, not a real financial loss when he scammed them. Jeremiah loved leaving some dick-swinging, Rolex watch–wearing businessman like Daniel to come to the startling realization that he'd been finessed, despite believing in his own brilliance and superiority. All the money and gatekeeping in the world hadn't kept out the ruffians. Someone had managed to take advantage of him. Worse, it had been someone he'd believed was beneath him.

Jeremiah's dad would crack up when he'd regale him with stories about his exploits and tell him how he'd suckered money out of some rich asshole, although his dad never had the patience for these kinds of cons. Pops much preferred stealing credit card numbers, writing fake checks, or selling stolen cars. In fact, stealing credit cards is what landed the old man his latest stint in jail. He was now serving ten years in a New Jersey prison, unless he managed to get some time off for good behavior.

Fat chance of that. His Pops probably had a new scheme going behind bars.

"Xander!" Anna exclaimed, breaking into Jeremiah's thoughts. "Good morning!"

"Mornin'," Xander growled, practically staggering into the dining room. He was wearing sunglasses even though he was indoors. He pulled out a chair at the head of the table and sat down but waved away a plate of bacon and eggs that a servant immediately set in front of him.

"Just toast for now," he mumbled.

"So you decided to join us for breakfast after all," Anna continued. "After the state you were in last night, I wasn't sure if you'd make it down here on your own."

Xander pushed his sunglasses up, revealing bloodshot eyes. "Yes, I made it to breakfast, Anna, and I'm very hungover so I would appreciate it if you would keep the snark to a minimum, especially before I've even had my coffee." He shook out a dinner napkin and placed it on his lap.

"I'd drink coconut water," Daniel volunteered. "The electrolytes in the water are better for a hangover than caffeine."

"Thanks for the helpful hint, Daniel, but I'm going to drink my fucking coffee or my fucking head is gonna explode," Xander replied dryly as he raised his steaming coffee cup to his lips.

"Fuck," Harper said before bursting into giggles.

"Really, Xander?" the blond woman groaned. "She's like a recorder. You have to be careful what you say in front of her."

"Did you forget, Charlotte? Xander here doesn't think about those things," Anna said. "That would require consideration of other people."

Xander glared at his aunt over the lip of his coffee cup. "Give me a break, Anna."

"Fuck!" Harper shouted again, making her mother respond with, "Don't say that, honey. It's not a nice word!"

"Charlotte, can't you quiet her down? I'm on a business call. Jesus Christ," Mark grumbled.

"I'm trying, Mark. Why don't *you* try to quiet her down? Maybe get off the phone for once," she replied, nearly pouting. "We're supposed to be on vacation anyway, aren't we?"

"Yeah, Jim, I'm still here," he said, ignoring her. Mark shoved back his chair and walked out of the dining room.

"Fuck!" Harper shrieked even louder, laughing even harder, making everyone at the table wince.

"Harper, stop it!" Charlotte ordered. She turned to Elena. "I think she's done eating now. Just . . . just take her away from the table, please?"

Elena quickly nodded, dropping her fork and knife. She climbed to her feet and grabbed the little girl's hand. "Come on, *niña*. Let's head upstairs. We'll put on your bathing suit, and I'll take you to the pool."

"Yay!" Harper cried as she hopped out of her chair. She skipped out of the room, still holding Elena's hand.

"So, considering that our numbers have greatly dwindled, can we all safely assume that there will no longer be a winery tour today, Xander?" Daniel asked.

Xander took a bite of toast. "That would be a safe assumption, Danny boy."

"Well, if that is the case," Daniel said, wiping his mouth with a napkin, "I should get going."

"*Already?* Off to meet my ex-husband again?" Anna asked with mock innocence, making Jeremiah almost choke on his bagel. "Planning a late brunch?"

"Actually no, but I enjoyed drinks with Edward and his lovely fiancée last night. He sends you his regards," Daniel said with an icy smile. "The truth is that I'm heading back to the office."

"Why? It's Sunday," Xander said with a mouth full of toast.

"Yes, it is Sunday, Xander, but our stocks have been plummeting," Daniel said, rising to his feet, "and we just lost a major acquisition. It's an all-hands-on-deck situation. Now that most of your guests have also departed, will you be joining me?" Daniel raised his brows. "I was going to speak with Tyler this weekend to get an update on our financial prospects. I've also called in Sara and the communications team to discuss our media response to what happened yesterday. I've heard we've gotten quite a few calls already, asking for a statement."

Anna snorted. "Is anyone surprised?"

"If you can't come to the office in person," Daniel went on, ignoring Anna, "we could certainly patch you in remotely, Xander."

Xander leaned back in his chair and took another bite of toast. "I'm sure you guys have got it covered. Do what you've gotta do, bro."

"Right. I'll do what I have to do," Daniel said. His smile was so tight now that it looked almost painful. He nodded. "Well, everyone, enjoy the rest of your weekend. I guess I'll see you Monday, Xander."

Xander gave a halfhearted salute as Daniel pushed back in his chair and exited the dining room.

Anna shook her head in disgust at her nephew. "You could at least attempt to pretend you care about that company, Xander. Bridget left it in *your* hands. Not Daniel's hands or anyone else's. Are you not even going to try?"

"Daniel's a big boy, Anna. He's been there a lot longer than me and knows what to do." Xander slowly turned his withering gaze to his aunt. "And frankly, I'm not going to be lectured about Altruist by *you* of all people. OK? Thanks but no thanks," he murmured before taking another drink of coffee.

Anna blinked rapidly. Her cheeks bloomed pink. Despite the Botox, her lips tightened. She dropped her fork to her plate with a clatter and roughly shoved back from the table. "I'm done with breakfast as well. Are you, Jerry?"

Do I really have a choice? He nodded and gobbled the last of his bagel. "Sure, babe."

CHAPTER 26

"That little shit," Anna spat as soon as Jeremiah closed the door to their suite behind them. She turned to face Jeremiah with her fists balled at her sides. "How dare he talk to me that way! In front of everyone! Was he trying to humiliate me?"

"You mean Daniel? I wouldn't worry about it. He seems like a jerk anyway."

Even Jeremiah had felt the subtle jab of Daniel's comment about Anna's ex-husband and his new fiancée, and he hadn't even met the guy.

"No, I mean Xander!" she yelled.

Jeremiah frowned, now bewildered by what her nephew could have said or done to set her off this badly. Compared with all the other offensive things Xander had said that morning and yesterday, he'd thought Xander's retorts to Anna were pretty tame. Nevertheless, Jeremiah reached out and rubbed her tense shoulders. She groaned with relief and wrapped her arms around him. She rested her head against his chest.

"I cannot wait to get out of this place," she moaned.

So why was she still here? A quick walk up and down the halls would reveal a series of empty rooms; it looked like almost all the other guests at the mansion had left.

"But I have to stay," Anna went on, answering Jeremiah's silent question. "Xander and I have an agreement, and he's trying to wiggle out of it, but I won't let him. I'm going to pull him aside tonight before or after dinner, and I'm going to *remind* him of the promise he made me."

"It has to be done tonight?" Jeremiah asked.

"Yes, I've let this go on for too long. I'm running out of time."

Jeremiah frowned. "Time for what?"

"Nothing," she said before sighing gruffly and shoving away from him. "Jesus! I just want it finalized before I leave Maple Grove. All right? That's all."

"I get it," he said, although he really didn't. He wondered what their agreement was about.

She lowered her eyes, now shamefaced. "Look, honey, I'm sorry for snapping at you. I'm just so tense. A long, languid bath, then climbing back into bed for a quick nap would be lovely," she whispered.

"I would, babe," he began, "but I was just about to head out for a run."

Actually, he planned to go to Nicole's room first, but he couldn't tell Anna that.

Anna laughed. "I meant by myself. I'm too exhausted for any morning shenanigans," she said, giving him a light kiss.

The truth is that she'd been too exhausted to engage in any "shenanigans" in the past three weeks, which was just fine with Jeremiah. He knew sex was part of the job sometimes, but faking affection and sexual attraction never sat well with him.

Lately Anna seemed more interested in taking him shopping and dressing him up like a Ken doll. She'd then show him off at events, like he was a new Birkin bag or a nice pair of Christian Louboutin pumps she'd just purchased.

"Well, enjoy your warm bath and nap. I hope it helps," he said while backing away from her. "I should be back from my run in a couple of hours."

"Bye, darling!" Anna called to him before he strolled out their bedroom door.

CHAPTER 27

INSTEAD OF WALKING STRAIGHT TO THE STAIRCASE THAT WOULD take him to the first floor and then outside to the Maple Grove grounds for his morning run, Jeremiah took his detour. He wanted to check on Nicole, to find out why she hadn't come to breakfast. He'd also tell her about Anna's blowup and the mysterious agreement between her and Xander.

Those aren't the only reasons you're going to see her, a voice in his head chided.

OK, maybe he'd been mentally replaying that hot-as-hell moment between them last night and what she'd said before it happened. How she'd admitted she had "complicated feelings" about him.

Jeremiah also had complicated feelings about her that got much more complex only days ago. It was back in Manhattan after Jeremiah had finished his morning run. He'd just rounded the corner and slowed to a stop when he noticed a black SUV sitting idle in front of Anna's Park Avenue co-op.

Finding a car waiting there wasn't unusual. Jeremiah knew that more than half of the people who lived in the building had their own drivers; there was always some car parked out front, waiting for some kid in their prep school uniform or woman in her Upper East Side finery or finance bro barking into his cell phone to climb inside. But this time, as Jeremiah did his cool-down walk near the building, he spotted something in the corner of his eye.

As he watched the digital reading on his wrist that showed his decelerating heart rate, Jeremiah noticed the SUV's driver hop out, jog around the hood, and open the passenger door.

Jeremiah stepped into the shadow of the building's awning as someone called out, "Jeremiah O'Connor!"

Jeremiah instantly halted.

Hearing someone call his name . . . his *real full name* . . . made his heart rate monitor give an alert—a loud squeak that showed his heartbeat had sharply increased. He squinted at the man inside the SUV who'd called out to him.

In the light shining into the opened car door, Jeremiah saw a gray-haired man wearing a navy blue business suit with a white dress shirt open at the collar. The man sat on the backseat with one arm stretched out casually as he gripped the headrest. The man grinned.

"It *is* Jeremiah O'Connor. Correct?"

Jeremiah glanced over his shoulder to see if the doorman or anyone else was listening, if maybe Anna suddenly decided to stroll downstairs at that moment. But no one he recognized was standing nearby.

"Let's go for a drive, Jeremiah," the stranger said, beckoning him forward.

Jeremiah narrowed his eyes, trying to determine if he recognized the guy. Had one of his old cons managed to track him down to confront him about money he'd stolen? If that was the case, it would be better to turn right around and do another loop around the block. He was tired, but he might be able to escape the stranger and his driver if he had enough of a head start.

"Sorry, dude, unless you're an Uber, I'm not in the habit of getting into cars with people I don't know," Jeremiah said, putting back in his earbuds. He slowly began to back away. "You have a nice day though."

"*Who* I am isn't relevant," the stranger said, leaning farther into the light. His grin widened—almost Cheshire Cat–like—as Jeremiah stilled. "But the fact that I know who *you* are and what you do for a living is very important. Especially since I'm quite sure Anna Quinton doesn't know and would be highly disappointed if she found out the truth." The stranger patted the empty leather seat beside him. "Come on, Jeremiah. Hop inside. Let's talk."

Jeremiah gritted his teeth. He didn't like this guy. He didn't like this setup either. He could "hop inside" and get driven to some back alley where men with big arms and heavy fists could beat the crap out of him. But he couldn't run the risk of letting Anna find out who he really was or about his grifter past. It would screw up everything.

So he loudly sighed and climbed into the SUV. A minute later, they were stuck in gridlock traffic but the sound of blaring horns was muffled by the financial news playing softly on the SUV's satellite radio.

"Would you like some water?" the stranger asked, offering Jeremiah an Evian bottle. "You must be thirsty after your run."

"No thanks. I'm good," Jeremiah mumbled, taking cautious glances at the driver in the front seat and the passenger door and blackout windows.

The stranger chuckled, following his gaze. "Don't worry. We didn't lock you inside. You can leave whenever you want, Jeremiah, but I'd advise you to hear me out before you do. Believe me, I can make it worth your while."

Reluctantly, Jeremiah listened as the stranger made him an offer. He told Jeremiah about a "very important business deal" that was in danger of falling apart, and he wanted to keep tabs on the situation to make sure things proceeded smoothly. He said that he didn't want "certain parties" to interfere with his plans.

He told Jeremiah that during the birthday weekend, he wanted him to keep an eye on Xander Chambers and his assistant.

"His assistant, Nicole, in particular. I thought she was in my corner . . . that she was an ally, but I'm starting to wonder. I need to know where her head is at and make sure she doesn't get in my way."

The stranger offered him ten thousand dollars in cash for the job, handing it to him across the backseat. "And there's ten thousand more where that came from for whatever intel you can give me."

Jeremiah had accepted the money. *Hell, why not?*

Why not kill two birds with one stone? He was already getting paid by his client and one-night-stand Lisa to spy on Anna for one job. Why not spy on Anna's nephew and her nephew's assistant while he was at it? Besides, if he didn't discover anything, at least he'd still have an extra ten thousand bucks.

"All right. I'll do it. I'll need a way to contact you at the end of the weekend if I find out something though," Jeremiah said. "I'll need your name."

"Oh, don't worry," the stranger assured with a wink.

The SUV abruptly stopped. Looking out the tinted windows, Jeremiah spotted a familiar bagel shop, letting him know they were two blocks away from Anna's building.

"You don't need my name. You won't have to reach out to me. I'll know where to find you," the stranger said.

A minute later, Jeremiah climbed out of the SUV and shut the door. The car pulled off, blending in with the rest of midmorning traffic.

Jeremiah had planned to follow through with his agreement with the stranger, but that was before he found out that "Lisa" was really Xander's assistant, Nicole—the woman he was getting paid potentially twenty grand to spy on. That was before he'd arrived at the tent last night and spotted Nicole and the stranger engaged in a heated conversation and all hell broke loose at the birthday celebration a few minutes after. Both revelations gave him pause.

Was Nicole working for the stranger, too, like he claimed? Or had she been previously and was no longer following orders?

The problem was Jeremiah couldn't get a read on Nicole.

He could usually place people into categories, establish a profile of strengths and weaknesses. It came with the job. He wanted to know all that he could about his mark, what motivated them . . . what they secretly feared and, in turn, use that knowledge against them to get what he wanted. But he still couldn't get a handle on Nicole or who she really was, nor had he figured out exactly what he wanted out of her.

Information he could use against her or feed to the stranger? Another round of good sex? Both? Or maybe . . . just maybe something more?

That was the most confusing part.

Jeremiah had told Nicole the truth last night: he didn't like to walk into jobs where he didn't know the scope and the risk.

"That's how you get yourself killed, boy," Pops used to warn him.

Unfortunately, it was starting to look like this was one of those jobs.

Jeremiah continued walking toward Nicole's room but paused when he heard voices behind a closed door.

"They know!" a woman sobbed.

"Wait. Wait. Who knows? Just calm down, Charlotte," he heard a familiar voice say. It sounded like Xander. "Take a deep breath and repeat what you told me. I barely understood what you were saying."

Jeremiah quietly eased the door open. He peeked through the crack and found Xander standing near one of the bay windows. His arms were crossed over his chest. His brows were lowered. Charlotte looked even more distraught than Xander. Tears were in her blue eyes and wetting her cheeks. Her face and neck were red.

"Don't tell me to fucking calm down!" she shouted, making Xander raise a finger to his lips. "This is my life," she began in a softer voice, gesturing to a red envelope she held in her hand. "My marriage could be at stake!"

"I understand that," Xander said tightly, "but—"

"I'm telling you, they know. They know about us," she said in a harsh whisper that almost sounded like a hiss. "I don't know how, but they do! They know what we did."

What we did. Were they talking about Bridget Chambers?

"It happened years ago, Char."

"It doesn't matter. They know about Harper. That she's your daughter, Xander. You can read it yourself." He snatched the envelope from her and opened it. He unfolded the letter inside.

"They're going to release the information to the press if I don't tell the truth of what happened to your mother, Xander."

Xander silently read for a bit then looked up at her. "What does that mean?"

"I don't know! I was hoping you could tell me what it means. What the hell are they talking about?"

Xander slowly shook his head and refolded the letter. "I honestly have no idea."

"Then you need to figure it out, because this can't get out to the press and it certainly can't get back to Mark. I don't even want to imagine what he'll do. He's been so angry lately. And . . . and . . ." She broke down into sobs again.

Xander reached out and wrapped his arms around her. He held her close, kissing her brow and then her lips.

"It's OK. I'll get to the bottom of this. I promise. Don't worry. OK? I'll take care of it," Xander assured, gazing into her eyes.

Jeremiah stepped away from the door, quietly eased it closed, and continued on his way to Nicole's bedroom. Now he had even more information to share with her.

CHAPTER 28

A minute later, Jeremiah knocked on Nicole's door and waited, but no one answered. He knocked again.

"Nicole? Nikki?" he called out over the ballad he heard blasting on the other side of the door. She was definitely in there; she just couldn't hear him over the music.

Jeremiah tried the handle. It wasn't locked so he opened it, stepped inside, and closed the door behind him.

The music was even louder inside the room, playing on a Bluetooth speaker sitting on one of her end tables. A few of her dresser drawers were open and her suitcase sat open on the mattress. He could see some of her clothes neatly folded inside the suitcase along with a few toiletries.

It sounded like she was in the bathroom. A cloud of steam streamed out the opened door.

Jeremiah winced as she belted along with the songstress Mariah Carey. Instead of hitting the same high notes, Nicole sounded like a mewling cat. She was many things, but a singer she was not.

He rounded the corner and found her standing in front of her bathroom mirror. At the sight of her, all the urgency to tell her what he'd discovered that morning seeped out of him. Instead he chuckled silently and slowly shook his head in befuddlement.

She was in her underwear and brushing her teeth. White froth was around her mouth. Pink eye masks were beneath her closed eyes. The lacy bra and panty set she wore looked familiar.

Blue this time, he thought, giving her an appreciative, head-to-toe glance.

The set had been black that night at the Arlo.

She paused from brushing to use her toothbrush like a mic. She raised one arm above her and let out another belt.

This was the woman who he was supposed to gather intel on? Who the stranger thought might get in his way?

"Nikki," Jeremiah called to her, making her eyes flutter open.

Nicole saw him in the mirror's reflection and let out a startled shriek. She dropped her toothbrush into the sink and clenched her fists at her sides.

"What the hell! You scared the shit out of me!" she cried. "How long have you been standing there?"

"Not long. I just came in." He gestured across the room to her now closed bedroom door.

"Why didn't you knock?"

"I knocked, but you didn't hear me with the music and all the screeching you were doing. And why wasn't the door locked? Anyone could walk in."

"I've stayed here four times before and it's never been an issue until now, but thanks for the advice." She looked down at herself and seemed to realize for the first time that she was in her underwear. "Turn around so I can grab my robe."

He cocked an eyebrow. "*Really?*"

Was this another act, or was she serious?

"Yes, really!"

"I've seen you in your underwear before, Nikki. Hell, I've seen you in less."

"That was months ago *with* consent. This is not. Turn around, please," she ordered, twirling her index finger.

He rolled his eyes and slowly turned around to face one of the bedroom walls.

"Should I close my eyes, too?" he asked sarcastically as she grabbed her robe off the bed.

"That won't be necessary," she muttered.

In the corner of his eye, he saw her put on her robe and tie the belt around her waist with a knot. She pushed back her shoulders.

Too bad, he thought.

He'd liked seeing her that way. Not just in her underwear, although that was delightful, too. He'd also liked seeing her carefree and silly. He was starting to get a handle on the different versions of herself that she threw on like a costume throughout the day, but he liked this version the least. The stuffy, prim assistant persona didn't suit her.

"I'm done," she announced before wiping the toothpaste from her mouth with her sleeve. "So, what's up? Why'd you stop by?"

He turned back around. "I came here because I didn't see you at breakfast." He watched as she placed a folded T-shirt in her suitcase. "You aren't leaving, are you?"

She hesitated then nodded. "Yeah, I'm heading out today. I quit my executive assistant job with Xander, which was *long* overdue."

She'd quit her job? That was interesting. He bet the stranger would be eager to hear that.

"For the first time in a long time I decided to sleep in, since I had nothing else on my plate for once," she went on. "So I skipped breakfast. I was going to tell you and Elena the news before I left."

He frowned. "*Elena?* You mean the nanny?"

"Technically, she's the Danfreys' au pair. She's also like you," she whispered, leaving him to conclude what "like you" meant.

So he wasn't the only one working for Nicole at the mansion. There were other plants here as well.

"But why are you leaving?" he asked. "I thought the point of all of us being here was to help you solve your old boss's murder."

She shrugged and began to peel off her eye masks. Nicole walked back into the bathroom, tossing them into a waste bin. "I'm leaving because everyone else is leaving. Thanks to what happened last night at the party, everything is falling apart. All the plans I had are pointless. Why should I stay?"

"Because I thought you put a lot of time and effort into this. You got us all here, and everyone *isn't* leaving," he said, falling back onto her bed. He leaned back on his elbows and gazed at her as she pulled up her braids into a ponytail. "Anna and I are still here, aren't we?"

"*And?*" She shrugged again. "She wants to take advantage of the free food and the pool. I wouldn't blame her."

"She's not staying here for the food or the pool. I asked her about it, and she told me this morning after breakfast that she still has to talk to Xander. She mentioned something about an agreement they made that he reneged on."

Nicole perked up. She lowered her hands from her head and turned away from the bathroom mirror to face him. "What agreement?"

"I don't know. When I tried to get more details out of her, she stonewalled me," Jeremiah said, pushing himself up from his elbows so he could sit upright. "And while I was on my way here, I overheard the tail end of a conversation between Xander and that blond chick, Charlotte."

"Charlotte is Mark Danfrey's wife," Nicole explained, adjusting her ponytail. "He and Xander are buddies. Frankly, the whole dynamic between those three is confusing as hell. I think they both dated her at some point. Knowing you and a close friend shared the same woman would have to be weird."

"Well, they're still sharing her. Turns out her kid is Xander's."

"Hold up!" Nicole exhaled. She stepped out of the bathroom and leaned against the doorframe. She gaped. "Are you serious?"

He nodded. "Heard it with my own ears."

"I mean . . . there were rumors that Charlotte and Xander had an affair, but I thought . . . I thought it was just gossip. People being mean and petty. But she actually had *his child*? You really overheard her say that?"

"Yes." He hopped off the bed, rose to his feet, and strolled toward her. "And she said someone else knows. They sent her some letter."

"*A letter?*" Nicole murmured.

"Yep. It was in a red envelope. What?" he asked, noticing she was frowning now. "Have you heard something about it, too?"

"I'm not sure. Maybe." She bit down on her bottom lip. "Can you tell me more about it? Does she know who sent it?"

Jeremiah shook his head. "But they're threatening her and Xander that they'll tell the big secret about who Harper's real father is, if she doesn't tell the truth about what happened to his mother. She claims she doesn't know what they're talking about."

"What did Xander say when she told him that?"

"He said he didn't know what the letter writer meant either. Not sure if I believe him, though."

"Why not?"

He shrugged. "Just a hunch."

It was more than a hunch; Jeremiah was almost certain Xander had been lying to Charlotte based on his body language. Jeremiah trained himself not to show similar "tells" while running cons. The long pause before answering a question, like you're trying to come up with a believable answer. How Xander's eyes kept drifting toward the window, breaking Charlotte's gaze. And he couldn't stop swallowing, like his mouth was going dry.

"A hunch, huh?" Nicole said before gnawing her bottom lip again—a tic he found downright delectable but also intriguing. Was it her "tell," too? Did she know something about all of this that she wasn't saying?

"Dammit," she murmured, her shoulders slumping.

"What?"

"What you told me is some good intel. I thought my whole plan had no potential, and now things are moving forward again. That means I have to take my assistant job back with Xander. I can't quit yet," she groaned. "God, I thought it was over!"

"Oh, come on. Working for him probably sucks but it can't be that bad. Just dust yourself off, put some clothes on, and get back out there. Your hair looks better down, by the way," he said, reaching out and running his fingers through her ponytail.

She grabbed his hand to stop him and shook her head. "Jeremiah, come on. Don't do that."

"Don't do what?" he asked with mock innocence and a sly smile.

He noticed that she hadn't let go of his hand. She hadn't pulled away, either.

"You know what I mean," she whispered impatiently. "You're supposed to be Anna's new boy toy. Remember?"

"When it's required of me, but Anna's not here right now, is she? Or," he said, squeezing her hand back and not breaking her gaze, "do you want me to keep my distance because of those complicated feelings you mentioned yesterday?"

"We are *not* starting this again. What happened yesterday shouldn't have happened." She obstinately shook her head. "You and I both know none of this makes sense."

"But does it *have* to?" he asked, drawing closer.

It certainly didn't make sense for him. Nicole could be telling him the complete truth of why they were here or hiding more secrets but, at that moment, he didn't care.

"You ever just do what you wanted to do, Nikki? What you *really* wanted? No precalculation of pros and cons. No strategy. Just acted on pure impulse?"

"Yeah, that night back in March," she said matter-of-factly.

"And did you like it?" he asked as he began to undo the knot of her robe.

It was his job to notice the tells, to see the cues to let him know if what he was doing was working. He searched for her tells now.

Was he persuading her? Was he winning her over? She didn't ease away from him or bat his hands away this time. Her breathing was slow. She kept eye contact.

"Did you like just doing whatever the hell you wanted, Nikki?" he repeated.

"Yeah. Of course, I did," she said almost reluctantly, closing her eyes—another tell. It was as if she was physically shutting out the truth. She didn't want to see it. "But I shouldn't have, Jeremiah. *We* shouldn't have."

"Why not?" he asked as he opened her robe.

"Because I . . . because it . . ."

"It doesn't make sense?" He finished for her.

She opened her eyes again and glared up at him.

She was angry now. She'd obviously taken what he said more as a taunt than a question.

"Pressed the wrong button?" he asked.

She shook her head in bemusement. "All you do is press my buttons."

"In the right way—or wrong way?"

"I'm still not sure." She looped her arms around his neck and tilted back her head. "The even more confusing part is why you keep doing it. Is it because of the challenge?"

"I'm not sure either," he said, making her laugh. He wrapped his arms around her waist, feeling the warmth of her bare skin against the palms of his hands. "Part of it may be because I like you," he whispered.

It was the truth; he really did like her.

He had since that day at the coffee shop when she'd interviewed him. The chemistry between them only grew stronger at the bar the next day and was almost incendiary in their hotel room that night. He'd liked her so much that he'd blurted out his offer to meet up again the next morning, only to have her look at him, horrified, and reject him. And he liked her now, even though he still couldn't figure out the story behind this woman.

When he leaned down, she didn't ease away. She brought her mouth to his and kissed him just as fiercely as he kissed her, groaning as she did it. A minute later, she shrugged out of her robe, letting it pool at her feet.

"Wait," Nicole said abruptly, shoving him away just as he began to nibble her ear. "Stop!"

"What?" he asked breathlessly. "What's wrong?"

Her eyes were wide. Her mouth trembled.

"What's wrong, Nikki?" he asked again.

She looked away. She strode into the bedroom and he followed her. Jeremiah watched as she reached for the door.

He guessed he'd pushed her too far. It was one of the few times that his people-reading skills had failed him. But instead of opening the door and ordering him to leave, she locked it with a click and turned back around to face him.

"Nothing's wrong. I'm just taking your advice and locking the door for once," she said with a mischievous grin before hopping up and wrapping her legs around him. He held her as she kissed him again before carrying her to the bed.

Whoever walked by her bedroom was treated to the full playlist of Mariah Carey's greatest hits, muffling the noise from the couple inside.

CHAPTER 29

"You've got some long fingers," Nicole said an hour later, holding his hand within her own, examining it in the afternoon light coming through her bedroom window. "Do you know that?"

"Well, you know what they say about big hands," he replied, making her roll her eyes and laugh.

"That's not what I meant, Jeremiah, and you know it."

They both were naked underneath the bedsheets, lounging blissfully among the chaos that was now her bedroom. Her suitcase was tilted on its side on the floor where it had landed when they knocked it off the bed. Her clothes and the rest of its contents now spilled onto the Afghan rug.

Thank God Anna was taking a nap because Jeremiah was in no condition to walk back to their room right now. He wouldn't mind drifting off to sleep himself.

"Long, thin fingers," Nicole observed before bringing them to her lips and giving them a gentle kiss. "Like a painter. Or maybe a musician. Have you ever played the violin?"

"No, but I played the piano from the age of nine to twenty-two. Even studied music theory in college."

She stared at him in shock. "Are you joking?"

"Nope," he said, shaking his head.

His mother used to drag him to his piano lessons. She'd even envisioned him one day becoming a classical pianist performing in sold-out concerts.

"So why did you . . . I mean, how did you become . . ." Her words drifted off. She grimaced like she couldn't finish.

"A con artist?" He shrugged. "Because music isn't exactly a predictable or sustainable career. I was a good pianist, but I wasn't great. Auditions didn't lead to anything long term. I tried to make it work though, splitting my time between listening to kids bang away at piano keys three times a week and waiting tables. But my tips paid me more than teaching piano."

Back when he was a waiter, Jeremiah got his first glimpse at his other talent; he saw how he could charm his way into getting people, especially women, into opening their wallets. To pony up the cash for the more expensive bottle of wine. To order the dessert even though they insisted they "just couldn't eat another bite!" And the night would end with a sizable tip, occasionally with a note attached to the restaurant's copy of the bill.

> *Best dining experience we ever had! Five stars!*

> *When we come back, we'll make sure to sit in your section.*

It was also where he had his first run-ins with the wealthy dickheads who were abrupt, rude, and expected the waitstaff to practically kiss their feet for a ten-dollar tip.

"Every year, my student loan debt kept mounting. I kept paying, but the number got bigger, not smaller," Jeremiah went on. "And I could barely afford to pay my rent. So my dad stepped in. He could see I was drowning. He said it was time to join the 'family business' if I didn't want to live in a studio apartment in Newark, eating cereal and PB&J sandwiches for the rest of my life."

Ezra O'Connor, high school dropout, may have grown up in one of the roughest neighborhoods in South Boston, but he wasn't stupid. His father offered to teach him the hustle. He could see the potential in Jeremiah, too.

"You went to college and learned stuff. You know how to talk to people," Ezra had told him. "Plus that face you got makes it easier to win 'em over. They'll trust you. You lucked up that you got your looks from your mother and not this ugly mug," Pops said with a self-deprecating laugh.

Before she got knocked up with Jeremiah, his mom, Cecilia, had won the Miss Filipina International pageant. The former beauty queen and mother of four now ran a flower shop in Jersey with Jeremiah's stepdad and was still annoyed and disappointed that her eldest boy had followed in his father's crooked footsteps.

He should probably give her a call sometime. He hadn't spoken to her in several weeks, trying to avoid the lectures and dire warnings in Tagalog she gave him whenever they spoke.

"So why did you become an assistant?" Jeremiah asked, turning the tables on Nicole.

He'd talked enough about himself and probably said more than he should've.

"Is this always what you wanted to do? Was eight-year-old you making schedules and calling Ubers for other kids on the playground?"

She burst into laughter again. Her walls were down. She was soft and pliable now. "Are you really interested, or are you just messing with me?"

"What do you mean am I just messing with you? *Yes*, I'm interested! We're sharing, aren't we?"

"Well, the answer is no," she began, "I didn't always want to be an assistant. I thought I was going to win over some venture capitalist and start my own business with the funding. I drew up the business plan and everything."

"Yeah, I saw that you developed some software program back in high school. You got an award for it, didn't you?"

"What the hell?" Nicole's eyes widened and her mouth fell open as he rolled onto his back. "Did you do research on me?"

Shit. Had he blurted that out? Best to keep going. Couldn't backtrack now.

"After you told me your real name . . . yeah," he said with another shrug before giving her a light kiss. "I told you. I need to know who I'm working for."

That was true. But he could've stopped at her LinkedIn profile, Instagram page, or even the earnest blog post she wrote eight years ago back at Cornell when she was a business and comp sci dual major. But over the past two days, whenever he was alone, Jeremiah kept digging, learning more about Nicole. He knew she grew up in Maryland. Her favorite breakfast was bacon and egg chopped cheese. She had a cat named Nemo. She was also single, according to a Facebook status, but he wondered if there could be a boyfriend lurking somewhere since she hadn't updated her profile in almost two years. Nicole kept secrets but was she the type to cheat, too? Was that another reason why she gave him a fake name? Was it the real reason why she'd rushed out their hotel room the next morning? He was still trying to figure that out.

"I guess that's fair," she said. "Anyway, I became an assistant because of Bridget, my old boss. She came to college once for a roundtable. They were always doing that kind of stuff on campus. Bringing in big CEOs who were alumni or gave money to the college. They'd ask them to impart some knowledge to us undergrads. But Bridget was different. She was a self-made millionaire, which a lot of millionaires claim to be, but then you usually find out their daddies were rich or their grandparents gifted them a hundred thousand dollars to start their first business. Bridget started Altruist from the ground up with her own money. All by herself. And she was so . . . so compelling, Jeremiah. She believed in herself. In what her company represented. A lot of us in the audience were riveted by everything she had to say. I know I was. After the roundtable, I came up to her and told her about my business idea. About how I believed in it, like she believed in hers. I offered to show her my business plan if she was willing to invest."

Nicole laughed fondly at the memory as she rested her chin on his chest. He rested his hand on the small of her back while she shifted around, getting comfortable.

"I don't even know how I worked up the balls to do it. But she turned me down and said she'd offer me a job instead. She told me if I was really serious about running a company, I had to learn how to do it for real. Her assistant at that time was moving to Europe, and Bridget needed a replacement. It would be like an apprenticeship. She'd try me on a conditional basis, and four years later, I'm still here."

He frowned. "So you came to her for an investment . . . and she made you her assistant?"

"I was twenty-one years old and inexperienced, Jeremiah. It was a big leap! I wasn't offended."

"Did she *ever* offer to invest in your business?"

Now she was the one frowning. "Well, no, but—"

"But what?"

"Maybe she knew deep down I wasn't cut out to run a company. Or it was a bad business plan. Who knows?"

"So, you were good enough to serve her, but not good enough to lead a company?"

Nicole slowly eased out of his grasp. She shifted off him. "Where are all these questions coming from?"

"We're just talking, Nikki. Casual conversation."

"No. No," she insisted, "this isn't just talking. Why are you asking me this stuff?"

He could tell he'd pressed another hot button with her, but he couldn't resist tapping it again.

"I'm just trying to understand you. You seem really loyal to this woman—you worked for her for four years and now you're doing all this to try to avenge her. But she couldn't even give you a couple hundred grand to start your own business? She took her chances. Why couldn't she let you take yours?"

Nicole pursed her lips. "Don't you have to get back to Anna?"

Her wall was back up. He figured she'd erect it again once things started to get uncomfortable. He recognized that trait in her now.

He watched as she threw back the sheets and climbed to her feet. "Are you asking me to leave?"

"In the most roundabout and nicest way possible, yes," she said while striding across the room, grabbing her robe from the floor and putting it back on.

"Look, Nikki," he said, sitting up in bed, "I wasn't trying to offend you. Again, just trying to understand."

"What is there to understand? Why do you even care?" she asked, screwing up her face. "About me or my relationship with Bridget? And don't tell me it's because you need to know who you're working for. I don't think you're asking most of your clients their life stories. Are you . . . are you trying to run a con? Seduce me like you're seducing Anna to squeeze something out of me? More money, maybe."

His heart rate kicked up as she gazed at him. This was not going well.

"Oh, I get it." He chuckled coldly, playing off his mistake. "I pissed you off, so now you're trying to piss me off too. It's working, by the way."

"No, Jeremiah. I'm serious! Is that why you did research about me? An article about me in high school. What is that about? You wanted to profile the mark?"

"Of course not!"

"Then why the hell are you asking me all these questions?"

He leaned back against the headboard. "I told you already. I just wanna know more about you."

"*You want to know more about me?*" She barked out a laugh. "Jeremiah, I don't even know your real name."

"For fuck's sake, we've been through this. I already told you my real name! It's Jeremiah."

She opened her mouth to reply but he spoke over her.

"My name is Jeremiah O'Connor. Want to know my dad's name? Ezra O'Connor. He's in prison. My mother's name? Cecilia Manalo. I have two brothers. Nineteen and eleven. One sister who's sixteen. They all still live in Ho-Ho-Kus, New Jersey, where I grew up. I studied music at the University of New Haven. Want to know anything else?"

His rapid-fire answers seemed to take the bluster out of her. It snuffed the fire in him, too.

Why the hell had he told her all of that? With little prying, he'd given her all the keys to his past and real life that he usually guarded so fiercely.

What the hell is wrong with you, boy? He could hear his dad rasp in his ear.

The tightness in Nicole's face disappeared. Even her body language changed.

"*Ho-Ho-Kus?* That can't be real."

"Jesus Christ, I swear to you, it's real!" He sat up in bed and sighed. "Look, we're just getting to know each other, Nikki. I'm getting to know you because I like you! That's all. No other reason. No ulterior motives," he answered honestly.

He still wanted to know what she liked and what she hated. Why had she believed in Bridget more than she believed in herself? What was her childhood like? What did she want for the future? He wanted to know all he could about her for himself, not for the stranger.

"Look, I'm . . . I'm sorry," she muttered. "I don't mean to come off so . . . so . . ."

"Suspicious. Mistrustful. Insulting," he finished for her.

"All that," she said sheepishly. "It's just the nature of everything that's happening here at the mansion this weekend has my antennae up, even if it may not be justified. Even if you don't deserve it." She walked back to the bed and sat down beside him. She met his gaze and gave him a peck. "The truth is I like you, too," Nicole confessed. "I just don't want to make a fool out of myself."

"And you won't," he whispered. "So, are we done fighting now? Can we call a truce?"

She gradually nodded. "Sure."

The bedroom went quiet. The Mariah Carey playlist finally ended.

"So," he began, "in the spirit of our truce, I've got one last question for you. And I'd like you to answer without getting angry or offended."

"Okaaaaay," she answered slowly, looking suspicious again. "What's the question?"

"Are you dating anyone? I mean . . . is there a potentially pissed-off boyfriend hiding somewhere?"

She burst into laughter again. "You're really asking me this now?"

"I'd just like to know, Nikki. You know about Anna, but that's part of the job. This isn't."

She shook her head. "No, Jeremiah, I don't have a boyfriend."

"Good," he said before grabbing her around the waist and dragging her back against him, making her squeal, snort, and giggle before he kissed her again.

CHAPTER 30

"We have to move it along, darling!" Anna sang later that evening as she fastened diamond studs to her earlobes. "Are you almost ready, Jerry? We cannot be late for dinner tonight."

"Are you still planning to ask him about your agreement?" he asked, closing the buttons of the Armani shirt she'd bought him specifically for this weekend.

Hiding under four hundred dollars' worth of cotton were scratches on his back that Nicole had left that morning.

When he returned to the guest suite sweaty and flushed from his "run," Anna hadn't asked any questions. Even when he begged off giving her a kiss, claiming that he was too gross and needed to take a shower first. It was in the shower that he noticed the welts near his shoulder blades. Instead of being annoyed that Nicole had left behind something so obvious that he'd have a hard time explaining it to Anna, he smiled at the memory of their time together.

None the wiser, Anna now sighed, more engrossed by her reflection in the makeup vanity mirror than by Jeremiah as she ran her fingers through her hair.

"Yes, but privately. I won't let him wiggle out of it this time. Strangely enough, though, my nephew claims he has something important that he wants to discuss, too, so he wants everyone there on time."

"Do you know what he wants to talk about?" Jeremiah asked.

She turned away from the mirror and shook her head. "Who knows with Xander."

She then turned back to her reflection and tugged open one of the vanity drawers. She retrieved an eyebrow pencil. He noticed, beneath the lipsticks and tubes of mascara, a red envelope.

So she got one too, he thought as she applied the finishing touches to her look. *Interesting.*

He'd have to find a way to surreptitiously text Nicole at dinner and tell her.

They left the bedroom a minute later. When they neared the staircase, Jeremiah saw Nicole climbing up the steps in the opposite direction while staring down at an iPad. He noticed she'd gotten rid of her ponytail and was wearing her hair down the way he liked.

He told himself to control his features, to not show a hint of interest in her and keep his expression blank, but it was more of a struggle than usual. She practically glowed.

"Nicole, don't tell me you aren't eating dinner with us," Anna said.

"I'm afraid not, Ms. Quinton." Nicole shook her head. "I'm having supper in my room. Xander said he wanted to keep dinner small tonight. Intimate. Just friends and family."

So she'd told the prick that she wasn't quitting her assistant job, after all. Good. Jeremiah would hate to see her give up now, after all she'd done already.

"Well, that was rude of him," Anna said. "You're the one who planned all of this. The least he could do is—"

"It's fine, Ms. Quinton." She waved her hand. "I have work I should be getting to, anyway."

By work, she meant digging through the Danfreys' room in search of the letter that Jeremiah had told her about that morning. While they were downstairs at dinner, Nicole hoped to find the letter, read it, and take a picture of it if it proved to be evidence related to Bridget Chambers's death.

"I see," Anna said. "Well, you will be missed, Nicole. You seem to be the only one who can keep Xander under any semblance of control nowadays."

Nicole laughed. "I'm sure tonight will be uneventful. Enjoy your dinner, Ms. Quinton. Jeremiah," she said before giving him a brief smile and nod goodbye before climbing the last stair and continuing down the hall.

He turned and watched as she walked away.

Nicole was getting good at this. Good at stealth and lying, and he had seen her comfortably alternating personas. She'd given up on the idea of starting her own business, but he wondered if she'd ever considered running cons. He guessed the one good thing that came out of her boss kicking the bucket was that Nicole might finally be willing to do something for herself. He could see that drive in her, that hunger. Maybe he should forget about his deal with the stranger and take her on as a partner instead. Show Nicole the ropes. They would work well together; they certainly had so far. And he wouldn't mind having her around more often.

Pump the brakes there, boy, his dad's voice in his head cautioned. *Just because she's about to quit her bullshit assistant job doesn't mean she wants to run away with you and start the life of a full-time criminal.*

Besides, he hadn't had a partner since his dad went into the pen for his ten-year prison sentence. He hadn't trusted anyone else enough.

But still, he thought as his gaze lingered on her, *there might be some potential here.*

"Jeremiah," Anna called, making him turn around to face her, "did you forget something?"

"Huh?" he asked her vaguely.

"I noticed that you were looking back there. I assumed it was down the hall. Did you leave something in our room?" she asked.

He paused and then patted his pockets. "My phone. I thought that I . . . that I left it." He took the phone out of his pocket and smiled. "But it's right here. My apologies, babe."

She nodded. "We should get going. They're probably waiting for us."

CHAPTER 31

A FEW MINUTES LATER THEY STEPPED INTO THE DINING ROOM AND Jeremiah paused at the entryway, feeling the weight of the mood immediately. Xander was already sitting at the head of the table, looking grim. The top of a red envelope peeked out of his shirt's breast pocket. Charlotte and Mark sat on one side of the table. The chairs facing them were empty.

When Nicole said Xander wanted to keep this dinner intimate, he'd meant it.

"What is he doing here?" Xander asked, glaring up at Jeremiah. "I told you to come alone, Anna."

Jeremiah raised his brows in surprise. Well, this dinner was starting off with a bang.

"You did no such thing!" Anna said indignantly. "You told me to come to dinner, and that is what I did. I've brought Jeremiah with me because he is my guest and your guest, too."

"But I don't want him here. I don't know if I can trust him," Xander said, jabbing his finger at Jeremiah.

"What?" Anna cried.

"Hey, I can leave if you want to keep this dinner private," Jeremiah said, holding up his hands in surrender. "It's not a big deal."

"No, Jerry, it *is* a big deal!" Anna said, stepping in front of him. "Quite frankly, I've had it up to here with my nephew's rudeness and treatment of us . . . of *all* his guests this entire weekend. And I, for one, refuse to come here to dinner just to be subjected to it again."

"Who gives a fuck whether I'm being rude or if your little boyfriend's feelings are hurt!" Xander bellowed. "There's a shark in the henhouse, and I wanna know who it is!"

"Xander, what the hell are you talking about?" Mark asked, screwing up his face. "Why would a shark be in a henhouse?"

"Goddammit! You know what I mean!" Xander shouted.

"No, I don't," Mark said. "None of us do. You're not making any sense."

"Of course he isn't. He's probably drunk or high again," Anna sniffed.

"I am not drunk or high," Xander said through clenched teeth. "You know what? Fuck it!" He slapped his hands on the table, making the silverware rattle. He slumped back in his chair. "Fine. Let him stay. What I have to say, I'll say in front of him, too, then. Whatever. Let's eat."

Anna and Jeremiah walked farther into the dining room. The whole time, as one of the servants swiftly arranged another table setting for him, Jeremiah kept his eyes trained on Xander's red envelope.

Honestly, if not for the fact that Jeremiah was gathering information, he would have left, regardless of Anna's protests. He'd had it up to here with these self-entitled rich pricks. But instead he played the good little boy toy and silently pulled out a chair for Anna closest to Xander. He took the chair beside her.

No one spoke. Even when the first course arrived, their strained silence continued. The clink of silver against porcelain and dribble of the wine being poured into glasses by one of the staff was amplified in the quiet room.

Jeremiah noticed that before they finished their potato-leek soup, Xander had already downed two glasses of Cabernet. He beckoned for the staffer to pour him another as they cleared the table for the second course.

The guy was drinking like he was on a mission to get trashed. Jeremiah wondered if they were about to get part two of the drunken performance from last night at the birthday party.

After their plates of tiramisu artfully garnished with a sprig of mint were placed in front of each of them, Xander barked, "Close the door!" to one of the staffers.

The older man ushered the servers out before quietly shutting the double doors to the dining room behind them.

Mark loudly cleared his throat. "Well, we made it to dessert. What did you wanna talk about, Xander?"

Xander downed his sixth glass in two gulps and eyed Jeremiah. He then glanced at Anna. "You sure you still want him to stay? This could get ugly. I'm not going to hold back just because you're my aunt."

"Hold back?" she asked. "Hold back from what?"

Xander removed the envelope from his pocket and threw it on the table. "I found this on my Porsche, under one of the windshield wipers, a couple of days ago. It was addressed to me. Someone managed to dig up information about me. Information about my past, and now they're threatening me with it. And I wanna know who sent it."

"Well, it wasn't me. I got one, too," Mark said before taking a sip from his wineglass.

Charlotte blinked in shock. Xander and Anna whipped their heads around to face Xander's oldest friend.

"You got one, too?" Charlotte asked.

Mark nodded, looking unphased. "Yeah, at the gym. Found it in my bag. I didn't see who left it."

"*What?*" Charlotte cried. "You didn't mention it to me!"

"Why would I?" Mark asked with a shrug. "Anyway, it was about some old shit that happened back in college. Stuff that doesn't even matter anymore." He snorted. "They thought they could scare me by blackmailing me with it."

"What 'old shit from college'?" Charlotte asked. "What are you talking about?"

Mark glanced at Xander then looked around the table. "Me, Xander, and some of our frat brothers used to . . . well, we used to invite girls to parties and do . . . stuff. Sometimes drugs were involved. Again, we did it back when we were nineteen . . . twenty. We partied! So what?"

"Why in the world would someone blackmail you with that?" Charlotte asked.

Instead of answering her question, Mark took a sip of wine and then a bite of his tiramisu, going conspicuously silent.

"You're not gonna tell her?" Xander asked. "It's not a big deal. Right?"

Mark glared at his friend.

"Fine. Since he won't explain, I'll explain it then." He looked pointedly at Mark's wife. "Because the drugs were roofies, Charlotte. OK? We put roofies in the drinks of girls who came to the frat house. We used to hold a vote on who to do it to."

"We just did it to loosen them up," Mark argued. "Stop trying to make it sound nefarious, Xander. It wasn't like that!"

"Yeah, well, one girl dropped out of school when she figured out what happened to her. Do you remember that too, Mark? She threatened to have us prosecuted but our parents hired this big bad lawyer to make it all go away."

Mark didn't respond. Instead he cleared his throat and took another drink of wine.

Wow, these guys really are assholes, Jeremiah thought.

He'd crossed paths with lots of lowlifes during his years of running cons, but these two were a distinct set of bottom-feeders.

"But none of this is as important as figuring out who's blackmailing us. Why they're holding this stuff over our heads now." Xander turned back to his aunt. "Anna?"

She sputtered. "What? Why are you looking at me?"

"Don't play stupid. You know you sent those letters!"

"Why on earth would I send them?" she asked, pointing at her chest.

"Because you've been on my ass, begging me to end that contract since Mom died. I told you, your debt wasn't to Mom but to the trust. The lawyers can't just forgive it! And I know Mom told you what happened with me back in college. How she had to pay people off. Obviously you decided to switch from begging to threatening now that you're tired of waiting to see if I can get you out of the contract. 'Tell the truth, or I will.' Are you fucking kidding me?"

"How *dare* you!" Anna yelled. "I got a letter just like you did. In a red envelope. It was in my mailbox but had no postmark. I was threatened, too!"

Jeremiah stilled. The red envelope in the vanity table drawer . . . so it did contain one of the infamous letters like he thought.

"Right. How convenient," Xander now said with a lofty eye roll.

"Oh, to hell with you, you little shit! This is the first time I'm hearing about your letter, and I have no reason to lie about mine. How could I have delivered these letters, anyway? Did I personally go to your garage and put it under your windshield wiper? Did I sneak into Mark's gym in disguise?"

Xander eyed Jeremiah again. "I know you didn't leave them yourself. You couldn't have. Maybe that's why you don't mind your new boyfriend being in the room. He already knows what's going on because you had him do your dirty work!"

"I swear to you I have no clue what you're talking about," Jeremiah said.

And the truth was, he didn't. Someone was playing them, causing havoc and making them turn on one another. He suspected who that person was but hoped his hunch was incorrect. Because if he was right, that meant Nicole had lied to him—again.

"I don't believe you. And I don't believe her, either," Xander said, jabbing his index finger at his aunt.

"Well, if we're throwing out random accusations, I think Charlotte did it," Anna said. "She's close to you both and would have ample opportunity to leave the letters with either of you."

"That's bullshit," Mark snapped. "Charlotte clearly has no idea what the hell is going on! My wife isn't involved in this."

"I am now," Charlotte said softly.

"No, you're not, honey. I'll take care of it. We'll weather this storm, and it'll all blow over." He balled up his dinner napkin and dropped it on the table before shoving back his chair. "If my secret comes out, I'll hire a PR firm for damage control. I don't give a shit about any threats. This conversation is over."

"No, it is not!" Xander yelled.

"Yes, it is! We shouldn't be talking about this stuff here with other people around and your staff on the other side of the—"

"Will all of you be quiet and listen to me for Christ's sake?" Charlotte screamed, clenching her fists, startling everyone. "I *am* involved in this, and I need to know what you did, Mark! What *all of you* did, because now it affects me. I got a letter, too. They threatened me, too!" Tears pooled in her eyes. "I didn't know why, but it obviously has to do with what happened to Bridget Chambers. What happened to her the night she died. That's what they meant . . . what the letter threatened you about, right?" she asked, scanning the room, peering at their stricken faces. "What we *all* were threatened with. 'Tell the truth, or I will.'"

The table went unnervingly quiet.

Jeremiah thought of the expression "It was so quiet, you could hear a pin drop." He bet if he had a pin, he could prove it true.

"They want us to tell the truth!" Charlotte said. "So what really happened to her? Do any of you know?"

"They threatened you?" Mark squinted at his wife. He placed a hand on her shoulder. "Threatened you with . . . with what, honey? You haven't done anything."

Charlotte lowered her gaze.

"Char, what . . ." Mark frowned. "What did you do?"

She didn't answer him. Instead she broke down into tears and shot up from the table, sending her chair careening to the hardwood floor. She ran toward the double doors and yanked one open, fleeing into the hallway.

"Charlotte! Charlotte, wait!" Mark yelled before running after her.

The room went silent again. Jeremiah sat awkwardly in his chair, wary of what would happen next. They all stared at one another.

Xander shook his head before turning to his aunt. "You know this all could've been avoided if you would've just fessed up."

"For the last time," Anna began in a low growl, "it wasn't me!"

She punctuated her point by grabbing her wineglass and throwing the leftover Cabernet into Xander's face.

Xander reeled back and Jeremiah's mouth fell open. They watched as Anna stomped out of the dining room.

The two men gazed at each other for a few seconds. Xander licked wine off his lips, then wiped his face with his dinner napkin. "Well, I'm going for a fucking swim," he said before staggering to his feet and walking out of the dining room.

Jeremiah looked around the now empty table, at the half-eaten plates of tiramisu, knocked-over chairs, and red wine now staining the white tablecloth.

He took a deep breath. "Better go check on Anna," Jeremiah murmured aloud before also rising from the table.

CHAPTER 32

Jeremiah found Anna in their bedroom. The four suitcases she'd brought with her for their three-day trip sat open, along with all the dresser, vanity, and night table drawers. When he stepped through the door, he saw that she was gathering bottles and compacts from their bathroom counter, almost swiping them into her arms before running toward the bed. She cursed under her breath as a few items clattered to the floor.

"Anna?" he asked, drawing her attention.

"Oh," she said, almost guiltily as if he'd caught her doing something shameful. She continued her way to the pile of clothes and suitcases now assembled on their bed. "Grab those for me, will you, darling? I need to put them in my bag."

He walked across the bedroom and picked up a blush compact and tube of lipstick. He dropped them both inside her Louis Vuitton makeup case and watched as she began to ball up blouses and hurl them into one of her monogrammed duffel bags.

"Mark is wrong, you know," she began out of nowhere. "This isn't just going to blow over, and unlike him, no glitzy PR firm can clean up my mess."

Jeremiah sat on an empty spot on the bed and gazed at her as she continued to pack. "What did you do, babe? What are they blackmailing you with?"

Her movements slowed. She met his eyes. "If I tell you, you'll leave. I know why you're here, Jerry. I know the truth."

His face went blank. How had she found out? Who told her that Nicole had hired him?

She blinked back tears. "If you knew what I did . . . that the money is running out . . . that I . . . that I won't always be able to take care of you, you'll disappear."

So, that's what she means. Anna wasn't talking about the deal he made or that he was a con man.

Jeremiah relaxed, reached out, and hugged her. "Well, now I know, and I'm still here. May as well tell me the rest."

She leaned her head back and gazed up at him. "I suppose. If whoever is trying to blackmail me has their way, you'll find out soon enough. Everyone will." She stepped back from him. Anna stayed silent for a bit, as if carefully considering her words.

"Bridget and I started Altruist together," she finally began. "Did you know that? A lot of people forget that. They think it was all her. That she brought me in when the company got big, but the truth is, I was there at the beginning when she was trying to make ends meet as a single mom making these little holistic tinctures and face creams. It was back when she was still living in that crappy double wide in Selbyville and selling her wares over the internet. I was the successful sister. The one who was married with the condo and the nice accounting job. I agreed to help her build her business." She gave a small smile. "I handled the bookkeeping and sourcing since Bridge was never good at that kind of stuff. I didn't think anything would come of it, but hey, she was my sister. I figured why not indulge her until she gave up and moved on to something else. But Bridge didn't give up. She was sharp. She learned quickly. She was so driven and competitive. Sometimes . . . sometimes she could be outright ruthless if people got in her way. It was a side of her I hadn't seen before but . . . it worked. The company did well. Really well, Jerry."

She closed the zipper of her vanity case.

"When Altruist grew, I left my accounting job and joined full time as COO. The company was soaring, but everything else in my life was falling apart. I tried to be like Bridge and just focus on the work, but my marriage was suffering. Edward wanted to have a baby, but I kept putting it off. I told him it wasn't the right time. Year after year, I said the same thing. Finally he realized the time had passed and decided what we had wasn't working anymore. He left me. The divorce was *hard*. I started taking pills. Dating lots of men. Some nights, I couldn't remember who'd I even been out with. Then . . . then money started to come up missing. At the company, I mean. It was right before Altruist was set to go public. More than a quarter of a million dollars had disappeared from one of our accounts."

"Disappeared?" Jeremiah repeated, now frowning.

Anna looked away from him then. "I swear I meant to put the money back. I was going to put the money back! But I had to pay divorce lawyers and alimony. I was in treatment for pill addiction. Bridge figured out what happened and confronted me. I confessed because I was so tired of hiding. I couldn't recover with a burden like that on my shoulders.

"Bridge said she wouldn't press charges or do an investigation as long as I stepped down. I'd make the excuse that I wanted to take an early retirement. She said I also had to pay her back—triple the interest on what I stole as punishment for betraying her. I told her that I stole money from the company, not her. She said it was basically the same thing. She didn't care if it took me a decade or twenty years to pay the money back, but I had to do it or she'd have me criminally charged. So I agreed to everything. I signed a contract to pay her the money, and I left the company I helped build . . . that I chose over my own marriage. And she promoted Daniel to replace me. I made more than five million from the sale of my stocks when Altruist went public. More money than most could live on, but . . .

triple interest on a six-figure debt," she said then gave a rueful head shake. "That's a lot of money, Jerry—along with all the other debts I owe. I'm still paying that fucking money back to her. I probably will until the day I die."

Jeremiah wanted to ask Anna why she hadn't considered downsizing if money was so tight? Get rid of the Park Avenue apartment, drivers, and South Beach vacations. Stop chasing boy toys who only wanted her for her money. Get another corporate job to make more cash. But he already knew the answers to those questions.

The rich felt like they were owed their charmed lives; they couldn't fathom voluntarily going without them, even for the sake of survival.

Anna looked at Jeremiah again. "That's what the letter was about. They'd tell the world why I really left Altruist if I didn't tell the truth about what happened to Bridget. And I can't have that. I could still have charges brought against me for embezzling. It's still within the statute of limitations in the state of New York. I looked it up."

He tilted his head. "Do you know what happened to her, Anna? Do you know if your sister was murdered, or if it was just an accident?"

"No, but I have my suspicions. My nephew and I are more alike than he'd admit. He's just as capable of betraying his mother as I am, but on a much grander scale," she whispered before turning away from Jeremiah and heading back to the bathroom. "But he'll never confess what he did, so all our secrets will come out as punishment." She grabbed what was left of her things on the counter. "I'm leaving tonight. I'm boarding a plane and leaving the country. I'd hoped to do it with a promise that my debts were forgiven, that Xander would let me move on without that money hanging over my head, but I guess not. My nephew is obviously of no help. I'm taking the little money that I have and leaving. It's every man and woman for themselves."

Jeremiah raised his brows. *"Leaving the country?* Where are you going?"

"I'm not sure yet, but I can't stay here. I don't care what Mark says. This is going to end in some spectacle, either on the twenty-four-hour networks, in a police precinct, or both, and I have no interest in seeing how it all turns out. I can't go to jail, Jerry. I refuse. I'd rather disappear." She threw more items into one of the suitcases. "You can come with me if you'd like."

Jeremiah hesitated. "I would, Anna, but . . . but I—"

"It's fine." She waved her hand. "If you don't want to go on the lam with me, I understand. Besides, I suspect we've run our course. I know from past experience that these types of relationships have a limited shelf life. And your eye is already starting to wander."

He shook his head. "What are you talking about?"

"Xander's assistant, Nicole, is quite an attractive girl, isn't she? I've seen how you look at her. I saw it today before dinner and by the pool yesterday," she said, making his heart stutter to a stop then start up again.

"I . . . Anna, I—"

"Don't deny it. I'm foolish about many things, Jerry, but I am not blind."

He didn't respond. He had no idea he'd been that obvious.

Jeremiah was losing his touch, making lots of mistakes, and maybe he did have Nicole to blame. She threw him off his game. He now watched as Anna strolled to the neighboring room to get the rest of her things.

"At least you didn't steal my money like the last one did," she called over her shoulder. "Goodbye, Jerry."

He stood in the bedroom a few seconds longer, listening to her pack. His mind was reeling from everything he'd witnessed at dinner and thereafter. Had all this really happened in a mere two hours?

That's when he heard it—a high-pitched scream that made him jump in alarm. Anna came rushing out of the adjoining room, clutching a pile of caftans against her chest.

"Did you hear that?" she asked with widened eyes. "A woman just screamed."

He didn't respond, but instead ran to the bedroom door, whipping it open. He had to check on Nicole and see if she was the one who screamed.

"Jerry! Wait! Where are you going?" Anna shouted after him. "Don't leave me here!"

"Just lock the doors, Anna!" he yelled. "I'll be back. Don't open it for anyone if it isn't me," he said before heading straight to Nicole's room.

CHAPTER 33
NICOLE

NOW

"NICOLE! HEY, NICOLE!"

I turn away from the monitors where Asia is on-screen and nodding as Bill gives her direction for the next scene they're about to shoot. Gail and Clive are smiling and waving at me eagerly.

I wave back and return my attention to the monitor, but I pause when I realize a few other people are with them. They have a cameraman and sound guy standing behind them. In front of them stands a woman in a red polo shirt and white khakis with buoyant, heavily spritzed hair that probably could withstand hurricane winds. She's holding a mic. The FCTV LA acronym is stitched over her left breast.

Damn. It's a news crew.

"Nicole, could you come over here for a sec?" Gail asks, beckoning to me.

Trepidation trickles through my veins like ice water. I want to pretend like I can't hear them or see them but it would be futile at this point. I hesitate before hopping out of my chair and rising to my feet. I walk toward them.

In the past year, I've done more than a dozen interviews, but it never gets any easier. I'd brace myself for press junket interviews in several months to a year from now, but this is coming a lot earlier than expected. I'm not prepared to talk to reporters today, especially not an on-camera interview.

"Nicole," Gail says as she wraps an arm around my shoulder, "this is Kelly, a news anchor from FCTV LA. We're giving her and her crew a sneak peek of the production."

"Hi!" the reporter says, extending her hand to me.

Reluctantly I shake it.

"It is such a pleasure to meet you, Ms. Underwood," the reporter goes on. "I've been following your story and everything that happened at Maple Grove, even before the Netflix doc was released. Fascinating story! And now it's going to be a movie. How exciting!"

I nod, unsure of how to respond to such enthusiasm.

What would be appropriate to say? *"Thank you. Yes, making a film about murder and violence I witnessed firsthand is very exciting. It's good to be here!"*

"Nicole," Clive begins, "they just want to ask you a few questions about—"

"No," I say firmly, shaking my head. "Sorry. Not today."

The reporter blinks her fake lashes and lowers her mic to her side. She turns to the producers. The three have a silent exchange before Clive steps forward.

"Gail," he says, turning to his companion, "why don't you and Nicole have a quick convo while I show the news crew around the set?"

Gail nods. "Of course, Clive! Show them around the beautiful grounds. I'm sure it'll make for amazing footage for the broadcast."

We watch as Clive ushers the news crew away. When they disappear from view, Gail drops her arm from around my shoulder and turns to me.

"Now Nicole," Gail begins in a measured voice—the same voice that my therapist often used during our sessions, "I can only imagine how trying it is for you to have to talk about your experiences, but I can assure you most of the questions she plans to ask are about the movie . . . the production. The rest—maybe one or two questions—is ground that other news stories have tread before. Those are questions you could practically answer in your sleep."

"Yes, I understand all of that, Gail. But it's been a long day and even on my best days, I wasn't good at doing interviews on camera. I've only had one meeting with your PR department. I've barely memorized talking points."

"I'm sure you'll be fine, Nicole."

"No, I need more prep," I say, knowing how frantic I sound. "I need a few more weeks. I don't want to—"

"Nicole, can I be frank with you?" Gail interrupts, dropping her voice to a whisper. "We were so excited to make this movie. We knew, in our heart of hearts, that we had to get your story to the big screen, and we would be the ones to do it," she says, pointing at her chest. "But to do that, Clive and I had to pitch this film to the studio with a rather lean budget. We thought we could keep it fairly small and still get a good product, but the cost of this movie has become," she pauses and scrunches her nose, "a bit more robust than we originally expected. Bill is a phenomenal director. Stellar! No complaints. But he came with a high price tag. And then there's the rewrites and reshoots. Not to mention that we start fight scenes and special effect sequences soon. And we haven't even gotten to the editing. Possibly more reshoots. The budget just . . . well, it just keeps growing!" She ends her sentence with a panicked squeak.

I continue to listen but my frustration only builds. I'm failing to understand how any of this is my problem, let alone my fault.

"The studio is starting to look closer at the film for all the wrong reasons," Gail says. "We'd really like to get some *positive* buzz about the production. That's why the news crew is here. We want to drum up some anticipation for the release. Get the studio . . . get people excited! You know? Can you help us with that, Nicole? Just a little bit?"

I take a deep breath. "I want to help. I truly do. But I'm not sure an interview with me would get you guys the results you're looking for. So far, to be real with you, most of them have backfired on me."

I remember the first network interview I did. I'd seen the anchor on my television screen almost every Thursday night while I made myself dinner and drank a glass of wine after work. I loved her show. It was surreal to have her sitting right in front of me.

But being there in that studio got to me. The bright, hot lights. The makeup artist who was constantly blotting my face between takes. ("You're looking a little dewy on camera, honey," she said with a pinched smile.) The boom mic hovering over my head and the cameras pointed at my face.

Despite the media prep before the interview, I was nervous. I stumbled over my words. I shifted around anxiously in my chair. But I didn't know that my nervousness would be interpreted by those watching my interview as an admission of guilt. A sign that I was to blame for everything that happened that weekend. In public opinion—overnight and without any evidence—I was judged and found guilty.

Gail nods again. "Understood. And that's unfortunate, Nicole. It's unfortunate for the both of us because," she pauses to loudly exhale, "I absolutely hate to have to do this, but I must remind you that in the contract you signed granting us rights to adapt your story for film, you agreed to participate in promotion for that film. Press junkets and prerelease promotional opportunities, including news coverage like the interview we're asking you to do today."

My stomach drops.

"So, I'll tell Clive to bring the news crew back, huh? I'll give you a few minutes to freshen up, but honestly you look great already!"

Gail rubs my arm in a fake attempt at reassurance, and I almost shove her hand away. I bite my lower lip, trying my best to tamp down my fury as she pulls out her cell phone.

"Clive, she's willing to do the interview," she says before glancing at me. "Yes . . . yes, of course! Bring them back when they're ready. No rush. We'll be here waiting for you." She presses the button on screen to hang up and faces me. "So glad we were able to come to an agreement."

I don't echo her sentiment. Instead I lean toward her.

"I will do this, but if she asks any questions that are out of line, I'm walking off. I don't care what the hell my contract says."

I then turn and march in the direction of the bathrooms so I can pull myself together for the interview I don't want to do.

CHAPTER 34

"Hi out there, FCTV LA viewers! This is Kelly Ramos and I'm here today in Hollywood on the set of the film *Murder in the Valley*. I'm having a sit-down with Nicole Underwood, the woman who inspired this upcoming blockbuster. Great to talk with you today, Nicole."

I paste on a smile and try not to shift in my chair. "Great . . . great being here," I say. "Thanks for having me."

"Well, Nicole, we are so looking forward to the film *Murder in the Valley*. We understand that you were brought on as a consultant."

I can feel beads of sweat forming on my forehead and under my armpits. "Yes, I'm here to help make sure they get the story right. Well," I pause, "as right as they can."

"*Really?* How's that?" Kelly asks, inclining her head.

I take a deep breath. It's an easy question. I can answer this one.

"Uh, I've been consulted a few times on the script, and umm, I've talked to Asia . . . Asia Wilkerson, the actress who's playing me. We've talked about my experiences. How I felt as everything happened. I mean, well, during the events that are shown in the film. Our conversations have helped her flesh out the role."

"Have you talked to the other actors as well?" Kelly asks.

"Sure," I say, although I avoid Troy, the actor playing Xander, whenever I can.

"And have the other survivors of that deadly weekend been consulted for this film?"

I feel my body temperature rise slightly at that question. More beads of sweat. Even my hands are starting to get clammy. I take another deep breath and lick my lips. "Uh, I don't know. I m-m-mean I don't think so. I haven't seen them on set."

"Do you stay in touch with them? With the other survivors?"

My eyes dart to Gail and Clive, who are standing behind the cameraman. Gail gives me a nod and a thumbs-up. I force myself not to give her the finger.

"A couple," I answer, trying to keep my voice even.

"But not little Harper Danfrey, I assume," Kelly says with an exaggerated frown.

My eyebrows furrow and so do Clive's and Gail's. I guess even they're now bemused by the direction this interview is taking. Why is the reporter asking this?

"I understand that her family sued the filmmakers to keep the film from being made. They settled on her character not being included or even mentioned in the film," Kelly goes on, "out of respect for—"

"Cut!" Clive yells while making a slicing motion with his hands. "Cut."

"Keep going, David," Kelly says to the cameraman, not breaking her gaze or her grin. "We can just edit that out."

"No, you *are not* going to edit that out! This is not what we agreed to, Kelly," Clive says.

"I wasn't involved in the litigation, so you'll have to take that up with the filmmakers," I answer.

I'm surprised my voice is so calm because my heart is racing. I clench my hands in my lap to keep them from shaking.

"But you're profiting off the film, aren't you?" Kelly asks. "You received money for the rights. You've been hired as a consultant.

You have no opinions on the lawsuit for a film that shows the murder of—"

"I'm done," I say, rising to my feet and ripping off my mic. "Can you remove this, please?"

"I'd really appreciate it if you gave me an answer, Ms. Underwood. Out of respect for little Harper Danfrey."

But I don't answer her. I refuse to be baited any further. This woman doesn't care about Harper. She wasn't the one who had to look that little girl in the eyes after all that happened back then.

"Can you remove this, please?" I repeat to the news crew members standing around. "Or I rip it off."

The sound guy quickly steps forward and removes my mic and mic pack as Kelly gives a self-satisfied smile. I begin to walk away.

"Nicole," Gail calls after me, "I'm so sorry. Those are not the questions we agreed to. I had no idea she would do that!"

Didn't she? Anyone could've seen this coming. I want to believe that Gail was too trusting and naive, that she didn't intentionally set me up, but it's just as likely that she and Clive would try to orchestrate a combative interview like that to create buzz around a film that's ailing. If they did, mission accomplished.

ELENA

(SUNDAY, THE NIGHT OF THE MURDERS)

CHAPTER 35

You still haven't told her???
Elena seethed with annoyance as she read the text on-screen.
No. Haven't had the chance. Obvs, Elena typed back to her bestie and former roommate, Ines.
Why not? You said you were going to talk to that chick HOURS ago, Ines's text read.
"Look, Elly!" Harper cried, pointing at the television excitedly. "It's Sebastian!"
"Uh-huh," Elena murmured while sitting on the floor, still staring down at her phone.
All day she and Harper had been connected at the hip. Now it was after eight o'clock. The little girl had finished her dinner hours ago. Her parents were dining separately tonight—yet again. This time with the few remaining guests at the mansion. Harper had brushed her teeth and was now in her twill and lace PJs, lying on her belly on the rug in front of their double beds, watching on the wall-mounted flat-screen the live-action version of *The Little Mermaid* for the hundredth time.
Harper didn't look remotely tired, but Elena hoped the little girl would go to sleep soon without fuss so that she could sneak out and

do what she hadn't been able to do today. She had to track down Nicole, like Ines kept insisting, and tell her what she'd overheard last night.

Yesterday, after she'd put Harper to bed, Elena had strolled downstairs to grab a snack, hoping to find one of those mango-glazed, curry shrimp hors d'oeuvres that she hadn't managed to snag from one of the waiters before the birthday party came to its abrupt, chaotic end. When she'd reached the bottom of the stairs, she saw Nicole shouting something over her shoulder to someone before gathering the fabric of her gown and stalking off.

Elena had called out to her and tried to get her attention, but she must not have heard her because the other woman had kept walking in the opposite direction.

To be honest, Nicole had looked a little tipsy at that moment, but Elena figured she would be, too, after what had happened at the party. Who wouldn't want to drown their sorrows after witnessing such a shitshow?

Elena continued down the corridor toward the kitchen but paused when she heard more voices. One sounded familiar. They were both coming from her left, from the outdoor gardens.

She crept across the hall and eased closer to one of the glass doors, careful to hide behind the heavy curtains and stay in the shadows. She saw Mr. D and another man standing in the moonlight near a row of hydrangea bushes several feet away. Both had tumblers in their hands. Mr. D's companion was smoking a cigar. Elena also noticed that no other people were around.

"He's been that way since college," Mr. D said with a chuckle. "What did I tell you? He's a predictable fuckup."

"Yeah, I've gotta give it to you. You were right," his companion muttered. "I just didn't expect him to do it this spectacularly, this fast."

This man was much older than Mr. D. Like all the other guests at the party, he was wearing all white. Elena didn't recall seeing him before that night.

He sat down on one of the stone benches facing Mr. D and took a puff from his cigar. He then sent up a plume of smoke into the humid night air. "That dumb bastard is torpedoing that company in record time without even trying. I thought that his assistant might save him. That she was starting to feel bad for him or guilty and maybe work her magic and make him seem less like the mess than he really is, but I guess even she can't work a miracle. Lucky for you . . . lucky for the both of us, he's doing exactly what we hoped he would do."

"It's not luck. I don't invest in luck, Patrick," Mr. D corrected before taking a drink from his glass. "I need to know the odds are in my favor before I make a move. I wouldn't have bought all those shares in your company if I didn't think we were going to win in the end. That you were going to buy Altruist. I knew with that bitch gone that it would play out this way. They'd take your offer for the company more seriously once they saw what Altruist was like under that idiot's reign."

"Yeah, well, that's still luck. You didn't know what was going to happen to her. You didn't know she would have that accident."

Mr. D lowered his glass and began to smile, making his friend Patrick incline his head and raise his bushy eyebrows.

"Did you know?" Patrick asked.

"Of course not," Mr. D answered without hesitation—then winked, making Elena's stomach drop.

"Well, I'll be damned," Patrick whispered, tapping off ash from his cigar. "So the rumors are true. Xander really did do it."

Mr. D didn't respond and instead continued to stare off into the distance.

"I admire his pluck. Guess he got tired of being in Mommy's shadow," Patrick went on. "Didn't know he had it in him."

"Oh, please." Mr. D. snorted. "You really think he's capable of pulling that off by himself? That he would come up with it in the first place? Let alone plan it? That moron?"

Patrick leaned back on the bench and stared up at him. "So you talked him into it?"

Was this Patrick guy prodding him into a confession? It seemed like it. He was being subtle, though.

Mr. D took another drink. "Not exactly."

"What does that mean? *Not exactly?*"

Mr. D went quiet again, seeming to contemplate his answer. "My junior year in college, one of my frat brothers had a girl he dated for about a month that he just could not shake off. He tried to do it nicely, but she wouldn't take the hint. He told her outright that he just wasn't interested anymore, and they should see other people, and she made a big scene at the student union. She broke into tears and begged him, practically on her knees, not to leave her.

"He didn't know what to do, so I told him I could help him out. I'd been through something like that before and I knew what to do. He didn't ask any questions. At that point, I think he was just ready for it to be over. A week later, she broke up with him. He never heard peep from her again."

Patrick frowned, probably as befuddled as Elena was about what any of this had to do with Xander Chambers and his mother's murder.

"People don't need to know the details. Just the results. If I told my frat brother my plan, he would've balked and tried to back out of it or just screwed it up. So, I took care of it."

"How?"

Mr. D started laughing. "I pulled her aside at a party and told her that she should go to the school's clinic and get checked out. My frat brother thought he might have herpes, but he was too embarrassed to tell her."

"Herpes? You told her he had herpes? That was . . . a choice. So what did you do this time?"

Elena held her breath and leaned closer to the window, waiting for his answer.

"The 'how' doesn't matter, Patrick. But he got what he paid for, even if that dumb fuck had no idea what the money was really intended for. I told him it was a 'business investment,'" Mr. D said, making air quotes, "in his future."

"Jesus," Patrick said, shaking his head in shock.

"Please, he's been bitching about his mom for years. He said that she never loved him. That she treated him like a burden his whole life. Deep down, he knows he's better off without her. He's happy with the results, even if he claims it's not what he wanted. We're all better off in the end—you, me, and him. Aren't we?"

Elena had crept away on tiptoe quickly after, and then returned upstairs.

The next morning she'd tried to tell Nicole about Mr. D's conversation in the garden. She'd dragged Harper there with her after breakfast, but found Nicole's door locked. She'd knocked over and over again, but no one answered. She heard music on the other side and called out Nicole's name, shouting to be heard, before pressing her ear flat against the door. She lurched back when she heard the moans on the other side. Obviously she'd caught Nicole at a bad time.

It's not your fault she didn't answer the door, Ines now texted Elena. **You did what you were supposed to do. You got paid. Bien? You can always tell her later what you heard. Text her or email her later.**

No puedo hacer eso, Elena typed. **We're not supposed to text or email each other unless it's an emergency. That's part of our deal. She doesn't want anything traceable.**

Ay, FFS!!! Ines texted with an angry face emoji.

Ines had been the one to find online the job for a "seasoned au pair" and gave the listing to Elena. She knew Elena was tired of pulling double shifts at McDonald's and desperate for cash to pay rent and for her college classes.

"But I've only babysat my cousin Arturo and a couple of kids in my neighborhood back home. I didn't live with them. I wasn't an au pair," Elena had explained after she read the listing.

"¡No seas estúpido, estúpido! They don't know that!" Ines had rolled her eyes and waved her hand dismissively. "Just lie and put a fake name and my number down as a reference or whatever. I'll tell them you were the best au pair ever. 'Why, Elena was practically a member of the family by the end,'" Ines had said in a posh British accent that made them both burst into laughter. "It'll work out fine. Rich people are gullible. ¡Es fácil! Just email them and see what they say."

It had worked out, of course—but not in the way Ines had thought. The more Elena told her friend about her new job and what it required—the secrets and the spying, the more Ines told her to just "take the money and run."

It's just one more night, Elena texted back to Ines. **I can catch her later or I'll prob see her at breakfast.**

No me gusta! No me gusta nada! These people could be dangerous, Elena. GET OUT OF THERE!!!

Elena winced as if she could hear Ines's all-caps warning being shouted into her ears.

A few days ago, Elena would have dismissed Ines's alarm and paranoia. She'd been around the Danfreys for months. Mrs. D wouldn't hurt a fly; she couldn't even raise her voice to her own three-year-old. Mr. D, on the other hand, would lose his temper sometimes, but Elena had seen worse when her Uncle Rafe's favorite *fútbol* team got soundly beaten during the last World Cup.

But then she thought back to the conversation Mr. D had last night. He'd basically admitted to planning a woman's murder. What would he do to Elena if he found out that she'd been hired to do surveillance on him and his wife this whole time?

"Elly, get off the phone!" Harper cried indignantly as she climbed to her knees, bursting into her thoughts. "Watch *Little Mermaid* with me."

Elena lowered her phone to her lap and eyed her. "Thanks to you, *niña*, I don't need to watch the movie. I know all the lines by heart after seeing it so many times."

"I'll tell mommy and daddy," Harper threatened, wagging her head and dropping her hands to her skinny hips.

They both remembered the last time Elena had been admonished by Mr. D for being on her cell phone.

"We pay you to supervise our daughter. Not to multitask," Mr. D had told her, making her tuck her phone back into her pocket, shamefaced. She resolved that day to never pull her phone out again in his or Mrs. D's presence.

"*¡Ay, cotilla!* You narc!" Elena now said in a mock growl, reaching out and grabbing Harper. She began to tickle her, making the little girl break into giggles. After a minute or two, she pulled Harper to her feet.

"OK, kid," she said, grabbing the remote from the floor and turning off the television, "time to hit the sheets."

"No!" Harper whined.

"Afraid so, *niña*. It's bedtime." She rose to her feet and carried Harper to the bed. She pulled back the sheets and duvet, waited for Harper to climb underneath them, then tucked them around her tight, just like the little girl preferred. She turned off the overhead lights and the nearby lamp.

"Night-night, Elly," Harper said drowsily with a yawn.

"Good night, kid," she whispered back.

CHAPTER 36

THIRTY MINUTES LATER, ELENA WAS SITTING ON THE EDGE OF THE bed, wearing earbuds and FaceTiming with Ines in the dark while Harper slumbered.

"I still think you should just send her an email or somethin' and just get out of there," Ines said on-screen.

Her former roommate was back at their old apartment, sitting on the ratty beige sofa they'd gotten from Goodwill because it fit their living room and only cost twenty bucks. She was painting her toenails hot pink.

"*Eschúchame.* You heard what he said, Elena." Ines raised the nail polish wand and paused to blow on her foot, ruffling her fringe bangs. "I don't think he was just talking shit, either. He meant what he said, and what he said was crazy. *Como* Jeffrey Dahmer. I know I'd be scared if I were you."

"He's not like Jeffrey Dahmer, Ines," Elena whispered back, so she wouldn't wake up Harper. "I think I'll be OK."

"But you don't know that. He could—"

"Look, I'm going to have to get off the phone soon to sneak out and try to find Nicole. Besides, we've been talking about this nonstop. Can we like . . . talk about something else? *Anything* else?"

Their conversation wasn't making her feel any better; it was only making her anxiety worse. "What did you do this weekend? Did you finally go on a date with that guy you met at the park last week? *Me dice.*"

"Oh, yeah! *El guapo.*" Ines sucked her teeth then giggled. Her face brightened. "He took me to the movies and then out to dinner."

As Ines began to tell Elena about her date, Elena caught something in the corner of her eye. She noticed a light suddenly blaze bright in one of the windows thirty feet away, across the courtyard. Then another light turned on, then another. She knew they were the windows to the Danfreys' room, which happened to be directly across from theirs.

Just that morning Harper had waved at her mother from their balcony and shouted hello through the opened window.

"Elena. Elena, did you even hear what I said?" Ines asked, making her return her gaze to the phone screen.

"No, sorry. I think Harper's parents are back from dinner," she mumbled as she rose from the bed and slowly walked toward the sliding glass doors leading to the balcony. She paused when she saw Mrs. D run past one of the windows. Elena then saw Mr. D race after her with his arms outstretched a few seconds later, making her frown.

"Why are you looking like that?" Ines asked, now frowning too. "*¿Qué pasa?*"

"What the hell is going on over there?" Elena whispered, now thoroughly invested in whatever was playing out in the Danfreys' bedroom.

She took out one of her earbuds. She still couldn't hear them, but she could see a flurry of movement behind the windows. She saw an object fly past one of the windowpanes. Then another. Then she saw a lamp hurled, and Mr. D ducked to keep from getting hit.

"Ay! She just threw a lamp at him."

"*What?*" Ines asked, now gaping on-screen.

A few seconds later, Mrs. D yanked open one of the double doors leading to their balcony.

"With him? With him of all people, Charlotte! How could you? How could you fucking do this to me?" Elena heard Mr. D shout.

"Don't you touch me!" Mrs. D yelled back through strangled sobs. "Stay away from me, Mark!"

Elena watched as Mrs. D slowly backed toward the balcony railing. The au pair stole a glance over her shoulder at Harper who was starting to stir a little in her sleep. Could she hear them, too?

"You've been lying to me all this fucking time!" Mr. D said, reaching for his wife again. "You told me it was over between you two. That he meant nothing to you!"

"¿Qué pasa? ¡¿Qué pasa?!" Ines shouted desperately. "What's going on, Elena? Why aren't you answering me?"

Mrs. D lurched back from her husband. Elena dropped the earbud in her hand and reached out instinctively, wanting to warn the other woman to be careful, to stay away from the edge of the balcony. She could sense what was about to happen next.

Mrs. D's arms windmilled wildly but she couldn't regain her bearings or grab onto the railing in enough time before she went cartwheeling over the side. Elena screamed along with Mrs. D as the woman went tumbling to the ground twenty and some odd feet below.

"Elena, why are you screaming?" Ines shouted on screen. "Tell me what's happening!"

But Elena couldn't tell her. She couldn't find the words. She stared in horror with her hand clutched over her mouth as Mr. D raced to the edge of the balcony and looked over the side to see where his wife had landed. His eyes were wide and his mouth was grim.

"Elly?" a little voice called behind her.

Elena whipped around to find Harper sitting up in bed, rubbing her eyes.

"You woke me up," the little girl said, yawning and smacking her lips.

"Elena! Elena, say something!" Ines yelled.

"Uh, I have to go," Elena blurted out before hanging up on her friend. She turned around to face Harper.

Her heart was pounding so hard and so fast she suspected that if she opened her shirt it might jump out of her chest like one of those animated hearts in the old cartoons. It would be a big, red throbbing thing that would scare both her and Harper. Her hands were shaking. She could barely hold on to the phone in her left hand.

"What you lookin' at?" Harper asked curiously, turning toward the window.

"N-n-nothing! Nothing, *niña*," Elena said as she whipped the curtains closed.

Under no circumstances could she let Harper see what had happened to her mother. Elena wouldn't forgive herself for frightening or scarring the little girl for life like that. Elena forced a smile and ordered her limbs to stop trembling, for her rapidly beating heart to slow the hell down.

"I-I-I'm sorry I w-w-woke you up," she stuttered. "I was watching a video on my phone and . . . and shouted out."

"No phone, Elly," Harper said sleepily, yawning again as Elena ruffled her hair and sat down beside her. "Daddy said so."

"I know, kid. Enough YouTube videos for me tonight." She set her phone on the night table. "Now back to bed, OK?"

She tucked her into the duvet. As she did she could hear her phone buzzing insistently. It was likely Ines calling her back, asking her what had happened and why she hung up on her. But Elena was still struggling to reconcile what she'd witnessed.

It was an accident. A horrible accident. Mr. D hadn't pushed her, but Mrs. D had still gone over that banister. She was dead.

Or maybe not, Elena thought. It was a steep fall, but Mrs. D might have survived it. If Elena called the paramedics now, they might still save her. She pressed the button on-screen to ignore Ines's call and eased back to the window. She stared over her shoulder to see if Harper was back to sleep. The little girl's eyes were closed. She was breathing heavily again. Elena then slowly parted the curtains open to look outside.

Mr. D was gone. She couldn't see him on the balcony across the way or in any of the open windows. She glanced over her shoulder to check if Harper was back to sleep, then slowly unlocked the double doors leading to the balcony and eased one of them open. She stepped into the warm night, feeling a light breeze on her face and hearing the singing crickets beneath her. It seemed as if a spotlight shined above her, but she knew it was only the full moon.

"*La luna llena*," her abuelita would say was the time when people acted wild. "*Como lobos*," Abuelita would whisper. *Like wolves.*

As she crept farther onto the balcony, Elena could hear cicadas in the distance and the sound of lapping water, like someone was swimming in the pool. But who could possibly be doing laps right now? Hadn't they heard the scream?

Maybe not underwater, she surmised.

Elena inched toward the edge of the balcony and peered over the side. On the stone pavers below lay Mrs. D. Her arms were outstretched. Her left leg was turned at an odd angle. Her eyes were wide open and unblinking like she was staring at something beneath the bushes below. In the bright moonlight and the floodlights of the property, Elena could see blood spreading from the corner of Mrs. D's mouth and near her brow into the grass.

Seeing her like that, Elena almost broke into a sob, but she caught herself and bit down so hard on her bottom lip she thought it might bleed. She raced back inside with her tears pooling in her eyes. She grabbed her phone, knowing as she dialed that she was no longer calling 9-1-1 with the hope of saving Mrs. D, but to investigate a crime scene.

CHAPTER 37
NICOLE

NOW

I can't do it. I just can't.

I've tolerated weird or outright miscastings. Actors using strange accents. Random rewrites and a romantic storyline that I had no idea would be included in the film. I got bullied into doing an interview I didn't want to do. But I refuse . . . I absolutely refuse to watch Charlotte's death scene.

As soon as the stunt crew starts to set up the rigging for the body double of the actress playing Charlotte on one of the mansion's balconies, I decide I'm done for the day. I've already seen the film's Charlotte run down the hall in terror from her husband over and over again after she makes her tear-filled confession about her affair with Xander. They shot it from different angles while trying out at least five different screams. It's all getting to be too much.

And it's the first murder scene on the shooting schedule. I'll have to watch some of the other deaths tomorrow.

"You sure you don't want to stay for at least the practice run?" Lacey asks me as I gather my purse and script. "It's pretty awesome to watch the stunt team at work."

"No, I should head back to the hotel before the traffic on the 101 gets too bad," I say. "I can watch the stunt work on another day."

Lacey nods and waves. "Well, see you tomorrow!"

"Bright and early," I say with a false smile before nearly running off set.

I step off the hotel elevator an hour later. I swipe my key card over the door lock to my room and the green light flashes. I shove the door open.

My throat feels achingly tight. So dry that my breaths come out in searing bursts. For the entire car ride I kept replaying the image of the actress running down the hall, trying desperately to escape her husband, only to be cornered in her bedroom.

I knew what had happened to Charlotte that night but, thankfully, hadn't seen it myself. Now I could no longer say I was so lucky.

I close the hotel room door behind me and rush across my suite to the small fridge underneath the television console.

I've been good these past several weeks, not snacking on the food in my hotel room because I was told explicitly that it wasn't comped by the producers or the movie studio. I didn't want to end up getting billed ten dollars for a Perrier or fourteen bucks for a bag of pistachios. But tonight, I don't care. Fifty bucks worth of salty, fatty snacks is just what I need right now.

I drop to my knees and start to reach for the overpriced bottled water in one of the door slots. But like a magnet, my hand is pulled to the tiny bottle of Smirnoff vodka instead.

I want to drink away the vision of that actress running and screaming down the hall as well as the memory of the terse phone call I had months ago with Harper's grandmother—Charlotte's mother.

"Is this some kind of a joke?" the older woman asked me over the phone.

"No, Mrs. Kaminski, it's not a joke. I wanted to offer Harper part of my option from the film, and I worked it out with the filmmakers so that she could get a percentage of—"

"Yes, I read your email that was forwarded to me by my lawyer. I saw your offer, Ms. Underwood, and that doesn't change my conviction about not having my granddaughter mentioned in your little film. I won't be bribed."

"It's not a bribe, ma'am."

"Then blood money? Was this an attempt to pay us back for Charlotte's death? You really think six figures will accomplish that? If it were up to me, you and your coconspirators would be in jail, Ms. Underwood."

"Look, I'm very sorry for what happened to Charlotte. If I could change—"

"And yet here you are making money off her demise. Making a spectacle of it on an IMAX screen." She paused. "Please don't reach out to me or my lawyers again, Ms. Underwood. If you do, I will take legal action. Maybe this time the police will actually arrest you." She then hung up.

I now screw off the lid to my Smirnoff and guzzle the vodka inside. I slap my chest as I start to cough. I almost choke. When the coughs subside, I wipe my mouth with the back of my hand.

It still burns, but at least the throat dryness and ache are gone. It's gradually replaced by a heat that spreads throughout my chest. I reach inside the fridge and take out a mini bottle of Jim Beam, a mini bottle of tequila, and a bag of chocolate-covered almonds. I stroll back to my queen-sized bed, kick off my shoes, grab the remote, and turn on the TV. I eat two almonds and open the bottle of whiskey.

Two hours later, I'm solidly drunk and have a sugar hangover. The empty mini bottles and bags of candy and potato chips lie on the bed beside me while late-night television blasts on my flat-screen TV.

I guess drinking myself into oblivion was my objective all along. If I can't sleep, maybe I'll pass out instead.

As I listen to late-night talk shows, I finish off the bottle of tequila and scroll through my phone. There's a text from my film agent. Another text is from my friend, Gretchen, back in New York who's staying in my apartment, cat sitting while I'm in LA. Gretchen has attached a video snippet of her and Nemo.

"He misses you! Say hi to mommy," Gretchen says on my phone screen, making a disinterested and bemused Nemo wave one of his paws at the camera.

I thump my head back against my headboard and nearly burst into tears at the sight of his furry orange face.

I miss my home. I miss my cat. Why did I come out here? They could have easily done the film without me. It's not like anyone on the production team listens to me, anyway.

The only thing I've successfully managed to do is get overwhelmed with regret and traumatize myself all over again. Harper's grandmother could have saved her breath with the guilt trip; I'm doing a sufficient job of dragging myself over hot coals on my own. I knew watching the reenactment of painful, tragic events was going to be challenging, but I highly underestimated just how bad it would be.

I keep scrolling and notice a call from Mom from earlier that day that went to voicemail. I click on the message and accidentally end up calling her instead.

"*Hello?*" Mom answers sleepily. I can hear a ruffling noise like she's raising her head from a pillow. "Nikki? Do you know what time it is? Why are you calling me this late?" There's a pause. "Wait. Did something happen again? Oh, my God! Are you OK? No one's dead, are they?"

"I'm . . . I'm fine. No one's dead, Mom. I didn't mean to call you. Sorry. I was just trying to check my voicemail," I say between sniffs.

"*Huh?* Then why does your voice sound like that?"

I wipe my face. My eyes brim over with tears that are making my vision blur, and I clear my throat. "Sound like what?"

"Nikki, are you drunk?" Mom asks. "Your voice is slurred."

"N-n-no." I take a guilty glance at the discarded bottles on the mattress.

"Honey, what's wrong? You don't sound good."

"It's just hard out here, Mom." I grab one of the pillows and tug them against me like a teddy bear. "I'm ready for this to be over."

Mom grunts on the other end. "Hmph, having a movie made about you ain't all it's cracked up to be, huh?"

"Not really. It's just making me examine lots of things, you know? Things that I thought I already examined in therapy. I thought it would be my way to tell my story the way I wanted to tell it. Not only is that not the case, but I don't even know if my version makes me look any better."

"*Better?* Better how? I thought you just wanted them to tell the truth."

"I mean *justified*, Mom. Does the truth justify what I did? I understood my rationale back then, but I can't rationalize it a year later, knowing everything that I know now."

Mom goes quiet. "You can't change what you did, Nikki," Mom finally says. "All you can do is move forward the best you can."

"But I can't move forward without closure, Mom." I sink down the headboard to the mattress. I close my eyes. "I thought this movie production would do that."

"Well, honey, maybe the type of closure you're looking for doesn't exist. Or the movie isn't the closure you need." She yawns. "Look, I've gotta get up early for work, baby."

"I know. Like I said . . . I'm sorry for calling you. I didn't mean to."

"It's fine. I don't mind you calling me when you're down in the dumps. Just climb under those covers and sleep off whatever you were drinking tonight, though. Don't head out and get kidnapped or hit by a car. All right?"

"I won't get kidnapped or hit by a car," I say with another sniff. "'Night, Mom."

"Good night," she says then hangs up.

I stare at the television, watching as one of the late-night shows switches over to the late-*late*-night shows on TV. The host begins his opening monologue as I take Mom's advice and shove the bottles and trash aside and pull down the white plush comforter on my bed to climb beneath it, still wearing the clothes I wore on location today.

I grab my phone and am about to place it on my night table but pause when I think about what Mom said.

Maybe the type of closure you're looking for doesn't exist. Or the movie isn't the closure you need.

I roll onto my back and find myself dialing another number. It's someone I haven't spoken to in quite a while. I half expect to find the number disconnected but it rings, to my surprise. An automated voice tells me to leave a message, then the line beeps. I hesitate for an achingly long time before I finally decide to speak.

"Hey, it's me," I say limply. "I know . . . I know I'm probably the last person you would ever want to hear from, but I'm drunk with little else to do here at the lovely Monarch Beverly Hills Hotel. They're shooting the movie here in LA, but that's not why I called. I know you don't really care about the movie. I just wanna say I'm sorry. I'm sorry for what happened to you. For what you had to witness. I know the experience changed me. I can only imagine what it did to you. No, I do imagine. And it haunts me. I don't expect you to ever forgive me. To be honest, I'll never forgive myself, either, but I had to say it anyway. I'm sorry. It was long overdue, and I'm ashamed it's taken me this long to tell you."

I hang up and finally set down my cell. When I do, I turn off the lamp and close my eyes. I'm still cradling the pillow and can hear the distant sound of audience laughter as I drift off to sleep.

CHAPTER 38

The next morning, a little after 8:00 a.m., I step out the hotel and wince at the achingly bright California sunshine that is the stuff of song ballads and TV commercials, but which is pure torture for me right now, thanks to my Category 4 hangover. I can't believe I drank so much last night. I found three mini liquor bottles on the bed but I'm sure the maids will probably find a couple more underneath it.

I vaguely remember making a couple of drunken phone calls last night before I nodded off. I had to check my phone history to see who it had been and spotted a 12:28 a.m. call to Mom. When I saw who I'd called fifteen minutes later, my eyes almost bulged out of their sockets. I saw that the call had lasted less than a minute. I struggled to remember what I said.

Had I blurted anything out that I would regret later? Even now, standing outside the hotel waiting by the valet desk, I'm still drawing a blank.

My car pulls up and Kabir, the driver that the movie studio assigned me, steps out and opens the door for me. I don't climb onto the SUV's back seat as much as collapse onto it like some movie starlet leaving a club after a hard night of partying.

My head is pounding. I'm still searching for my sunglasses when Kabir slams shut the passenger door behind me, making me cringe at the sound and reach for my temples.

At least it's darker here than out there, thanks to the tinted windows. The steady drone of air conditioning is comforting, too. I pretend it's one of those white noise machines that helps you mentally shut out the world. When Kabir takes off, I put on my seatbelt and settle onto the buttery leather upholstery.

We're headed back to the private property in Encino where they're going to start shooting the murders.

"Wild night?" Kabir suddenly asks, making me raise my head from the car window I've been leaning against while we make our way down iconic Sunset Boulevard.

"Huh?" I ask dazedly.

"I asked if you had a wild night last night?" I can hear the smile in his voice.

"You could say that," I mumble.

Does raiding the refrigerator minibar count?

"There's meds and water to wash it down in the compartment back there," Kabir says, glancing over his shoulder at me. I can see his brown face and aquiline nose in profile now. "If you need it."

It's sweet of him to pretend like I don't.

"Thank you," I croak, flipping open the lid to the center armrest. I find extra-strength Tylenol, a cache of small, bottled waters, and even eyedrops—like the Fairy Godmother of Bad Decisions left it in the compartment just for me. I pop two tablets into my mouth and guzzle them down with water.

We're on the 101 now. I don't know if the Tylenol kicked in yet, but my headache begins to wane a little. I close my eyes and drift off to sleep, but I wake up nearly thirty minutes later when I feel the SUV slow down. I look up and, through the tinted windows, I see the vineyard in the distance, the posts and green vines marching up the hill like squat little soldiers.

Kabir makes a right onto a pebbled road, kicking up dust and filling my ears with the crunch and ping of rocks under tire treads and the SUV's undercarriage. We pass a series of trailers parked on both sides of the road.

As we near the mansion and sail along the paved driveway, I see the extras are all wearing white, with their maxi dresses and linen jackets blowing in the wind as they walk toward the mansion with feathered, glittery Mardi Gras masks in their hands. Despite the crew members and the equipment being carried toward the mansion's yawning double doors, a wave of familiarity sweeps over me.

I look down at the car floor. By my feet is the script. It fell out of my bag when I climbed into the SUV. I pick it up and see that it's flipped to an open page.

Nicole turns to find the gun pointed at her. She holds up her hands in surrender and slowly begins to back away.

NICOLE
Please don't kill me! Please don't!

She considers her life and regrets. The things she will never get to do. On-screen flashes a montage of memories: loved ones, her childhood, and a flashback to when Xander first mentioned the birthday weekend.

NICOLE
You don't have to do this! There's still time. We can fix this! Please!

"Jesus," I whisper with a shudder, then drop the script onto the seat beside me.

This is why I got so drunk last night. It wasn't just because I wanted to finally get some sleep or because I was depressed and feeling remorse; it was also because I was trying to fortify myself to get through today. I was trying to prepare myself for the big finish. The grand finale. I'll have to watch some of the hardest scenes in the entire film over the next few days.

The SUV comes to a stop, and I can feel my throat going dry. I reach for the armrest again, in search of another water bottle, but when I look down my hands are bright red. Slick with blood. Kabir opens his door and closes it behind him. I shut my eyes, silently urging myself to calm down. The blood isn't real. I know it isn't real. It's just my memories playing tricks on me again.

I hear the rhythmic thud of his heavy footfalls on pavers while he walks to the rear of the SUV. My door slowly opens and so do my eyes. My heart sinks when I find Xander standing in the open doorway, staring down at me. His disfigured face widens into a gruesome grin.

"Well," he says, draping his blood-soaked arm casually over the door frame, "are you just gonna sit in there all day, Nicole?"

I let out a terrified squeak, close my eyes, and open them again to find Kabir's handsome face creased into a frown as he gazes at me worriedly. "Is everything OK, Miss Underwood?"

Gradually, I nod. "Y-y-yeah. I mean, yes. I'm . . . I'm fine."

I screw the lid back on my water and Kabir steps aside as I climb out of the SUV.

Two crew members carrying boom mics pass me. They jog up a short flight of brick stairs leading to the mansion's double doors. I only hesitate a second longer before following them through the shadowy entryway, wary of what awaits me inside but ready to face it nonetheless.

NICOLE

(SUNDAY, THE NIGHT OF THE MURDERS)

CHAPTER 39

Nicole was packing the last of her clothes in her suitcase when she heard the scream over the music streaming through her earbuds.

She paused and stepped back from the bed, tugging the earbuds from her ears, wondering if maybe it was the wind outside her windows, shrill laughter, or someone's television turned up too loud. Or perhaps she had imagined it and hadn't heard anything at all.

Nicole tossed her earbuds and phone aside, listening more carefully. She started to walk toward her door and step into the hall to see where the noise might have come from, but stopped short when she heard pounding footsteps. They were rapid, like someone was running along the corridor. Then they gradually tapered off.

Had the person gone down the stairs?

She slowly approached the door and unlocked it. Nicole started to ease it open but heard the pounding footsteps again. This time they were drawing closer, like someone was running down the hall toward her room.

Panicked, she slammed the door shut and locked it. She backed away and watched her door handle turn back and forth.

"Nicole! Nikki! Are you there?" Jeremiah shouted, knocking over and over again. "Open the door!"

She unlocked it, threw the door open, and he charged inside. He gazed down at her, then looked over her shoulder at the bedroom behind her.

"Are you all right?" he asked. "I thought I heard you screaming."

"I'm OK. I'm fine," she whispered as he dragged her into an embrace.

"Shit! I thought something had happened to you," he said, not letting her go.

Instead of pulling away, she pressed her face into his shoulder and wrapped her arms around him, touched that he'd been so worried about her, that he'd come looking for her. "I heard the scream, too, but it wasn't me. I couldn't tell where it came from. I guess it wasn't Anna?"

"No, but someone was definitely screaming." He gradually loosened his hold and stared down at her again. This time he looked less concerned than wary of her for some reason.

"What?" she asked, furrowing her brows.

"What the hell is going on?"

"What do you mean? Why are you asking me?"

"Don't play stupid. What happened at dinner tonight . . . whatever is happening now, did you do this? I mean . . . did you cause it?" he asked, pointing to the open door. "Was all this part of your grand plan for the weekend? Did you want them to turn on each other?"

Nicole hesitated then shook her head. "I don't know what you're talking about."

Jeremiah searched her face. "You're lying. You're lying to me *again*. I can tell."

"No," she insisted feebly, taking a step back from him then another. "I'm not lying."

"Come off it, Nikki. You can bullshit them, but don't you dare do it to me! You wrote those letters, didn't you?" he pressed. "Did you know about what happened with Xander and Mark in college, and that Anna stole money from the company? Did Bridget tell you that stuff before she died? You said you always wondered about the rumors about Xander and Charlotte. Were you trying to use that stuff to blackmail them? To get them to tell the truth about what happened to Bridget?"

"*Did* they tell the truth?" she asked almost greedily, seeing her first light of hope in weeks. Had her three months' worth of plotting and scheming finally worked? "Did one of them confess?"

He squinted at her and shook his head. "No. No one fucking confessed. All they did was start shouting at one another. They were at each other's throats down there."

She stubbornly pursed her lips. "OK, *and*? Am I really supposed to feel bad for them, Jeremiah? If they plotted to kill Bridget—"

"Goddammit, Anna didn't kill her sister! She said she had nothing to do with her death and I believe her, and now she's talking about fleeing the fucking country because of the threat you made! And you heard that scream just like I did. They're getting desperate and things are going crazy. Whatever your plan was, it's not getting the results you wanted because this shit is spiraling out of control."

"This wasn't my plan. I swear I didn't write those letters."

He shook his head. "Bullshit. It's all bullshit!"

"No, it's not."

"Tell me the truth. Tell me the truth, or I'm done with this. All of it."

She opened her mouth and, after a few seconds of hesitation, closed it.

"I cannot believe this." He slowly shook his head again and laughed coldly. "You had the balls to accuse me of trying to con you when you've been conning me . . . conning *all of us* this whole damn time. I told you that if you couldn't be straight with me, I wasn't going to do this. I'm done," he said before turning to walk out the door.

"Wait!" she said, running after him, grabbing his arm. "Wait, please! Listen, it wasn't supposed to be this way. I swear to you. They were just supposed to get a . . . a little push. That's all! That's what we agreed to. Nothing like this."

"*We?* Who's we, Nikki?"

Once again, she tried to force out the words, but they wouldn't come. She couldn't tell him. She couldn't say it.

"Right," he muttered in the face of her obstinate silence. He snatched his arm out of her grasp. "I'm out of here. Good luck with . . . whatever hell this is."

Nicole watched as he walked out of the bedroom door. She walked back to her bed and sat down with her head bowed. She had never felt so alone in her whole life.

Nicole had kept so many secrets . . . bore this burden alone for so long that it was almost impossible to let go of it now. To share it with someone else. She was only trying to do what she thought was right, but somehow she'd gotten lost along the way. She kept telling herself to "focus on the objective," to not be shaken from achieving her goal, but now the stakes were too high. She'd wanted resolution, not chaos. Nicole wanted out of this, too.

"Jeremiah!" she called after him, rising from the bed a few minutes later.

Maybe he hadn't left yet, like he said he would. Maybe she could still catch him before he left.

She strode toward the door and swung it open. She began to walk down the hall, toward the other end of the corridor where she would find his and Anna's suite. She knocked on one of the French doors, then tried the handles but they were locked.

"Jeremiah!" she shouted, knocking again but no one answered.

She headed back down the hall, returning from where she came. Had Jeremiah not gone back to his room and just taken the staircase downstairs? Was he outside? He'd have to wait for a ride, even if he insisted on fleeing the mansion tonight. Maybe she could catch him before the driver arrived.

As Nicole walked, she noticed that the corridor was eerily quiet. No screams or voices. Just the sound of her lone footsteps.

Where is everyone? she wondered as she passed her bedroom.

Pretty soon the sound of her own thudding heartbeat was louder than her footsteps. The breaths coming through her parted lips were like shouts in the vacant hallway. The hairs on the back of her neck began to stand on end.

Her primal senses urged her to go back to her room—to lock her door and hide behind the bed for cover—but she pressed on.

Finally she heard pounding footsteps again as she neared the end of the hall and approached the top of the staircase to head to the first floor. Was Jeremiah coming back? Had he changed his mind?

"Jeremiah, is that . . ."

Her words faded when she saw Jeremiah not walking but running up the stairs toward her at top speed. He collided with her, knocking her onto her rear end and making her shout, "Hey!" in surprise. She barely got her bearings again and was about to ask him why he'd shoved her, before he grabbed her hand and yanked her to her feet.

"Get up! Get up now! We have to run."

"Huh?" she asked, now even more confused.

He began to drag her in the same direction she'd just come. She could barely get her footing on the slippery tile. Her arm and shoulder were starting to hurt from how hard Jeremiah was pulling her.

"Wait! Stop! Why are we running?"

"Because your fucking boss is down there, and he has a fucking gun!" Jeremiah shouted as he continued to drag her. "Come on!"

Nicole heard the words but, like the scream, she wondered if once again she'd heard it correctly. *"What?"*

That's when she saw Xander standing several feet in front of them, climbing up the stairs. He was in his swim trunks, soaking wet, and breathing in long, ragged gasps like he'd been running himself and had stopped to catch his breath. And Xander was, indeed, holding a handgun.

Her stomach dropped at the sight of it.

Where the hell did he get a gun?

She then remembered the weapon display in his study downstairs. She could envision the blank spot in the display case where the handgun would normally be.

"It's all your fault," Xander said. His voice was eerily flat and emotionless. His face was blank and pale except for his eyes, which were wide and now so rimmed with red that they made his brown irises look almost black. "All the lies. All the fucking lies and manipulation. She's dead now . . . they're *both* dead now—and it's all your fault!"

Jeremiah didn't have to drag her any longer. They ran hand in hand down the hall toward her room. When they got inside, Jeremiah slammed the door shut and locked it. But seconds later, Xander started ramming the door like a Big Bad Wolf eager to get at the plump little pigs inside.

"Go!" Jeremiah shouted to Nicole, shoving her behind him. "Get your phone. Call the cops!"

She nodded shakily and ran across the room to search for her cell phone. She checked her night table and whimpered when she realized it wasn't on its charger. She searched the top of her dresser, but it wasn't there either.

Where did I leave it?

Then she remembered she'd been listening to music. She'd tossed it and her earbuds onto her bed. She searched the sheets and found both her phone and earbuds sitting on the duvet under the lid of her suitcase. Just as Nicole grabbed her cell, the door burst open, making her scream.

"Charlotte's dead because of you!" he yelled as tears streamed from his eyes.

"*What?* Charlotte's dead?" she gasped.

It couldn't be true, could it?

Nicole watched as Xander raised his gun. But instead of pointing it at her, he pointed it squarely at Jeremiah, astonishing them both.

"... and because of Anna," Xander went on, like he hadn't heard her. "Because of those fucking letters and what they said! Mark killed her, and he tried to kill me, too, but the bastard drowned before he could do it. Bet he wished he took those swimming lessons his mom signed him up for in high school. Mark drowned in my own fucking pool." He laughed but it sounded more like a hiccup . . . like he was choking on his own saliva. "They're both dead. Are you happy now? Was it worth it?"

"Xander, please don't do this," she urged, easing around the bed. "It's not his fault."

"No! No, it *is* his fault!" Xander yelled, not lowering the gun though his arm was shaking. He stepped farther into the room. "Don't you fucking defend him, Nicole! They should've left well enough alone. They—"

"I'm not lying to you, Xander. Jeremiah had nothing to do with this," she said walking toward him. "It was . . . it was all me. I did it."

"Nicole," Jeremiah said sharply, turning to glare at her.

He'd been pestering her to tell the truth, but she could see the warning in his eyes, urging her that now was not the time for bravery, let alone a grand confession. But she couldn't let him take the blame.

"If you put down the gun, I'll . . . I'll tell you everything," she said, drawing closer. "I promise. I'll tell you everything that I did for the past few months leading up to this. All the secrets I kept . . . all the stuff I did behind the scenes."

"Nikki, what are you doing?" Jeremiah grabbed her to pull her back. "Stop! He's going to kill you!"

"No, he won't," she whispered, wiggling out of Jeremiah's grasp.

Although she was only about 50 percent sure of that, her chances were still better than Jeremiah's right now.

Nicole didn't want to die, but she couldn't let an innocent person be killed instead, particularly someone like Jeremiah whom she'd dragged into this under false pretenses. She couldn't allow him to take a bullet for her.

She'd talked Xander out of his rages in the past, so maybe she could do it again tonight. But this wasn't tickets to the Met or a messed-up lunch order that he was bitching about.

"Just . . . just put the gun down, Xander," she urged with as calm a voice she could muster at that moment. "Or at least let Jeremiah go."

"Shut up! Just shut up!" Xander bellowed. "You all think I'm stupid, don't you? That you can manipulate me like Mark did. He said he found a way to finally get Mom off my back. I didn't ask any questions. But I should've! I should've! Mark knows investments. I just thought it was a business deal. That . . . that I could finally invest in something lucrative and be a big success. I'd show Mom I wasn't the fuckup she always said I was. I wouldn't need her help anymore. But I didn't know where the money was going," he rambled. "I didn't know what it was for—and Mark knew that. He knew! I'm not going to be manipulated again!"

His hand was shaking even harder now. The tears were coming faster. He was practically gasping through the sobs.

Every part of her said to run. To seek refuge behind the bed. To sprint to the closet and shut the door, but she took another tenuous step toward Xander.

"I don't think you're stupid," she whispered. "I just think that you're angry and scared. But . . . but I'm telling you, it's OK. I—"

She couldn't say for sure what happened next. That's what she would tell the police when they questioned her later that night and again several times after that. Each time her recollection would change. It had all happened so fast that Nicole couldn't distinguish between what she'd seen in her periphery and what she'd imagined happened in order to fill in the gaps of her memory.

She wasn't sure if Jeremiah had once again reached out to pull her back, or if he attempted to place his body in front of hers to protect her, or if he charged at Xander to take the weapon away from him, but Nicole knew for certain that it was Xander who fired the gun.

She heard the two quick pops. In shock, she looked down at herself to see where the bullets had landed, wondering why she didn't feel any pain and waiting for it to come. That's when she heard Jeremiah tumble to the floor behind her. She turned to find him lying on his back and blood pooling from his chest onto his white shirt.

"Oh, my Lord! Sweet Jesus!" she screamed, falling to his side. She held her hand over the wounds, which were near the center of his chest, but she couldn't staunch the bleeding. It gushed over her fingers, coating her hands with a glistening red.

There was so much blood.

"He was . . . he was coming at me," Xander said limply. "I-I had no choice. I had to shoot."

But Nicole was barely listening. Instead she watched as Jeremiah's eyes began to roll behind his drooping lids.

"It's OK," she whispered down to Jeremiah, keeping one hand on the wounds and raising the other to his cheek. She could barely make out his face with all the tears flooding her eyes. She sniffed. "I-I-I'll call for h-h-help. The E-E-EMTs will take care of you. Just . . . just keep your eyes open, OK? St-st-stay with me."

Jeremiah's mouth opened like he was trying to say something, but nothing more would come out than a soft groan.

"They're gonna arrest me, Nicole," Xander said behind her, now frantic. "Before you call 9-1-1, we . . . uh . . . we have to get our stories straight. I was . . . I was just defending myself. From him . . . from Mark. If you tell them—"

"I'm not telling them anything!" she shouted, glowering up at him.

"Don't desert me," he said desperately. "Don't desert me like the others. Don't desert me when I need you the most."

She slowly shook her head. This man was absolutely delusional. She would've laughed at the absurdity of the moment if Jeremiah wasn't bleeding out on the bedroom floor.

"I am not cleaning up any more of your fucking messes. You *shot* him, Xander! He's dying. And I hope you go to jail for it. I hope you rot there."

Just then, Nicole swore she could hear the far-off wail of sirens. Was it her imagination or had someone else heard the gunshots and called 9-1-1? She couldn't be sure but she turned to pick up her phone from the floor where it had fallen. She started to speak to the operator just when she heard another pop and a subsequent thump.

Nicole turned and found Xander lying halfway in the bedroom, halfway out. His body blocked the doorway. When the EMTs arrived five minutes later, his body would have to be dragged out of the way so they could load Jeremiah onto the stretcher, but Nicole wouldn't be spared the vision of her former boss. She wouldn't get the image of his disfigured face and his pleading eyes out of her mind. She'd see it even in her dreams.

CHAPTER 40

Nicole would discover much later that Xander hadn't lied. Charlotte Danfrey was dead after taking an unfortunate tumble from one of the second-floor balconies. Mark Danfrey had drowned during a fight with Xander in the Chamberses' pool. Now Xander was dead, too, after a self-inflicted gunshot, and Jeremiah was hanging on to life by the thinnest of threads.

She'd answered the police officer's initial questions of what had happened leading up to the shooting and asked to ride in the ambulance with Jeremiah, insisting to the cops, EMTs, and anyone else who would listen that she had to stay at Jeremiah's side.

"I'm . . . I'm his . . . his . . . uh, girlfriend," she'd blurted out as they loaded his stretcher into the van. "I have to go with him!"

"I'm sorry, ma'am, but no. There's no room!" one of the EMTs shouted back at her.

"I mean. Fiancée! I'm his fiancée! Jeremiah and I just . . . we just got engaged," she lied, feeling desperate tears pool in her eyes once again. "Please, let me stay with him! Or at least tell me what hospital you're taking him to. Please?"

The EMTs shouted the hospital's name to her before slamming the door shut.

She winced as the sirens blared. She bit down hard on her bottom lip, stifling a sob as she watched the ambulance drive away with lights flashing.

"You're engaged?" Nicole vaguely heard someone say behind her.

She turned around to find Elena standing on the mansion's entryway stairs. The au pair held Harper in her arms. The little girl was still in her PJs, although wrapped in a pink blanket. Her legs were wrapped around Elena's waist and one arm was looped around the young woman's neck. She was sucking her thumb. Her blue eyes were wide as she gazed at the spectacle of lights, sounds, and people around her.

Nicole wondered how much the toddler understood what had happened, of how much her life had changed that night. Her mother was dead, and both her real father and the man she'd known as her father were gone as well. In a matter of hours, Harper Danfrey had been made an orphan.

"*It's all your fault,*" she could hear Xander's disembodied voice echoing in her thoughts. She shook her head to answer Elena's question and to push Xander's voice away.

"No, we're not engaged. I just . . . I just told them that so they'd let me in the ambulance." She looked past the police cars and the officers circulating nearby on the driveway where the ambulance had sped away less than a minute ago. "I don't know if he's going to make it. I wanted to be there with him if . . . if he . . ." She couldn't finish the words. "I didn't want him to be alone."

Elena walked down the stairs, still clutching Harper in her arms. "The gunshots." Her voice trailed off, too.

Nicole nodded. "Xander shot Jeremiah before he shot . . ." She paused and looked at Harper, who was staring at her with rapt attention. She cleared her throat. "Before he . . . uh. He took care of himself," she whispered. "Xander blamed him for what happened, and now Jeremiah is—"

"But Mr. D was the one who did it. He's the one who killed his mom," Elena argued.

Nicole did a double take. "*What?*"

"Yeah, I tried to tell you this morning, but you were . . . well, busy. I heard Mr. D talking about it with one of his friends. Some other guy who came to the party. This guy named Patrick, I think. Mr. D said he set it up so that Xander paid for it but didn't know what Mr. D was going to do with the money. Mr. D planned the whole thing."

So that's what Xander had been rambling about when he said Mark had manipulated him.

"*He said he found a way to finally get Mom off my back. . . . But I didn't know where the money was going.*"

Mark had tricked Xander into paying for his own mother's murder. Normally Nicole would never believe that anyone could possibly be that stupid or naive to be fooled on such a grand scale, but she knew Xander. Xander was absolutely that naive and stupid.

Nicole glanced over her shoulder at the two body bags that were being loaded into the van by what she assumed was the medical examiner's office.

Mark had paid the ultimate price for his subterfuge and conniving. Unfortunately, Charlotte had paid, too.

"I'm tired," Harper murmured. She rubbed her eyes then yawned. "I want to say night night to Mommy and go back to bed, Elly."

"I know, *niña*," Elena whispered, kissing her brow and gently rubbing her back. The little girl's eyes drifted closed as she rested her head on Elena's shoulder.

Nicole grimaced. She didn't know who faced the harder task: her, as she waited alone at the hospital for word on Jeremiah, or Elena, who would be left with the task of explaining to an innocent three-year-old that both of her parents were gone.

"Look, I have to go," Nicole said, reaching out to touch Elena's arm, "but you can stay here as long as you want. You and Harper. The house is at your disposal."

"Thanks, but . . . no thanks." Elena slowly shook her head. Her eyes scanned the property, pausing on the police cruisers and the men and women in uniform that were now swarming around them. She then glanced over her shoulder at the yawning double doors to the mansion. "I can't take her back up there. I tried to cover her eyes on the way down, but I bet she saw some of it, even if she didn't realize what she saw. If the police say it's OK for me to go, I'm going to take her to a hotel. I grabbed what I could and packed us a bag while we were up there," she said, before glancing down at the leather duffel bag sitting on the stairs beside her, "because I know we can't stay. We'll stay at the hotel tonight, and I'll figure out what to do after that. Her parents left me a contact list in case of emergencies. I guess I'll call her grandmother."

Nicole nodded as she began to back away. "Well, expense the hotel room to me. Whatever you need. I'll pay for it."

Of course, you will. Because it's all your fault, she could hear Xander whisper in her ear as if he were standing right next to her.

She closed her eyes, silently willing the voice to go away, then ran in the direction of where she'd parked the Subaru she'd rented for the weekend, but stopped short when she realized she didn't have her car keys. They were back inside her bedroom, which was now a crime scene surrounded by technicians and yellow police tape. Nicole still had her cell phone, though. She hadn't let go of it, even in all the chaos. So she opened an app to get a car to the hospital, excusing her way through the crowd of officers as she did it.

CHAPTER 41

WHEN NICOLE ARRIVED AT THE HOSPITAL, SHE FOUND HERSELF IN A glass-enclosed waiting area filled with people, some who looked just as shell-shocked as she did. A few stared at her openly as she stepped through the sliding glass doors.

She looked down at herself and realized for the first time how gruesome she appeared to everyone else. Her hands were coated in blood that had started to dry and crust over so that it looked vaguely like she was wearing red gloves. The front of her T-shirt and pajama bottoms were smeared in red as well.

"*Ma'am?* Ma'am, where are you bleeding? What happened?" a nurse in blue scrubs asked as she rushed across the waiting room toward her. "I need help over here!" she shouted across the waiting room, waving at two medical assistants that stood near steel double doors.

"No! No, I'm not bleeding," Nicole quickly explained, making the assistants and nurse pause. "My friend was shot. It's *his* blood," she clarified. "The ambulance brought him here. His name is Jeremiah. Jeremiah O'Connor, and I'm Nicole Underwood. His . . . umm . . . his fiancée," she said, hoping the lie would work this time. "I wanted to check on his status."

One of the nurses at the front desk said that Jeremiah had been taken into surgery. Nicole tried to sit down in one of the empty chairs as she waited for news from a doctor or nurse on how the surgery was going, but instead she started pacing up and down the waiting room's linoleum tile, too restless to sit.

Nicole was a doer. A problem solver. She didn't sit on her hands and wait around for something to happen, but what was happening beyond the emergency room's double doors was well beyond her capabilities.

She went into the bathroom to scrub off as much blood as she could, watching the residue swirl down the porcelain sink. But worse than the blood was the armor that she'd usually throw on at moments of crisis. It was gone now; Nicole could no longer wear it for protection. She was laid bare.

As she sat in the waiting room, her phone kept buzzing, making her grimace. She guessed word of what had happened at Maple Grove had already begun to spread. Nicole pulled her phone out of her pocket and glared at the screen.

WHAT'S GOING ON??? Why aren't you answering any of my texts? Did we get a confession?

She gritted her teeth, muted notifications, and slammed the phone face down on the empty chair beside her in frustration and disgust.

As one hour passed into the next, the events of that night replayed like a movie in her head. She could see Jeremiah running up the stairs, barreling toward her then grabbing her hand. She could see Xander, bare-chested and soaked with pool water, pointing the gun at Jeremiah. She then saw Jeremiah lying on the bedroom floor, bleeding, trying desperately to speak although only pained gasps would come out of his mouth.

It wasn't supposed to happen this way. This wasn't the plan, she thought desperately.

Nicole squeezed her eyes so tightly shut that the lids were starting to hurt. Or maybe they were already sore from all the crying she'd done that night.

She rose to her feet and started pacing again. Trying her best to work out all the nervous energy and angst but to no avail. Her throat only tightened more. Her stomach felt queasy. She ran toward the automated doors leading to the parking lot, feeling like she was being strangled by the sobs that were fighting to get out of her.

She needed to breathe. She desperately needed some air.

Nicole made it to a nearby bush in just enough time to vomit. Only after she finished did she feel like she could breathe again. She sat down on a concrete wall, wiping her mouth with the back of her hand as she sobbed.

She could feel herself unraveling, but there was nothing . . . *no one* to hold her together, to keep her in one piece.

She returned to the waiting room and grabbed her cell. She took a deep breath before dialing her mother's number.

"Hello?" her mother answered sleepily. "Nikki? Why are you calling so late? What's wrong?"

Nicole sniffed. "Mom, something . . . something happened. Something really bad, and I . . . I need you. I need you, Mom. I don't want to be alone up here." Even her voice was trembling.

"*What?*" her mother shouted. "What happened, Nikki? What's wrong? Where are you, honey?"

"I'm at the hospital in the Hudson Valley. It's not far from the mansion. Xander's dead, Mom. He killed someone and tried to kill my . . . my friend. And I don't know . . . I don't know what to do. I don't know how to fix this."

Her mother went silent on the other end of the line for what seemed like a full minute. "It's OK, Nikki. I'll be there. I'm putting on my clothes now. Give me the address of the hospital and I'll be there in a few hours. Just . . . just hold tight, honey. OK?"

She gave her mother the address and waited. She waited for the doctor to come with news. She even made sure that the nurse at the front desk who started the new shift knew she was there.

"Yes, I understand, Ms. Underwood, and I know how long you've been waiting," the woman said in a measured voice and with a slow nod, like she was used to being harassed with these types of questions all the time. "Someone will come out to give you an update when they can."

She waited for her mother, getting text updates from her on the road.

I just hit Kent Island and should be in Delaware soon, her mom wrote at 12:48 a.m.

Stopping for gas. I'm down to a quarter of a tank. Shouldn't slow me down too much, she wrote at 2:19 a.m.

On the New Jersey Turnpike, she wrote at 4:25 a.m. **Getting closer.**

She watched other patients leave and new patients take their place in the emergency room's plastic chairs. As the hours passed, Nicole fought to stay awake, but the anxiety and panic of the night gave way to exhaustion, and she could feel sleep tugging at her like an insistent child. Her head began to droop despite her best efforts. Her eyes drifted closed. And she slept.

CHAPTER 42

"Nikki? Nikki, I'm here, honey," her mother whispered.

Nicole opened her eyes to a gentle tap on her shoulder. She found the waiting room now flooded with sunlight. It was the next day. Monday morning. Her mother was standing in front of her, gazing down at her worriedly.

The older woman was still wearing her pink hair bonnet that she'd been sleeping in when Nicole had called her. A smear of blue toothpaste clung to her chin. Nicole could see that underneath her mother's long cashmere sweater she was wearing a silk nightshirt and wrinkled jeans.

Her mother rarely, if ever, left the house without looking impeccable. The fact that she'd come all the way here, after obviously not taking a second glance at the bathroom mirror, warmed Nicole's heart. She rose to her feet and hugged her mother fiercely, catching the older woman off guard at first, but within a few seconds her mother wrapped her arms around her and held her close.

Relief washed over Nicole like an incoming tide; she was no longer alone. After a while she stepped back and saw that her mother was crying.

"Oh, Mom," she groaned, wiping her mother's tears with her thumbs. She winced as her own eyes began to water again. "Don't cry! You're gonna make me cry, too, and I've been doing it for the past five hours."

"Sorry," her mother said with a sniff. "Seeing you like this is just a lot, honey."

Her mother reached into her purse and pulled out a packet of tissues. She took out one from the packet and blew her nose before plopping down into one of the chairs.

"I was so scared driving here. You haven't called me in the middle of the night like that in . . . in *years*. Not since you did that sleepover at Casey Nelson's house and told me to come pick you up because you found a cockroach in your sleeping bag." She reached out and grabbed her hand. "Now tell me what happened, Nikki. What do you mean Xander is dead? Did that boy really kill someone?"

Nicole sat in the chair beside her and reluctantly began an abbreviated retelling of what had happened last night, leaving three people in body bags.

"Oh, my Lord! And how are you holding up, honey?" her mother asked.

"I'm . . . I'm fine. Fine now, anyway," Nicole lied with a tight smile that looked more like a wince. She squeezed her mother's hand reassuringly, then returned her hands to her lap, clenching them into tight fists.

How long was this surgery going to take? It had to be going on at least six or seven hours now. Had the doctor come with news about Jeremiah while she was asleep?

No, she thought, shaking her head. *They would have woken me up for that.*

They knew how long she'd been waiting; how eager she was to hear news.

"Are you sure you're OK?" her mother pressed.

"Well, not OK," Nicole admitted, "but I'm better now that you're here."

Her mother looked her up and down, pausing a beat on the bloodstains on her clothes and the heavy bags underneath her eyes. She didn't seem convinced.

"I bet you didn't get much sleep." She then scanned her eyes around the waiting room. "It's like a bus station here with all this noise and people coming and going. Have you eaten anything? I can grab you something from one of the vending machines."

Nicole slowly exhaled and began to rub her knees over and over again. Was it her imagination or was it getting colder?

"No, thanks. I haven't had much of an appetite, Mom."

"Well, the gift shop should be opening soon. You want me to get you some fresh clothes? Let me buy you a new shirt at least."

"No, Mom, I don't need clothes. I don't need food. I don't need sleep either. I just want to sit here and wait. OK? Is that all right?"

"Well, don't get fussy," her mother said, slapping her purse onto her lap. "I'm only trying to help."

Nicole rolled her eyes. The relief she'd felt at having her mother near was starting to fade; maybe it wasn't such a good idea to ask her mom to travel here to keep her company. The older woman couldn't help questioning and hovering. Couldn't her mom just *be* here with her? Support her?

"Mom, I swear I'll eat, wash, change clothes, and sleep when I get home *after* I get an update on Jeremiah." Nicole leaned to her side over one of the chair's arms to gaze around the waiting area's front desk where two nurses sat. She hoped to catch a glimpse of what was going on beyond the double doors leading to the bustling ER corridor.

"*Where* is the doctor?" Nicole lamented. "I've been here since last night and no one can give me an update?"

Her mother reached out and placed her warm hand over Nicole's again, catching her by surprise. "You're really worried about this Jeremiah fellow, huh?"

Nicole nodded. "He could die, Mom."

"Why haven't you ever mentioned him before, baby? Is he a friend of yours?"

Nicole hesitated and nodded again. "Yes."

"A close friend, I guess, if you've been waiting here so long for him," her mother said softly.

Nicole frowned. Before she could reply, one of the steel doors opened. She saw a gray-haired white guy wearing scrubs and a white coat step out and whisper something to one of the nurse attendants at the front desk. She pointed across the room in Nicole's direction. Nicole watched as he nodded and walked toward her. As the doctor drew closer, she saw that he looked as exhausted as he felt.

She held her breath, bracing herself for bad news . . . for the *worst* possible news that the surgery hadn't worked and Jeremiah had taken his last breath on the operating table.

"Hello, I'm Dr. Thornton. Are you Nicole Underwood? The patient Jeremiah O'Connor's fiancée?"

When he asked his question, Nicole's mom gasped audibly. She whipped around in her chair and turned to face Nicole with wide, questioning eyes.

Nicole ignored her mother's reaction and nodded.

"Yes, I'm Nicole. How is he, doctor? Is . . . Is he OK?"

"It was touch and go for a while. The bullets missed his heart and lungs by mere centimeters. He required a major transfusion for the blood loss, but we got the bleeding under control. He's stable but sedated. He's being transported to the ICU."

She fell forward in her chair and braced her elbows on her knees, nearly collapsing. She dropped her head into her hands. Who knew that good news could be equally overwhelming?

Her mother reached out and gently began to rub her back.

Gradually, Nicole lowered her hands, blinking through her tears. She sniffed. "Can I . . . can I see him?"

The doctor nodded. "We'll also need some medical directives from you. He's doing better now, but in case Mr. O'Connor takes a turn or if any other major decisions have to be made, we need to know how to proceed. If we should resuscitate or if—"

"No. No, I can't do that, Doctor. I can't make those decisions. His mother would be better. She's in New Jersey."

Cecilia in Ho-Ho-Kus, Nicole now thought, remembering the town's odd name from that conversation she had in bed with Jeremiah yesterday morning.

Jesus. Had it only been yesterday? It already felt like a lifetime ago.

"His mom should make decisions like that. Not me."

The doctor nodded. "Do you have her contact information? Could you get her on the phone? Or would she be able to come here?"

"I'll make sure that she does."

The doctor assured Nicole that she should be able to see Jeremiah in a couple of hours at most.

While she waited, Nicole managed to find a phone number with a Google search for Cecilia Manalo in Ho-Ho-Kus. She paced again—this time in the ICU waiting area—as she listened to the phone ring on the other end. Just when she was about to hang up, she heard the line click.

"Hello!" She heard a young woman shout over noise in the background. It sounded like a television broadcast, maybe the morning news.

"Hi, may I . . ." Nicole paused. She could feel her throat going dry. She loudly swallowed. "May I please speak with Cecilia Manalo?"

"Ma! The phone's for you!" the young woman on the other end yelled.

Nicole grimaced, realizing the woman who answered may be Jeremiah's little sister.

"Who is it?" she heard a voice ask in return. It sounded farther away.

"I don't know. She didn't say."

Nicole then heard a clatter, like the phone was being dropped on a table or countertop.

"*Hello?* Who is this?" a woman answered a few seconds later. She had a slight accent. "If you are trying to sell me something, I don't want it. You're wasting your time."

"No, ma'am, This isn't a sales call. I'm a friend of Jeremiah's. Jeremiah, your son. My name is Nicole."

There was a long pause. "My son doesn't live here. Why are you calling about Jerry? He got arrested, didn't he?" She muttered something in another language. "I told him that he would—"

"He's not arrested or in jail. He's in the hospital. Uh, Jeremiah was shot, ma'am."

"*Shot?* Jerry was shot?" the older woman repeated, like she hadn't heard Nicole correctly. "What do you mean he was shot? Is he . . . is he—"

"He's alive!" she rushed out, not wanting to scare the older woman any more than she already had. "He's stable. But he's at a hospital. In the ICU. I'm the only one here, and they need someone to make medical decisions for him." She gnawed her bottom lip. "I thought that should be you, ma'am."

Nicole heard another clatter, then more voices in the background.

"Hello?" someone answered. It sounded like the young woman from earlier. "My mom says my brother Jerry is at the hospital. Can you tell me which one, please?"

Nicole gave her the hospital's name and the address along with his doctor's name.

"It's OK, Ma! I got the address. She said Jerry is OK. He's not dying, Ma. Stop crying!" his little sister assured the ranting woman in the background. "Matt can drive us there. He's putting on his shoes now."

Nicole started to lower the phone from her ear. She'd made the call. Jeremiah's family would be at his side soon, she hoped, but Nicole paused when she heard the girl whisper, "Do you know how my brother got shot? I mean . . . was he in trouble again? Are the cops there? What did he do?"

"He wasn't in trouble. He didn't do anything wrong. He was . . . he was trying to save me when it happened," Nicole said.

That's right. He was trying to save you, and now he's here because of you, Xander's voice whispered gleefully into her other ear, making her cringe. *This is all your fault, and you know it.*

"Save you? *Jerry* did that?" The girl sounded surprised. "Hmm," she murmured. "OK, Ma! Yes, I'm coming!" she yelled before abruptly hanging up.

Nicole lowered the phone from her ear. When she turned around, she saw her mom silently watching her.

"I'm ready to take your advice," she said, looking down at herself. "Let's go to the gift shop and buy some clothes."

It was one thing to wear bloodstained clothes in the ER waiting area; it was another thing to wear it in the elevators or wandering around the other wards. Nicole didn't want to terrify the expectant moms making their way to the maternity wing or elderly patients coming in for physical therapy.

Soon after arriving in the ICU waiting area in her newly purchased oversized T-shirt and drawstring pajama pants, the nurse behind the desk motioned for her. "Ms. Underwood?"

Nicole shot to her feet. "Yes?"

"You can see Mr. O'Connor now."

Minutes later, she and her mother walked down the hall to his hospital room. Nicole took several deep breaths as she did it, bracing herself for what she was about to see, reminding herself that no matter what state Jeremiah was in, at least he was still alive. She read the number on the door plaque, confirming that it was the right room, then began to step inside, but paused when she realized her mother was no longer at her side. She turned to find the older woman lingering in the hallway behind her.

"I'll wait here and give you some privacy," her mom whispered.

Nicole nodded then walked inside the hospital room. Most of the bed was hidden by a sterile white curtain. She heard the beep of his heart monitor and the soft hush of the ventilator before she saw Jeremiah, but when she stepped around the curtain and laid eyes on him, she breathed in sharply.

His normally tan skin looked sallow and waxen under the hospital track lighting. Nicole drew closer and gazed at his face, which was mostly hidden by the tubing around his mouth. His wavy dark hair was pasted to his scalp. She wanted to reach out and push it back and smooth the tendrils into place. She wanted to lean forward and place her hand over his, but she was wary of touching him. Of disturbing him any more than she already had.

You've done enough, haven't you? Xander's voice whispered in her ear.

She opened her mouth to speak to Jeremiah. To reassure him. To apologize, but nothing would come out. What could she say? What would be suitable at a horrific moment like this? All he had asked her was to be honest with him. And she couldn't even do that.

She silently backed away from the bed, from him. She stepped around the curtain and back into the hall. Nicole looked at her mother, who was leaning against the hospital wall and watching a couple carrying a flower vase and helium balloons walk by.

"We can leave now," Nicole whispered.

"Huh?" her mother asked. She pushed herself away from the hallway wall then frowned. "*Already?* But you were only in there a couple of minutes, Nikki. I thought you would want to—"

"Let's go please, Mom," she said firmly, heading to the elevators, not looking back.

CHAPTER 43

An hour later, Nicole sat in the passenger seat of her mother's BMW. She absently wiped her nose while gazing at the passing scenery as her mother drove them back to the mansion. She needed to grab her things . . . her purse, keys, and suitcase, and retrieve the rental car she'd abandoned on the Maple Grove lot.

Both women remained silent during the drive, although Nicole could practically hear her mother shouting a multitude of unasked questions telepathically.

But seeing Jeremiah in that hospital bed, with his IVs and all those tubes and machines surrounding him or attached to him, had been a hard knock after a series of blows Nicole had already endured today and last night. She was too emotionally exhausted for heavy conversation. Unfortunately, her mother didn't pick up on those vibes.

"Engaged," her mother said, nodding her head like she was listening to a song on the car radio. "You're engaged and didn't tell me."

Nicole rolled her eyes. "Mom, seriously, out of all that's happened, *that's* what you want to talk about?"

"Nicole Underwood, I bit my tongue. I bit my tongue all damn morning! I held your hand and let you cry on my shoulder, but I'm not biting my tongue anymore. How could you get engaged to a man I've never met?"

"Mom, I'm not—"

"That I've never even *heard of*?" the older woman pressed on, shouting over her. "And the first time I see him is when he's unconscious in a goddamn hospital bed. Here I was, thinking you weren't even dating, and you had a full-blown engagement with—"

"Mom, calm down! Jeremiah and I are not engaged. I just said that so the hospital would let me in his room to see him. I'm not a relative and I figured that was the closest to it—short of lying about being his wife."

"But he's more than just a friend. A boyfriend then?" her mother asked slowly, furrowing her brows.

"No, he's not my boyfriend. We barely know each other, to be honest."

"*Barely know each other?*" Her mother squinted. "Nikki, you called his mother. You lied about being engaged to him and was crying over him in the waiting room and ICU. Why the hell would you do all that for someone you barely know?"

"I just had to."

"Had to?"

"I can't explain it, Mom. It's complicated."

Because the answer was complicated, just like everything else she'd done in the past few days . . . in the past few months. She knew instinctively that saying her reasoning and motivations out loud now wouldn't make it any easier for her mother to understand. The more she thought about it, the less she understood herself.

"Well, maybe y'all can figure out all that complication when he wakes up. You two can talk about it when you go back to see him again."

"I'm not going back," she whispered.

"What? Why in the world not?" her mother cried.

"His family is coming. It should take them a couple of hours at most to get here from New Jersey. I'd just be in the way. They can take care of him now."

"But don't you wanna—"

"Mom, I'm the reason Jeremiah is there. I can't look his mother and sister in the eye knowing that. I can't look *him* in the eye. I just can't. OK?"

Her mother gave her an uneasy side glance before returning her eyes to the road.

"Whatever you say, Nikki," she murmured as they turned onto the gravel road leading to Maple Grove.

Nicole half expected to see the dozen or so cop cars and medical vans there, but she spotted only two village police cruisers this time. Besides the two cars, the only remnants of last night in front of the imposing exterior of the mansion were a few lines of yellow police tape tied to the columns near the double doors, which were now fluttering in the wind like party streamers. In addition to the cruisers, she also spotted a black Lincoln Town Car with blacked-out windows parked out front.

Nicole's mom gradually came to a stop on the driveway near the entrance, behind the Town Car. Now they both were frowning, staring curiously at the vehicle.

"Whose car is that?" her mother asked.

"I don't know," Nicole said with a shrug. "Maybe one of the guests. Or someone from Altruist."

She wouldn't be surprised if the company—maybe Daniel himself—had sent a few of its lawyers and public relations Svengalis to the crime scene to assess the situation and figure out how to spin such a gruesome catastrophe so that Altruist suffered the least amount of blowback. But they faced an uphill battle, and, for once, it was no longer Nicole's job to clean up.

A minute later, she and her mother climbed the stairs to the mansion. Nicole tried the door handle and found it unlocked. As she pushed the door open, she was met by a cop who strode across the marble tile, his heavy footfalls echoing to the high steeple ceilings as he walked. He held up his hand, making Nicole and her mother instantly halt in the doorway.

"Not another one," he grumbled. "Hey! Hey, this is a crime scene. You can't just walk in here and—"

"Yes, of course! I'm so sorry, officer. I wasn't trying to just walk in. See, my name is Nicole Underwood. I was here last night. I . . . uh . . . I worked for Xander Chambers. I was here when he . . ." She paused and winced. "When Xander killed himself. I just wanted to grab a few of my things from upstairs. My purse. Car keys. So I can go home."

The officer glared over Nicole's shoulder at her mother. "And who are you?"

"Juanita Underwood," her mother said, raising her chin and meeting his glare. "I'm her mama."

"She drove me here," Nicole quickly explained.

"Yeah, well, you can go upstairs with an escort. She'll have to wait outside. But first I'll need to see some ID so I can verify who you say you are."

"I would, officer, but like I said . . . my purse is upstairs. My wallet and my ID are in my purse."

He narrowed his green eyes and hooked his thumbs in his belt. "Then you have a problem, don't you?"

Nicole heard her mother loudly suck her teeth behind her, showing her frustration. Nicole was getting just as annoyed. Dealing with a rude cop was the last thing she needed right now, but she'd try her best to remain calm.

"Is there an officer upstairs? Maybe one of them could—"

"You can let her inside, Officer Tatum," a familiar voice said, making Nicole's gaze dart down the corridor beyond the great hall.

She found Bridget Chambers standing in the doorway of one of the sitting rooms.

CHAPTER 44

"Oh, my God! Oh, my God!" Nicole's mother screamed as Bridget strolled toward them. "Tell me you see what I'm seeing! That you see her right there in front of us, or am I going crazy, Nikki?"

Nicole turned to find that her mother's eyes were wide with terror and shock, like she'd just encountered a ghost.

"Yes, I see her, too. It's OK, Mom," she assured, placing a hand on her shoulder. "Everything is OK."

Bridget sported a tan, thanks to a private island in the Caribbean where she'd been quietly hiding for the past several months. She'd also cut her hair into a windswept bob. She wore an orange silk sheath dress and canvas espadrilles.

Bridget looked as if she'd just strolled off a sunny beach with turquoise waters and white sand, because she probably had.

"This is my home, and they are my guests," Bridget said as she approached the officer. "I'll take over from here."

The officer's face went red. This time he was the one who looked annoyed. "Ma'am," he began, "I was told to—"

"You and your fellow officers were told by Police Chief Nash to monitor and secure the crime scene," Bridget said, speaking over him. "And you've done a stellar job, Officer Tatum. I'll tell the chief when I speak to him later today. Thank you. I'll take over from here."

Bridget was smiling but her voice was firm. The officer finally caught on that she was not to be challenged, lowered his head, and angrily walked away.

"Bridget," Nicole whispered, stepping toward her, "what are you doing here? You were supposed to wait until I gave the all clear. This isn't what we agreed to."

"Agreed to?" Nicole's mother squeaked. "You . . . you knew she wasn't dead? That she didn't die in a car crash?"

Nicole sighed. Reluctantly, she nodded, making her mother's mouth fall open all over again.

"And you agreed to keep me informed," Bridget said. "I would've waited, Nicole, but I saw the video footage and news reports of what was happening here. You weren't answering any of my calls or texts. I had to find out what was going on, so I chartered a jet and took a flight as soon as I could to see for myself what was happening."

"Nicole," her mother said in a hoarse whisper, grabbing her arm, "what the hell is she talking about? What is going on?"

Nicole closed her eyes. "Mom, can you wait for me in the car while I talk with Bridget? While I get my things?"

"No, I will not wait for you in the car!" her mother yelled, making her open her eyes again. "I want you to explain to me—"

"I swear, I will explain everything to you, but just . . . just let me do this. Please, Mom. I know I'm asking a lot, but . . . but let me talk to her privately first. Just trust me."

Her mother let go of her and stared at her for a long time. "You're asking me to trust you? After all of this? After all that you've done and the lies you've told me?" she shouted.

At that question, Nicole had to look away. She could no longer hold her mother's gaze, now overwhelmed with shame.

Finally, her mother sucked her teeth again and shook her head in frustration. "Twenty minutes. I will wait for you twenty minutes, Nikki, and then I'm leaving. I swear to God," she muttered before turning and marching out the mansion's double doors. After her exit, Nicole turned back around to find Bridget gazing at her.

"Come with me, Nicole," Bridget said, gesturing down the hall. "We should talk."

"First off, I want to say that I'm sorry, Nicole. I didn't mean to frighten your mother," Bridget said, holding up her hands as they walked into the sitting room. Bridget made her way around one of the sofa chairs as she spoke. "I didn't know she'd be here. I thought you might come back . . . I just thought you'd be alone." Bridget looked her up and down. "How are you, by the way?"

Her former boss's face showed such intense concern that Nicole didn't know whether to laugh or to slap her.

"*How am I?* How am I?" Nicole sighed. "Well, I was held at gunpoint by *your son* before he shot my friend Jeremiah, then turned the gun on himself. Now, Jeremiah, who was only here because I hired him to gather information for *you*, is now on a ventilator. Xander's dead. Mark is dead, too, and—"

"And Charlotte and Anna. Yes, I know," Bridget finished for her with a solemn nod.

"*Anna?*" She didn't think it was possible to endure yet another shock. It felt like her heart did a few arrhythmic thumps before returning to his normal pace.

Nicole fell back onto the leather sofa like she'd been shoved onto it, and Bridget casually took a wingback chair facing her.

"What the hell happened to Anna? How . . . how . . ." Nicole murmured. Her voice drifted off into nothing.

"How the police explained it to me," Bridget began, crossing her legs, "is that it happened while Anna was fleeing the scene. The police saw her speeding away and didn't know if she was one of the assailants. They chased her, and she did a bad maneuver on one of the roads about a few miles from here. She made a sharp turn around a bend, spun out and . . . well, she hit a tree." Bridget sighed. "She died on impact."

The sitting room went quiet. Nicole swore she could hear the clock on the wall ticking.

"Anna's dead," Nicole said, feeling numb. "Your sister is dead."

"Yes." Bridget gave a slow nod. "I am aware, Nicole. And it's very sad. It's unfortunate but—"

"No 'but's! She's dead, Bridget, along with your son and two other people! Harper, your own grandchild, is an orphan now, and Jeremiah might be debilitated for the rest of his life because of this. Because he was shot twice in the chest!" She sat forward on the sofa. "How are you so calm and not devastated by all of this? Because I am! I'm falling apart! Do you realize what we've done?"

"Yes, I realize what we've done, Nicole. We did what the police could not." She rose to her feet. "Because you found out the truth, didn't you? We were able to solve the mystery of who hired a hit man to try to kill me, to sabotage my car that night in February and send it sailing off that road."

But the car hadn't really been sabotaged. And it really hadn't been a hit man, either; it was an undercover officer who was part of a sting operation set up by the New York State Police after getting wind that someone close to Bridget was trying to set up her murder. They got the tip from an inmate but didn't know for sure the identity of the person who tried to contract the hit. Police suspected it was Xander but couldn't prove it.

The "hit man" got in touch with a mysterious intermediary, but each time the individual refused to meet in person and would only communicate via email, text, and once through a homeless man who conveyed the message to the hit man for him—or her.

The police were left at a loss with such an elusive adversary. They hoped that once they went forward with Bridget's contracted "murder," her murderer would reveal their identity. They would finally gloat to the wrong person or give an outright confession, but it didn't happen. They remained hidden.

Bridget was faced with two options: admit defeat and "come back from the dead," or continue the ruse and let it play out until her killer or killers showed their hand. Bridget chose the latter, telling the cops a week after her "death" that she would carry on without them and take over the "murder" investigation herself, since they seemed incapable of finding out who wanted to kill her. Nicole—her ever loyal and dutiful assistant—agreed to help her. They decided they would hire a network of spies who would observe who Bridget believed were the top suspects. Nicole would also keep her eyes and ears open at the office and whenever she was around Xander, who Bridget suspected as well. They would give it three months and then call it off if they didn't figure out who was behind the murder plot. But Nicole had greatly underestimated what she had agreed to and what it would truly entail.

"Nicole, I am incredibly grateful to you. You did a great job. You got a recording of the plot from Xander's very own mouth."

Nicole furiously shook her head. "I didn't get it! There were no cameras in my bedroom, only in the other rooms. There's no recording, Bridget."

"No, there were cameras. Three of them, in fact. I had them installed in your room."

Nicole pointed at her chest. "You put . . . you had cameras in *my room*? You recorded me, too?"

Bridget had been watching her—just like the others? She'd seen her sleep. Brush her teeth. Talk on the phone with her mom. Bridget had witnessed all those intimate moments between her and Jeremiah as well.

"I cannot . . . I cannot believe you! You were watching me this whole time?" Nicole yelled. She closed her eyes, nauseated from such a violation by someone she'd trusted.

"Oh, Christ," Bridget grumbled. "There's no reason to freak out. I won't release *all* the footage. Just what's relevant." She loudly exhaled. "You aren't the only one who would be embarrassed about what was caught on camera. I even saw Daniel's little speech about how he should be CEO and what he really thought about my leadership." She gave a lofty roll of the eyes. "I told you I always suspected that he was a backstabbing piece of shit. That he was the one secretly working with Gallagher and feeding him information about Altruist. One of my hunches was right, but I was wrong with the other."

That was the other task Bridget had given Nicole: to keep an eye on Patrick Gallagher. It was obvious he was still trying to make a play for the company, and using whomever he could to accomplish it. Bridget didn't know for sure who it was. When Gallagher tried to win Nicole to his side with secret phone calls and gifts, Bridget told her to play along.

"See what he's up to," Bridget told her. "Let me know what you discover."

"But it turns out it was Mark Danfrey, not Daniel," Nicole now said. "Mark was the one who did it. Who orchestrated this whole thing. Daniel was innocent."

"Innocent," Bridget repeated slowly, inclining her head and making her bob sway. "That's open to debate. But regardless, you and I are innocent. At least in the eyes of law, as the video footage and audio shows. We needed those cameras in place as an extra insurance measure. Something for situations like what happened last night."

"An extra insurance measure?" Nicole shot to her feet. "Is that really it, or did you want to keep tabs on me too, Bridget? Did you *ever* trust me?"

"Of course I did!" Bridget exclaimed, having the nerve to look offended. "I wouldn't have confided in you . . . made all these plans with you, if I didn't, Nicole."

"What about the letters?" Nicole asked, glaring at Bridget. "That wasn't part of the plan either."

"We agreed they needed a little push."

"That was not a little push. It made the situation twenty times worse! They turned on each other because they didn't know who wrote them."

"Which was necessary to accomplish our goal," Bridget said tightly. "What do I always tell you? Focus on the objective. And you did. *We* did! You and I took the reins, and we steered this thing, Nicole." Her smile was so bright.

Seeing Nicole's horrified expression, Bridget quickly sombered. "Look," Bridget began again, "I know what has happened these past few days . . . all these months has taken a toll on you. Frankly, it's taken a toll on me, too. It was painful being so far away from everything and everyone I care about. I worried about you, Nicole. I worried about Xander. How he would handle all of this. I worried he would fall apart, and unfortunately, he did. I'm sorry for what happened to Anna, but frankly her life has been in disarray for quite some time, ever since her marriage ended. Who's to say she wouldn't have suffered this fate in the future anyway? That any of them wouldn't have? Please, stop beating yourself up. We've suffered enough. Thankfully, it all worked out in the end."

Nicole stared at Bridget, now dumbfounded. Nicole couldn't believe she'd admired this person. That she'd aspired to be like her one day.

"I have to go," Nicole said dazedly as she began to walk and almost stumble toward the sitting room entrance. "I need to grab my things. Mom is waiting for me."

"Nicole," Bridget called after her, making her pause and turn around and face her again. "You're an amazing assistant. The best. You did a great job. No situation is ever perfect. Take your wins where you can get them."

Nicole narrowed her eyes. How could Bridget describe what had happened here . . . losing her own son and sister as a "win"? But then again, now that Nicole knew the woman Bridget truly was, the description Bridget had used wasn't surprising at all.

Bridget was back from the dead. Her foes were now vanquished. She'd begin the work of taking back her company. Nicole had no doubt that her former boss would make out good in the end. Unfortunately, Nicole couldn't say the same for herself.

Nicole slowly turned back around and walked out of the sitting room, hoping she would never see Bridget Chambers again.

CHAPTER 45
NICOLE

NOW

"Roll camera!" Bill orders.

"Rolling!" Larry, the cameraman, shouts back.

"Roll sound!"

"Rolling!" another voice answers.

I watch as a clapper board appears on the screen monitors.

"Action!" Bill yells.

The clapper board disappears and Asia is now on the monitor in front of me. I adjust my headset.

Asia is sitting on the edge of a bed in a room that, according to the script, is supposed to be my old bedroom in Brooklyn, although the room I'm looking at on-screen is twice the size of my place.

Even with my generous salary, I never could have afforded a bedroom this big in New York.

Asia is also wearing a bandage around her head with dried blood for some reason. The makeup artists added scratches and bruises to her face as well. She raises her bowed head, and her mouth falls open in shock.

"Bridget, what . . . what are you doing here?" she asks.

A tall blond woman—the actress playing Bridget—steps into the frame. "I saw the news, Nicole. I had to come."

As she says those words, I settle back into my chair.

They're filming the moment when Bridget comes out of hiding. It was the last time I've seen or spoken to her without lawyers present after Altruist Corporation tried to enforce my NDA to keep me from talking about what happened at Maple Grove and the months leading up to it.

This scene has the least gore but I'm sure it will have the biggest emotional wallop when moviegoers see it, much like it had for me the day it happened.

I watch as Asia tells "Bridget" on-screen all the things that happened as a result of their conspiring together to uncover the murder plot against Bridget. All the people whose lives were destroyed or lost in the process.

Asia suddenly bursts into tears on-screen. She's crying so hard that it devolves into choking sobs, and I get a little teary myself watching her and remembering how I felt at that moment more than a year ago.

It wasn't only disappointment or shame that I experienced that day. It was also disillusionment. I'd finally understood that I'd been lying not only to everyone else, but also to myself. I may have been manipulated into it, but I'd done things that were, at best, underhanded and morally ambiguous, and, at worst, truly horrendous and diabolical to people who did not deserve it.

And why had I done all of this? To please my boss. To be her good assistant.

It feels so ridiculous now.

"Bridget" on-screen sits on the bed beside Asia and wraps her arm around her.

"Nicole," she whispers, "I know what's happened these past few days . . . all these months have taken a toll on you. It's taken a toll on both of us. But thank you for doing this for me. For taking the lead on everything. You planned it all from the beginning. When I was at a loss of what to do . . . how to handle it all, you took control of the situation."

I stare at the video monitors, leaning forward. Did I hear what I thought I heard?

"I couldn't have done any of this, let alone come up with the plan on my own. Bringing them all here together. Those letters you wrote. Getting that confession from Xander on tape. That was all you!"

I look down at the script and quickly flip pages, comparing what the actresses are saying on-screen to what I'm reading. The lines don't match. I don't remember them saying these lines when they did rehearsals yesterday, either.

When the hell did the lines change? Why is she saying that I wrote those letters? None of this is true.

I look around at the other crew members. They don't look confused like I am. I scan the scripts they're all holding. Do they have new pages that I don't have?

"But I no longer have to look over my shoulder, terrified that someone is out there trying to kill me, Nicole, and it's all thanks to you," the actress playing Bridget says as I jump out of my chair. "You can't—"

"Excuse me! Excuse me!" I shout.

"Cut! Jesus fucking Christ! Are you kidding me?" Bill yells before yanking off headphones. He turns away from the camera and glares over his shoulder at all of us. "Who just spoke? Who was it?"

"Don't worry. I've got it, Bill!" the second assistant director Lacey says as she rushes toward me. She's holding a finger to her lips. "Nicole, under no circumstances can you talk while we're filming. You have to be quiet or—"

"No, I will not be quiet! I want to know who changed those lines." I shouted, pointing at the bedroom where Asia and the other actress are rising from the bed, looking alarmed. "Who made that call?" I look around me. "You changed it so that I'm admitting to the letters . . . so that I'm admitting to setting up this whole damn thing! Who? Who did it? Why? *Why would you do that?*" I yell.

"I don't have time for this. I'm trying to make a movie here. Get her off my set," Bill says, before tugging back on his headphones. He leans around the camera and gives the thumbs-up. "Sorry, Asia . . . Melanie. You're doing a great job. Don't let this ruin your mojo, ladies. OK? Back to one. We'll pick up at 'I couldn't have done any of this, blah, blah, blah . . .' All right?"

"I'm sorry, Nicole," Lacey begins, motioning to a nearby security guard, beckoning him toward us, "but you heard Bill. I'm afraid you have to leave."

"Fine, I'll leave but I want to speak to Gail and Clive, and I want to speak with them right now! If I don't, I'm calling the FCTV LA news crew myself and telling them what I *really* think about this fucking production."

The security guard grabs my arm to escort me off set, but I yank it out of his grasp.

"I'm going, goddammit!" I yell before stalking off, leaving shocked crew members gaping and whispering behind me.

CHAPTER 46

I'VE BEEN BAKING IN THE CALIFORNIA SUN FOR THE PAST HALF HOUR, waiting for Gail and Clive to arrive. When they finally show up, I'm burning on the inside as well. My fury is giving me a migraine. My hands hurt from being balled into fists for so long.

I still don't understand why they changed those lines. Why do they have me admitting to planning everything? None of it makes sense.

Gail and Clive approach me with polite smiles but there's a wariness in their eyes and their posture, like they're bracing for me to start screaming or to throw something at them. Frankly, I'm so angry I just might.

"Nicole, we heard there was an issue on set," Clive begins.

I open my mouth to reply but stop when Gail blurts out, "We heard that you were asked to leave." She slowly shakes her head and cringes. "That is very, very disappointing, Nicole."

"Yes, I was asked to leave," I begin through clenched teeth, "but only because I wanted to know who changed the ending of the movie. Who decided that I should admit to being responsible for *everything* that happened?"

Clive squints. "I wouldn't characterize it that way."

"Well, I would!" I insist. "You have me admitting to writing the letters. You have me saying that I came up with—"

"But that's the thing, Nicole. *You* aren't admitting or saying anything. Your character is," Clive says. "That's very different."

"The character is me! It's me!" I point at my chest. "The story is mine."

"No, the story is *inspired* by your life," he says. "We clearly stated this when we showed you the first draft of the script. We also mentioned that we might undergo rewrites. And you said you were OK with that."

"But you never said you would outright lie! I wouldn't have agreed to this if I knew that."

"Oh, Nicole," Gail says, finally speaking up and reaching out to me. "It's not a lie. It simply puts a positive spin on what was originally a dark ending. When the change was suggested, it all made sense. Before, the film concluded with Nicole feeling aggrieved. She was alone and disillusioned by everything she once believed and trusted. Now she's done something good. Useful, in fact! She saved her boss's life."

"It'll be uplifting for the audience," Clive says.

"Absolutely!" Gail exclaims.

"Me admitting to being solely responsible for the death of four people is not uplifting. It's bullshit!"

"Well, our new executive producer thinks differently," Clive says as his ears turn pink. "And she gets the final say on this. We agreed to that, Nicole."

"What new executive producer?"

Clive and Gail don't answer me right away. Instead, they exchange a look. When they do, my shoulders fall. I instantly know the answer to my own question. I just can't believe she would do this, which is laughable. Once again, I underestimated her.

"It's Bridget, isn't it? Bridget Chambers is the new executive producer."

"I told you that the film was over budget, Nicole," Gail says. "This influx of funding from Ms. Chambers will help get us over the finish line."

"She threatened to *sue me* for telling my story," I say while blinking back tears.

"And she seems to have changed her mind on the issue," Clive says.

But they all knew Bridget hadn't changed her mind. She'd just decided not to pursue a lawsuit because she'd figured out another way to control the message and get what she wanted.

I shake my head in bewilderment. "So you fucked me over because she wrote a check? Is that it?"

"Excuse me!" Clive exclaims, puffing out his chest. Now his neck is pink, too. "*Fucked you over?* I'd argue, Ms. Underwood, that we've done the exact opposite! We flew you to LA and booked you at a four-star hotel the entire duration of this movie. We've let you have a voice throughout the production. We—"

"Clive," Gail says, placing a hand on his shoulder. He instantly goes silent. "Nicole, please try to see this as the glass half full instead of half empty. Now you'll be able to see your story on the big screen," she whispers, even as I close my eyes, refusing to show them how much they, Bridget, and this whole drama have wounded me. "This is a once-in-a-lifetime opportunity. You've won!"

I bark out a hollow laugh. "No, I haven't, Gail. She did." I then turn and walk away, no longer able to hold back the angry tears that spill onto my cheeks.

A half hour later, I'm being driven back to my hotel. My anger has given way to numbness. Kabir even notices the change in me.

"Are you all right, Ms. Underwood?" he asks, eyeing me in the rearview mirror. "I can turn up the AC if it's too hot in here for you."

I slowly shake my head. "I'm fine, Kabir. Thank you. I'm just . . . just a little tired. A lot tired, honestly. It's been a long day."

"I feel you. Only a few more days of shooting though and then you guys are done. Right?"

"No, Kabir, I think today was my last day on set. I'm done."

I can't go back there. I can't sit through any more blocking, rehearsals, and filming when I know what the ending of this movie will be and the lies it will tell the world about me. About everything that happened.

I can see Kabir's furrowed eyebrows in the rearview mirror, like he wants to ask more but I return my gaze to the car window. Fortunately he figures out I'm not in the mood to talk.

When I arrive at the hotel twenty minutes later, I walk through the lobby and head straight to the elevators, seeking the refuge of my hotel room and maybe the liquor bar in my fridge again. As I pass the reservation desk, I gradually slow my steps.

A tall guy stands at the counter with his back to me. I can't see his face, but the moment I spot him, the hairs stand up on the back of my neck. Goosebumps sprout on my bare arms. His posture and body frame seem eerily familiar. Even the way his dark wavy hair sweeps the top of his shirt collar has a familiarity to it.

Xander's ghost has chosen the worst possible moment to make a reappearance. Of course he does it when I'm at an all-time low. When I have no fight left in me. Will I be forever haunted by this man? Why am I the only one who sees him around every corner or in my dreams? I bet Bridget isn't haunted by Xander. Bridget probably hasn't given her son a single thought since his death.

He turns to face me, and I brace myself for blood and gore. For the swollen eye, disfigured jaw, and the broken teeth.

Instead, I see that it isn't Xander's ghost; it's Jeremiah. He has a beard now. His dark eyes widen as we lock gazes, and his handsome face slowly breaks into a smile.

"Hey, stranger," he says as he pushes himself away from the counter.

At the sight of him, I'm swept over by a series of emotions. Shock. Confusion. Relief. And finally, gratefulness. I'm grateful to see Jeremiah alive and walking around the hotel lobby, since the last time I saw him was when he was in a hospital ICU connected to a ventilator.

I don't return the greeting but rush toward Jeremiah and wrap my arms around him, catching him off guard.

"Huh," he says with a chuckle and wraps his arms around me, hugging me back. "That's a nice hello."

I can't help myself. I burst into tears and Jeremiah stills.

"So, you didn't just call me because you were drunk. You really are falling apart out here, aren't you?" He asks a minute later.

I slowly raise my head and look up at him. "Do you really have to ask?" I say between sniffs.

He leans down and gives me a light kiss, this time catching me by surprise. But I don't pull away. I kiss him back.

"Then I guess I came at a good time," he whispers.

CHAPTER 47

"Come in! Make yourself comfortable," I say a few minutes later to Jeremiah in my hotel room.

I've stopped crying and am trying my best to pull myself together. I already drew a few stares in the hotel lobby because of my outburst, although I have to admit that it felt good to get it all out. To be held by him as I did it.

I steal a glance at Jeremiah over my shoulder as he steps through the door and shuts it behind him. I want to make sure he's here, that I'm not imagining him like I've imagined Xander's ghost. Thankfully, Jeremiah doesn't shimmer and fade away like a mirage as he surveys my hotel suite.

I don't know how long he plans to stay, but he's definitely here for now.

I remove my luggage cases from the settee so Jeremiah can sit down. But instead of taking a seat there, he flops back onto my bed, bouncing on the mattress. I turn around to face him as he links his fingers behind his head and raises his eyebrows at me expectantly. "*What?* You said to make myself comfortable."

I burst into laughter. Relief washes over me as I see that, despite everything that happened between us that horrible night more than a year ago, and besides the additional facial hair, Jeremiah hasn't changed.

He pats an empty spot on the duvet beside him. "Come here, Nikki," he whispers seductively. "Join me."

I roll my eyes. Yeah, he hasn't changed at all.

"There is no way you came all the way here to LA just for that."

"No," he says, pushing himself upright and turning slightly to face me, "actually, I came all the way to LA because I got a long, rambling voicemail from you a few days ago at around four in the morning. I could barely make out what you said. All I heard was lots of 'I'm sorry's and a mention of the Monarch Beverly Hills Hotel. It was the most I've heard from you all year, so I figured something was up. You had to be in a bad place."

So that is what drew him here. Once again he was concerned about me, and knowing that makes me feel worse, not better.

I lower my eyes. I want to say "I'm sorry" again for how much I've wronged him, but I figure I've done it so much that it will sound hollow. Besides, it's too little, too late.

"I meant to call you . . . to reach out to you so . . . so many times," I say.

"But you didn't, outside of sending wire transfers. Was that all your money from the movie rights or did you save some for yourself?"

"I saved a little. Enough to live on and pay my rent. I wanted to give Harper Danfrey some of it, too, but her grandmother refused it. She said she doesn't want my 'blood money' and threatened to sue me instead."

"You didn't have to give any of it away."

"No, I did. You deserve that money. You and Elena deserve every penny. Money will never be enough for what we put you guys through."

He loudly grouses. "You didn't put us through it. Elena and I signed up for it. We took those jobs willingly."

"But you didn't know the full truth." I finally raise my eyes to look at him again. "You don't take jobs where you don't know the scope and the risk. You said that yourself. If you had known everything that was really going on, you would've walked out of there. You wouldn't have been there the night it all happened. You wouldn't have been shot, Jeremiah. We both know that. I wasn't completely honest with either of you. I kept secrets from you both. *Big* secrets."

"And I kept secrets from you, too," he says softly, making me frown.

"What are you talking about?"

He pats the bed again. "Come here. I've got a story to tell you."

I hesitate, then ease onto the bed beside him. He wraps an arm around me, pulling me closer. It's not lost on me that the last time we were like this was at Maple Grove when we were blissfully unaware of what would happen only hours later, how everything would change.

"Now hold off on judgment until the end," he says. "That's all I ask? OK?"

Gradually, I nod. "OK."

He then begins to tell me about the first time he met Patrick Gallagher on a sidewalk on the Upper East Side and the offer that the CEO made him. He tells me how he accepted the money to spy on me and Xander so that he could feed information to Gallagher, figuring what harm would come from having both Gallagher and me as clients at the same time.

When he finishes, I'm stunned; I hadn't expected a confession like this one.

"But it's still not the same as what I did to you. You only took the money to get him off your back. So that Gallagher wouldn't tell Anna the truth about you. And you didn't know it was me. You didn't know that I was the person he wanted you to spy on."

"No, I didn't . . . at first, but—"

"And when you found out who I was, you decided you couldn't do it. You weren't going to tell Gallagher anything. It was all—"

"Nikki, stop. Just stop. You're trying to excuse the fact that I took money from someone who wanted me to spy on you. You're trying to explain away that I kept it a secret from you when there's no excuse or plausible explanation—other than the obvious one: I betrayed you, like you betrayed me." He pauses. "And if you really want to know the truth, I don't . . . I don't know if things hadn't happened the way they did that weekend, if I wouldn't have gone through with it. Maybe I would've given Gallagher the info on you that he asked for. I kept going back and forth on it the whole weekend, but that bullet made my decision for me."

I go quiet. I can't hold his gaze any longer, so I ease out of his arms and crawl off the bed.

"Where are you going?" he says.

Nowhere. Absolutely nowhere. I'm just circling the drain, I think as I slide to the floor.

I lean my head back against the mattress as I stare out of the floor-to-ceiling windows facing the hotel's pool area where some guests are splashing around in the water. Their laughter and squeals are so dissonant to how I'm feeling right now it's as if they're mocking me. They're mocking what a trusting idiot I am. That I've been.

"Look, you're pissed at me. I get it," Jeremiah says behind me. "But I only told you so that you don't have to feel guilty anymore, because I wasn't honest about everything back then, either. I'm owning up to it now."

I don't respond but close my eyes and drop my face into my hands instead.

"Come on, Nikki. Say something. Anything," he says, climbing off the bed and sitting down on the floor beside me. "Call me a hypocrite. An asshole. I can take it."

I lower my hands and gaze at him.

"Jeremiah," I begin, "I'm more pissed at myself than I am at you. I'm pissed that I am so fucking gullible. That I could be so easily manipulated. You knew it and so did Bridget. I'm so—"

"Jesus Christ!" he groans. "You're still going to turn this back on yourself? Even though I'm the one who admitted I fucked you over." He shifts and turns to me, shaking his head in exasperation.

"You know what's so frustrating about you, Nikki? I couldn't put my finger on it a year ago, but I see it now. You take on other people's baggage like it's your job. Clear and simple. That's why you did all that stuff for Bridget. It's why you took shit from her son, Xander, for so long."

"Xander's dead because of me, Jeremiah. Because of what—"

"No, he's dead because he was a fucking moron who shot me and shot himself," he snaps. "The bastard expected you to clean up his mess, even at the very end. Like it was your job to serve him . . . to serve *them*, when you could run circles around their asses if you wanted to. Play them off each other. Play the game in *your* favor, not theirs, if you'd just let yourself do it," he says, glaring at me. "I may be a con artist and a scammer, but I know who I am. That boss of yours hides behind her CEO title but I bet, deep down, she knows who she really is, too. You, on the other hand, keep denying it. You hold yourself to these standards. You hold yourself back again and again, even when you know what you're truly capable of. That you could be as strategic and conniving as the rest of us."

I narrow my eyes. "I'm not strategic or conniving. I only did those things because I had to."

"Bullshit." He slowly smirks and leans toward me. "You're a manipulative liar."

I flinch at his words. "That's not funny."

"Neither is this penance you've been paying for the past year. They're all dead now. You can't change what happened. Things spiraled out of control that night, but we all played our parts in it. Including Xander. Hell, even Anna did. You gotta let it go, Nikki."

"I can't let it go! I feel bad about what happened. I can't just move on. I'm not like Bridget."

He rolls his eyes and grumbles again. "Which is why she's in New York, still the CEO of a major company, and you're on a hotel floor having a pity party."

"I get it. She won! OK? Did you come all the way here to LA just to rub it in my face? Because you could've saved the airfare. I know she won, Jeremiah. And she will always win. She's a helluva lot better at this stuff than I am."

"Dammit, no she isn't! That's what I'm saying. She only won with *your* help! She knew what you were capable of when you didn't. But now you know what you can do. The lengths you can go. And you're *not her assistant anymore.*"

The room goes silent. Jeremiah is making good points, as usual, but he doesn't realize that I'm not the confident, calculating woman I was a year ago. I don't have my armor anymore, and I don't know the path forward without it.

After a minute or so, he loudly sighs. "Look, I didn't just come here to give you a pep talk. I wanted to tell you in person that I may be going away for a while."

I sit up beside him. My body tenses. "Going away? Going where, Jeremiah? What . . . what does that mean?"

"You know what it means, Nikki," he says tiredly. "Notoriety has its drawbacks. Since all the media buzz around the murders, some of my old scam victims have popped up. I got a lawyer. He's good. He's trying to work out deals with most of them. Restitution for what I stole. But one won't take a deal. They said they're pressing charges. My lawyer warned me that my chances don't look good. I may have to serve some time in prison. Could be a few months, if I'm lucky—or a few years. Hell, maybe I'll end up in the same pen as Pops. We'll have a little family reunion."

I wince. My eyes start to water.

"Fuck, don't start crying again," Jeremiah mutters with a part laugh, part groan, and reaches out and drapes an arm around my shoulder. I rest my head against the crook of his neck and wrap my arms around his waist as the tears come, anyway, wetting the front of his shirt. I cling to him like the cops could burst through the hotel door and drag him away at any moment.

Although Jeremiah has committed his fair share of crimes, it doesn't seem right that he—out of everyone involved in what happened at Maple Grove—should be the one to go to prison. Why not me? Why not Bridget? The New York State Attorney General's office certainly tried to send me to jail. But, despite pressure from Harper's grandmother, the prosecutor hadn't been able to bring charges against anyone. The video footage showed Charlotte's fall, Mark's drowning, and Xander shooting Jeremiah and himself. The cops who pursued Anna saw her drive off that road.

Everyone who killed anyone was already dead.

"It's fine," Jeremiah now says. "I'm good with serving time if I've gotta. I did my scams, and I don't regret any of it. If this is my punishment—so be it. But I'll be damned if my punishment is self-inflicted. Life's too short." He cups my face. "Stop fucking around, Nikki. Take back control and show Bridget Chambers what you're really capable of. Make me proud, and make that bitch pay," he says before he brings his lips to mine.

The whiskers of his mustache and beard tickle my chin as I kiss him back and tug him toward me.

Jeremiah stays the night. Hours later, as he sleeps, I climb out of my hotel bed and grab my robe. I part the curtains and stare out my bedroom windows at the now vacant pool area below and the twinkling LA landscape in the distance playing against the midnight sky.

I've been so obsessed with controlling my story on-screen. Why have I completely given up on regaining control in real life? Have I been boxing myself in, like Jeremiah said? Is that the reason Bridget keeps beating me at every turn? Because I've been the one holding myself back?

Bridget has a lot more money than me. She certainly has more power than me, and white privilege, to boot. But is she smarter than me? Is she more cunning than I am when I need to be?

"No," I whisper.

Jeremiah's right. Maybe it is time to make that bitch pay.

CHAPTER 48

"NICOLE? NICOLE, IS THAT YOU?" DEIDRE ASKS.

I've just stepped off the elevators of Altruist headquarters in NYC and barely had the chance to get my bearings before she stands from the receptionist desk and waves at me, beckoning me toward her.

The two-foot-tall, chrome letters spelling ALTRUIST CORP stand out prominently behind her, along with a painting that's been added since I quit. It's a portrait of Xander in profile. I'd almost forgotten this version of him after being haunted by his macabre, bloody ghost for so long. Beneath the portrait on a gold plaque are the years of his birth and death, "1993–2025," engraved along with the words "Always in Our Hearts – from the Altruist Corporation staff."

I almost snort when I read it but catch myself before I do. Considering the havoc he wreaked during his brief tenure as CEO and president, I doubt anyone in the company misses him all that much, but it certainly makes for good PR to claim that they do. Bridget wouldn't want to seem like a callous mother who ignored the tragic death of her son during her grand comeback tour now that she was back from the dead and leading the company again.

"Hi, Deidre," I say.

"Oh, my God! It's been so long since I've seen you . . . well, outside of on my phone or a TV screen. I watched all your interviews and I'm so excited for your big Hollywood movie! How are you, Nicole?"

I take a deep breath. "I'm OK. Better now that I'm home and more time has passed since . . . well, since . . . ." I let my words drift off and I glance at the portrait.

She nods grimly. "I would imagine. It couldn't have been easy for you with all that happened," Deidre says slowly. "We held a memorial service in his honor last year. The catering was good. Coconut shrimp. Open bar." She drops her voice to a whisper. "One of the girls from payroll got drunk and talked about how Xander hit on her at an office Christmas party, and they made out in one of the copier rooms. It was so awkward." She scans me up and down. "You look great, though!"

"Thanks," I say, glancing down at myself.

I've traded the T-shirts and ratty jeans I lived in while in LA for business casual pants, a blazer, and high heels. It feels like I've put on my armor again, which I suspect I'll need for what I'm about to do.

"So, what are you doing here, girl?" Deidre says. "Visiting someone?"

"I have a meeting with the big boss. I'm scheduled to see Bridget at ten o'clock."

Deidre looks more than a bit shocked. "You . . . you *do?*"

I nod and smile. "Yes, I do."

I understand why she's surprised. Bridget seemed shocked as well when I called her out of the blue a couple days ago, telling her that I finally wanted to bury the hatchet.

"I've had a full year and a half to think about this, and I realize that I let my emotions get the better of me. You were the best mentor I ever had, Bridge," I said over the phone. "I shouldn't have reacted the way I did. I shouldn't have put the blame squarely at your feet. I'm sorry for that."

"It was all very hard for you, Nicole. Witnessing all that firsthand. Maybe emotions got the better of us both. I'll forgive you if you forgive me."

"Of course! We made a great team, Bridge. And to tell you the truth, I still regret just tossing all that away. I regret walking away from Altruist. I miss everyone there so much."

She seemed to pause on the other end for a long time. "Then why don't you pay us a visit?"

"*Really?* You'd be OK with that?"

"Sure! How about Thursday? Let's catch up."

I now wait in front of the receptionist desk as Deidre continues to gawk at me.

"OK," Deidre finally says. She lowers herself back into her office chair. "I'll . . . uh . . . let her new assistant know that you're here."

About a minute later, a young woman who looks a little younger than me arrives to escort me to Bridget's office. She's a replica of Bridget down to the windswept bob, chinos, and cashmere turtleneck that Bridget usually wears to the office.

"Hi, Ms. Underwood. I'm Megan, Ms. Chambers's assistant."

"Pleased to meet you. And call me Nicole," I say, extending my hand to her for a shake.

She seems to hesitate before shaking my hand. "Great to meet you, Nicole. I can take you to see her now."

I follow Megan through the maze of cubicles and desks that lead to Bridget's office, formerly Xander's office. I wonder if she's returned the office to its original state, before her "death."

"How was your flight?" Megan asks over her shoulder. "Ms. Chambers said you just arrived from LA yesterday."

"Actually, it was two days ago, and the flight was fine. Long but I only had one layover in Tucson."

"I love the West Coast," she says. "My family has a beach house in Santa Monica. We go there twice a year."

"Nice," I murmur as we walk through the maze.

While Megan prattles on with small talk about Southern California weather and its beaches, I notice several people staring at us. A few employees from the accounting department openly point at me and whisper as I pass by their cubicles.

I'm sure my return will be a popular topic in the office gossip sessions around the coffee dispenser later today.

I smirk on the inside. Just wait until they hear what I have in store.

"*Nicole?*" a voice calls out, making both Megan and I halt in our steps.

I turn to find Daniel gaping at me.

I'm as astonished to see him here as he is to see me, though unlike him, I don't show it. I know Bridget caught him on tape candidly bad-mouthing her and Xander and plotting his takeover of her company. And Daniel had to have heard enough about the investigation in the news to know that I'd been spying on him on Bridget's behalf the whole time that she was "dead."

But then again, Bridget keeps her friends close and her enemies closer. She'd keep Daniel on as COO to make sure he stayed in line. And despite all his bluster, Daniel could never go toe to toe with Bridget. He saw what happened to Xander, Mark, Anna, and poor Charlotte. He saw what she has done to me since I turned on her: the lawsuit threat and now the splashy announcement in *Variety* showing how she undercut me by becoming executive producer for the movie she didn't even want to be made.

He's sneaky, but cowardly.

"Hello, Daniel," I say.

"Wha-what are you . . . you doing here?" he stutters.

"I'm here to see Bridget. Why?"

"Well, I . . . I just thought . . ." He goes silent then clears his throat. "Never mind. Good to . . . to see you, Nicole."

"Good to see you, too," I say with a smile before turning back around. I wave. "Bye, Daniel."

CHAPTER 49

SECONDS LATER, MEGAN USHERS ME THROUGH BRIDGET'S OPEN DOOR.

I was right; she's returned the office to its original state. The gray paint, floating glass shelves, Matisse, and Basquiat have disappeared. Even the Hans Wegner Swivel Chair is gone. There may be a portrait of him behind the receptionist desk out front, but there are no photos of Xander in her office anymore. Not even him as a baby or a little kid. It's like Xander never existed.

"Nicole," Bridget says, rising from her desk chair as I step into her office.

She walks toward me with arms outstretched and envelops me in a big hug, like we're friends who haven't seen one another in years. It was the same warmth she showed me the first day we met. It's what drew me in; I had no idea what lurked underneath.

"It's so good to see you," she croons before stepping back and rubbing my shoulders. "Can Meg get you anything? *Water?* Maybe coffee or tea?"

"I'm fine," I say.

Bridget nods then turns to Megan. "Thank you, Meg. Looks like we won't be needing anything else. I've got this from here. Please close the door behind you."

"Yes, Ms. Chambers," the young woman says.

"Take a load off. Have a seat," Bridget says to me as Megan closes the office door. "Love the shoes, by the way."

"Thanks," I say as I lower myself into the seat facing her desk.

"It really is great to have you here again, Nicole."

She sits in the chair beside mine rather than the chair behind her desk. It's a tactic I've seen her use before to put folks at ease. When she's not Bridget, the Big Bad Boss Lady, but your good ol' gal pal Bridge.

The tactic doesn't fool me anymore.

"I wasn't expecting that phone call from you," she says. "It was a welcome surprise."

"Oh, you knew I'd come crawling back eventually," I say, fighting to keep the bitterness out of my voice.

She demurs with a slight chuckle. "I didn't know, but I hoped you would. Like you said—we made a great team. You were my right-hand man. I trusted you with everything, Nicole. All my secrets. I don't do that with just anybody."

Yeah, she trusted me. She trusted me so much that she videotaped me and my most intimate moments like everyone else at that mansion that weekend more than a year ago, but I don't point that out.

"Our relationship took years for us to build, Nicole. It hurt that you just threw it away."

Keep eye contact, I can hear Jeremiah's voice whisper in my head.

He coached me back in LA. As he snacked in bed on winter melon and cantaloupe that room service brought to my hotel room along with the rest of our breakfast spread, Jeremiah gave me tricks of the trade.

"Make sure," he said between chews, "when you lie that you keep your gaze steady and your breaths even."

"Don't I already do that?" I asked before snagging the fork out of his hands and taking a bite of melon.

"Sometimes. Most times. You're good. But you could always be better. And it's different when you're one-on-one with someone. She'll be looking for the lie. Don't make it easy for her to find it."

I now nod as I look Bridget straight in the eyes. I don't blink. I keep my breathing even. "I know. And I'm sorry, Bridge. Like I said, I want to start over."

"And like I said, I'm willing to forgive and move on." She reaches out and grabs my hands. "To be honest, you were, by far, the best assistant I've ever had, Nicole. You still are! Meg is great but it's not the same. She doesn't have that drive that you had. The precision. She can't get down in the muck with me and do what needs to be done. I wouldn't feel comfortable leaving her to supervise things in my absence like I did with you. I'd love to have you back at Altruist. If you're willing, I'd like you to be my assistant again."

And there it is. I knew she'd make the offer and extend it like a gift rather than what it really is: a way to have me serve her and do her dirty work because I'd done it so well in the past.

"But what about Megan?" I ask.

Bridget inclines her head and sighs gravely. "I'm sure one of the other officers could take her on staff. Maybe Daniel or one of the other chiefs. Or if not, I'd be happy to write her a recommendation. She can seek employment somewhere else. A talented, smart girl like her with the connections she has will be snapped up quickly, I'm sure."

"I see." I pretend to consider her offer. "Well, I would love to become your assistant again, Bridge."

She grins. "Wonderful! Then let's get you—"

"But I can't," I interrupt, making her smile fade.

"Why not?"

"Because I'm going to be so busy now that I plan to start my own company. I'm finally going to pursue the dream I've had since I was in high school. That I told you about when we met that day back at Cornell. Remember? And it's all thanks to you."

She slowly releases my hands and leans back in her chair. "To . . . *me*?" she asks with a frown, narrowing her hazel eyes.

"Why yes! Because you're going to be my angel investor. I think we can agree to maybe a fifteen percent equity stake. That seems fair, right? Of course, it would have to be a sizable amount of seed money to give you that. I'd say a five-million-dollar investment. Maybe five-point-five." I consider the numbers for a second or two. "Oh, why not just make it an even six million?"

Her face changes. I see her lips tighten as her cheeks bloom bright red.

"And now that we're both working on the film, you can tell the producers to change the ending back to what it was in the original script, where we *both* admit to playing a part in what happened that weekend at Maple Grove. Where you admit to sending those letters that unleashed all that chaos and ended in the deaths of four people."

I watch as she rises from her chair and strolls to her desk. She takes her seat behind it and crosses her legs.

"With you as executive producer," I continue, undeterred, "they'll have more than enough money to reshoot the scene."

"This is all very inventive," she says dryly from her perch behind her massive desk, "but it's in the realm of fantasy, Nicole. Six *million* dollars? There is no way I'd give you that. And why would I reach out to the producers to change anything?"

"But why would you not?" I ask with mock innocence. "You said it yourself that I'm the best assistant you ever had. That I was always willing to wade into the muck with you. That I was the keeper of *so* many of your secrets, Bridget. Why wouldn't you want to repay me for that?"

"That isn't repayment. That is extortion."

"No, it's showing appreciation for the work I've done. That's very different." I raise my brows. "And if you won't do it, then maybe I could get the funding from Patrick Gallagher."

Her eyes narrow even more at the mention of Gallagher's name.

"I paid him a visit yesterday. He was surprised to see me at his office, but he was willing to talk. Even invited me out to lunch. We had a good conversation at this Greek restaurant in the East Village. I told him my business idea and he loved it! He appreciates *everything* I have to offer and I'm sure he'd pay handsomely for it."

She gives me an icy smile. "So, is this what we've come to, Nicole? I hired you straight out of college. You had no experience as an assistant, let alone an assistant to a CEO. But I brought you on, anyway. This is the thanks I get? You think you're being—"

"If you're about to call me ungrateful, I wouldn't do that, Bridget. It's a bit of a trigger for me."

"Well, I get triggered with threats of blackmail. You're trying to blackmail me by threatening to tell all my secrets to that son of a bitch Gallagher because of a movie ending and for seed funding?"

"I'm not blackmailing you, Bridget. I'm just reminding you of what you said. Your words. How grateful you are to me. I didn't just take over while you were gone for three months. I slaved for you for four years without complaint," I say, rising from my chair. "I believed the bullshit you shoveled about duty and working hard and paying your dues, and I regurgitated it like cow cud without question. I watched you act underhandedly, punish those who dared to challenge you, and I rationalized it all. You were just a woman doing what she had to do to survive in the business world. And I would have happily continued to do it until . . . until that weekend woke me up. Until people actually died."

She crosses her arms over her chest. "Nicole, I didn't shove Charlotte Danfrey off that balcony. I didn't drown Mark. I didn't drive Anna's car into that tree, and I didn't shoot my son in the head. The letters I sent may have been somewhat of a catalyst, but," she shrugs, "what was in those letters was all true. They were liars, thieves, adulterers, and rapists. And I kept their secrets for years. Each of them made their choices. You included—especially when you decided to fuck that con man rather than do your job." She points up at me. "You, not me . . . *you* put him in harm's way, Nicole."

My mask of calm falters a little at that jab, but I push it back into place.

"Meanwhile, I was trying to figure out who wanted to kill me. I was simply protecting myself and my company." She slowly shakes her head. "If you do this, I will send legions of lawyers after you and Gallagher. I will assassinate you in the press so that your name is synonymous with serial killers. You will be penniless and broken when I'm done, and I won't accept any apologies the next time around. If you cross me like this . . . if you come for me, Nicole, I swear that you will regret it. Do not underestimate me."

"No, what I would regret more," I say as I walk toward her desk, "is going back to the way it was before. The rose-colored glasses are off now, Bridget. I'm not putting them back on. I know who you really are and if we're going to work together in any capacity, it's going to be as equals. I'm not underestimating you, but I'm also warning you to make damn sure you don't underestimate me. Because whatever pain you inflict on me won't equal what I could do to you with just a few email attachments and a phone call to Gallagher, the *New York Times*, or whoever is willing to listen. And what will it do to the Altruist brand? Your baby. That's always been what's important, right?"

Her cheeks are no longer pink; now her entire face is red.

"Do we have a deal, or do I go to Gallagher instead?" I ask.

She doesn't respond right away, but gradually she unwinds her arms from in front of her. The red in her face begins to fade.

"Let me think about it," she finally mumbles.

"OK, I can accept that. I know it's a lot to take in." I give a thoughtful nod. "I'll give you a day."

"*A day?*" she squeaks, shooting to her feet. "Nicole, you are completely out of line to—"

"Actually, make it 5 p.m. today." Just to piss her off and let her know she's not in charge anymore. "I look forward to hearing your decision. I really do hope you say yes, Bridget. Think of what a great investment opportunity this could be," I say as I walk to her office door. "I'll see myself out. Thanks."

I wave goodbye, smile, tug the door open, and walk out.

CHAPTER 50

ONE YEAR LATER...

OUR SUV SLOWLY MAKES ITS WAY DOWN WILSHIRE BOULEVARD. I can see that it is lined on both sides by metal barriers holding back screaming crowds. I can't touch the people through the glass and locked doors, but I swear I can feel their frenetic energy as they push and jostle to get closer, as the police officers shout and order them to stand back.

"Why are so many people here?" I ask as I lean toward the tinted windows.

"It's a movie premiere," Jeremiah says.

Now almost two months after his three-and-a-half-month stint in prison, he lounges casually on the leather backseat beside me. His parole officer granted him permission to travel to Los Angeles with me for the premiere, with the explicit request to bring back a few celebrity autographs.

"Don't a lot of people usually show up to these things?" Jeremiah asks.

"I guess," I murmur, although I'm surprised that all of them have come for the premiere of *Murder in the Valley*. I know it has some buzz and good reviews with movie critics who saw early screenings, but it's not a major Hollywood blockbuster. No superheroes.

No car chases. Just the story of an assistant whose life is changed during a murder-filled birthday weekend in the Hudson Valley, who comes to a few realizations about her boss, herself, and her purpose.

Or at least those are the talking points I've been using for my press junket interviews.

My cell phone buzzes in my purse. I pull my eyes away from the SUV windows and quickly dig it out to see the text on-screen.

"What's wrong?" Jeremiah asks, noticing my brows furrow while I read the text from Natalie. She's heading the team of programmers at my start-up.

We kicked off six months ago after we received our first round of funding—$3.5 million—from Bridget. The other $2.5 million is slated for next year. We've hired developers, programmers, and a marketing and publicity team. Things are moving so fast and are overwhelming, but it's been rewarding to finally see my dream come to life. A dream that I fought for.

"It's just Natalie updating me," I say to Jeremiah as I type a message back. "We're behind schedule on the app and the team has been pulling all-nighters all week trying to fix this bug. It makes me feel bad being out here for a movie premiere when I should be back there with them, debugging code myself."

"Nikki, you're the CEO. Delegate," Jeremiah says. "That's what CEOs do, right? It's just one weekend in LA. You'll be back in the trenches by Monday, and I'll be eating takeout by myself all alone in bed."

"You won't be alone," I say, giving him a quick kiss. "You'll have Nemo."

He chuckles. "Can't forget Nemo."

"Oh, stop," I say before checking my phone when it buzzes again. "He loves you and you love him too." I squeal with excitement when I see my latest email. "It's from Elena. She passed all her final exams!"

I quickly type my congrats. She'll graduate with her degree in psychology next month. I offer again to help find her a job or write her a recommendation if she needs it. I hope she takes me up on it. I want to see her succeed.

In the corner of my eye, I notice someone pointing at our SUV and a few women wave excitedly at us. I don't know who they think is behind the dark-tinted glass but they're starstruck regardless.

Farther down Wilshire, I can see bleachers with even more movie fans. They're holding up signs and waving at the line of other SUVs and a few limos in front of us, squinting and trying desperately to see who's riding inside of them.

I watch as the door to a black Lincoln Town Car at the front of the line opens. Asia, the star of the film, steps out in towering high heels and a tailored white suit, wearing no top underneath, putting her glowing skin and enviable physique on display. She's in her full movie siren glory, basking in the screams and cheers from the crowds. She waves at the stands and blows kisses to her fans before turning to smile and poses for the photographers posted behind the velvet rope.

She's in her element and it shows.

Her costar, Troy, steps out of the Town Car next and waves before his face goes bright thanks to the photographers' flashing cameras.

"This is not real," I say, slowly shaking my head in amazement.

"No," Jeremiah says, "it's real. It's a circus. But it's real."

Sooner than I anticipated, it's our turn to face the crowds and photographers. The SUV comes to a stop with our rear door directly in front of the red carpet. They're waiting for us to make our grand appearance.

"Do I look OK?" I ask, glancing down at myself. I adjust my skirt and wiggle my toes in my strappy heels. My hands flutter to my ears to check that I'm still wearing both earrings, that my braids are still pinned in place.

Jeremiah reaches up and grabs one of my fidgeting hands. He holds it and links his fingers through mine.

"You look great," he whispers against my ear.

I instantly calm and smile. "You do too."

He could be one of the actors on-screen tonight; in fact, I suspect that someday he will. In the past few months, starting mere days after he got out of prison, Jeremiah has gotten a few offers for guest role appearances in TV shows and even an indie movie. He told me over dinner last month that a famous New York modeling agency tracked him down and asked him if he was seeking representation.

"I told them I was flattered but my criminal record might be a problem. They said that it could help rather than hinder me from landing bookings. 'Clients love it when you have some edge,'" he said, quoting the modeling agent. He laughed it off and shook his head before taking a sip of wine.

"You might be good at it, though," I told him, assessing him objectively in the restaurant lighting. He'd given up his beard and was back to being clean shaven. "Your parole requires you to have a legal income, doesn't it? Maybe you could try acting, too. Work your musical talent into some role. You acted all the time as part of your job, anyway, right?"

He cocked an eyebrow and nodded thoughtfully. "You've got a point. I guess it'd be like trading one con for another." He took another drink. "I don't know. Maybe. I'll think about it."

He signed with the agency a week later and booked an Armani campaign a week after that. He's working on getting a film agent and manager now, too. A few have made him offers.

To his mom's relief, I think Jeremiah's days as a con man are officially over.

I watch now from inside the SUV as a man in a satin jacket and black pants walks toward our car door to open it so we can step onto the red carpet next. When I see his face in profile, my hold on Jeremiah's hand tightens. My breath catches in my throat.

"Oww!" Jeremiah exclaims, wincing at my death grip and staring down at our linked hands. "What's wrong?"

As the man on the other side of the glass turns and draws closer, reaching for the door handle, I see that he isn't who I thought he was. He isn't Xander coming back to haunt me.

I loosen my grip on Jeremiah's hand and loudly exhale.

I haven't seen Xander's ghost in quite a while, not since I returned to New York and had my one-on-one with Bridget.

Not that I haven't been looking for him. I expect Xander to pop up during my morning walks to Starbucks. I anticipate seeing his face in the crowd streaming toward me on the sidewalk. Sometimes I wonder if I'll spot him on the treadmill next to me at the gym. He'll give me his gruesome smile and ask me how I've been. Except I haven't seen Xander in a year. Not even in my dreams.

I guess Mom was right. It took a lot longer than I expected, but I finally got the closure that I needed by doing the hardest part: confronting Bridget and taking back the control I relinquished long ago.

"Nothing," I say to Jeremiah, breathing deeply again. "Nothing's wrong. Sorry. I'm just nervous."

He eyes me suspiciously but doesn't have a chance to ask more questions before the car door opens and the muffled shouts and screams hit us in a full wave of sound. Together they become a roar.

I step onto the carpet first and Jeremiah follows soon after.

I hadn't planned to stop for photos or to do any interviews; I know I'm not the one everyone is here to see. That's validated when I hear the photographers shouting "Asia, over here!" and "Troy, give us a smile, handsome!" But a clipboard-wielding woman rushes toward us. I can tell from the eager look in her eyes that she's about to ruin my plans.

"Ms. Underwood and Mr. O'Connor, stand over here, please," she says, pointing to a spot on the red carpet next to the actors.

I walk toward the spot and smile at the flashing lights, tightening my grip on Jeremiah's hand again.

"Couple more minutes, then we head inside the theater," he whispers into my ear, seeing how overwhelmed I am. He kisses my cheek. "Just a couple more."

I nod, resigned. I survived being held at gunpoint. I can survive this.

After five minutes, the clipboard wielder tells us we're done with photos and leads us past a line of reporters. We continue our way down the red carpet until someone calls out, "Nicole Underwood! Ms. Underwood! Can we talk to you for a sec?"

I turn to find a young woman waving frantically at me. A cameraman stands behind her, shining a bright light on Jeremiah and me. I hold up my hand and squint at its brightness, averting my eyes.

"Can we do a quick interview?" she asks.

I shake my head. "Sorry, no. We should get inside."

I haven't had a good history with reporters. And I already talked to almost a dozen in the past two days for the press junket. Even then it was because I was contractually obligated to do it and all the questions I answered were pre-submitted. I made sure they were about the movie only.

"Oh, come on, Nicole!" she whines, wagging the mic at me. She actually pouts. "Just one interview! It won't take more than a minute of your time. I swear! We want to know what you think about the film? Don't you want the chance to tell your story? To have your say?"

I exchange a look with Jeremiah and laugh. "I already have."

The reporter lowers her mic, now disappointed.

"You guys have a good night. Enjoy the movie!" he says over his shoulder as we continue down the red carpet and step through the movie theater's double doors.

CHAPTER 51

THE CROWDS ARE EVEN MORE DENSE IN THE MOVIE THEATER LOBBY, but I quickly spot Gail and Clive not far from the entrance, shaking the hands of men in suits who are probably studio executives. When the producers see me, they excuse themselves, grin, and stroll toward me like we're the best of friends, like they hadn't called me ungrateful or gone behind my back and almost allowed Bridget to buy her way into the film ending that she wanted.

"Nicole, hi!" Gail sings as she waves.

"It's so wonderful to see you!" Clive says with arms outstretched. He envelops me in a hug, and I don't fight it although I also don't return it.

"Good seeing you too," I say, giving a tight smile. I turn to Jeremiah who's standing beside me. "Jeremiah, meet Clive and Gail. They're the producers of *Murder in the Valley*. Gail and Clive, this is Jeremiah O'Connor. He's—"

"Oh, this gentleman needs no introduction," Clive says with a chuckle, reaching out to shake Jeremiah's hand. "After working on this film for so long, we feel like we know you, Mr. O'Connor."

"*Do you?*" Jeremiah said, giving his hand a shake. "Well, if that's the case, call me Jeremiah, and now that you've mentioned it, I've heard so much about you guys that I feel like I practically know you, too."

"Good things, I hope," Gail says.

"I'll never tell," Jeremiah says, giving her a seductive wink. Gail erupts into giggles as she blushes.

"Well, both of you enjoy yourselves tonight," Clive says, glancing over his shoulder and waving at someone across the lobby, near the concession stand. He leans forward and hugs me goodbye. "It looks like the movie is going to start soon. Nicole, it was a pleasure to see you again."

"Bye, Clive. Bye, Gail," I say as Gail kisses me on the cheek.

As Clive turns to walk away, he stumbles slightly and Jeremiah catches him before he tumbles.

"You OK there?" Jeremiah asks while he pulls him to his feet.

Clive nods, looking sheepish now. He brushes off the front of his jacket and adjusts his shirt. "Guess I tripped over the carpet there. Or maybe I had one too many glasses of wine at dinner."

"Maybe that's it," Jeremiah says, patting his back.

We watch a few seconds later as Gail and Clive walk away, joining another set of old white guys in suits.

"Prick," Jeremiah mutters.

"Yeah," I say, shaking my head and turning back to Jeremiah. "I'm glad the movie ending was fixed but it would've been nice for them to acknowledge what they did. To apologize even. Instead they just keep pretending like it never happened."

"Oh, you'll never get that apology," he says before reaching into his pocket. "This is Hollywood, after all. Backstabbing comes with the territory, but at least you have this to make you feel better."

"Huh?"

I frown and look down to see him holding a brown Hermès men's wallet.

"Why are you showing me your wa—"

It takes me a few seconds to realize what he means, what he's really holding. When I do, my eyes widen and I almost yelp in surprise, but I stop myself by clapping my hand over my mouth. I take a quick glance around us to see if anyone else noticed then look up and meet Jeremiah's gaze. There's a mischievous twinkle in his brown eyes as he starts to laugh.

"Tell me you did not just steal that man's wallet," I whisper.

"OK, I didn't steal his wallet," he says, examining the driver's license and credit cards inside. "He's got a Black Card. Nice."

"Jeremiah, you're not going to use those, are you?"

He could do a lot of damage with that Black Card.

"Of course not! You think I'm gonna risk going back to prison for that asshole? I told you, my con days are over." I watch as he turns and tosses the wallet into a nearby trash can. "I'm content with knowing how much he'll sweat when he realizes it's gone. Life's little victories," he says.

I shake my head. "You're incorrigible."

"And that's why you love me."

He's right—it is.

He wraps an arm around my shoulder. "Let's head inside. Remember. The movie is about to start."

We find our seats not too long after. My cell phone starts to buzz again. I take it out of my purse and examine the name on-screen. "It's Natalie again. I should take this. I'll be back before the opening credits. OK?"

Jeremiah adjusts in the seat beside me and nods. "Gotcha."

I head back into the lobby that is mostly deserted now; everyone else has taken their seats inside the theater. I press the green button on-screen to answer.

"Yeah, Natalie, what's up?" I ask.

As Natalie updates me on the programmers' progress, in the corner of my eye I see the actor Troy walking swiftly out the theater doors holding some young, mousy-looking woman by the elbow. I can tell from his fake smile he gives me as they pass and the terrified look in his companion's eyes that something is off.

He nearly drags her past the concession stand and they stop near one of the columns farther across the lobby. I assume it was to give them some privacy, but unfortunately for Troy, their voices travel across the empty space.

"Are you *trying* to embarrass me, Abby? Do you realize how important tonight is for me?" he says through clenched teeth, glaring down at her.

"Yes, Mr. Fletcher," she says, dropping her eyes to his Ferragamo-clad feet. "I'm so sorry, sir. I didn't mean to—"

"Enough with the sorrys, Abby. I don't want to hear it anymore. First, you fuck up and book me the wrong reservation tonight."

"But sir," she begins, "the restaurant said that they could take you. They just couldn't take a party of—"

"I don't care," he snaps.

I'm barely listening to Natalie now because I'm so engrossed with their conversation but pretending not to eavesdrop.

"And now I find out the masseuse I wanted later tonight isn't available. How the hell am I supposed to relax after all this if I don't have Diego? I have to head to Toronto tomorrow to shoot another movie and now I'll have all this tension in my shoulders and my lats! How can I work like that, Abby?"

"I know, Mr. Fletcher. I'll book you a masseuse in Toronto."

"Not good enough. It's not good enough!"

"After we deboard, I'll have a driver take us straight to the hotel and the masseuse will be waiting for you there. I'll give explicit instructions about the type of massage you prefer. I'll supervise it myself if you want. I'll make sure it goes smoothly, sir."

He shakes his head in disgust and points down at her. "Learn from this, Abby. I don't want fuckups like this to happen again. Understood?"

"Yes, Mr. Fletcher," she says with a solemn nod.

"I hired you as a favor to your brother. He said you wanted some Hollywood experience, but don't test my benevolence. I'm not a charity."

"I know, sir. I won't, sir."

He gives another headshake and loudly exhales, showing that his anger has simmered down to irritation. He then walks away.

As Troy heads toward me, I turn the opposite direction, pretending to be engrossed by one of the movie posters on the lobby wall as I talk on the phone. When he disappears behind the theater doors, I look back at Abby. The young woman hasn't raised her eyes from the floor. Her shoulders are slumped. Her head is bowed.

"Natalie, let me call you back. I'll check in tomorrow," I say into the phone. "I trust you. I know you have everything covered. OK?"

Natalie says goodbye a few seconds later and I hang up. I walk toward Abby. When she notices me approaching, she wipes away her crestfallen expression. She pushes back her shoulders and plants on a crooked smile.

"Hello, Ms. Underwood," she says.

"Hey," I say, offering my hand to her. "Are you Troy's assistant?"

"Yes, ma'am." She eagerly shakes it. "I've been with Troy for six months now. I've learned a lot."

"And you put up with a lot too, I bet." I eye her. "Are you OK?"

Her smile falters. She pauses then nods. "Uh, yes, I'm fine. I'm great! I'm really excited to see the movie."

"Abby, can I be candid with you?"

"Uh," Abby hesitates, "sure, Ms. Underwood."

"So," I say, taking another step toward her and dropping my voice to a whisper, "when you go home tonight, curse, cry, scream . . . do *whatever* you need to do to get through this. But understand your objective. Figure out what your next steps are, and focus on that. Network. Make those connections. Learn what you can. Don't stay longer on this job than you need to. He's using you right now, but don't ever forget, you're using him, too."

She blinks in surprise.

"And when you do leave this job—because you will—he'll finally realize how important you are to him, but by then he'll already be in your rearview. And he might even ask . . . hell, he'll *beg* for you to stay or come back when he remembers that not only are you the one who knows his exact coffee order and the PIN to his voicemail, but you also know all his secrets. He'll remember the dirt you've swept under the rug for him while you were his assistant. And all the while you were just biding your time because you knew you were too big, too smart, and too capable for this job, but you let him think you weren't because that's how the game is played. OK?" I say, reaching out and giving her shoulder a reassuring squeeze.

She gives a shaky nod then pushes back her shoulders. I can see a steeliness in her eyes now. "Yes, Ms. Underwood."

"Good, and call me Nikki," I say, before turning back around and heading across the lobby to the theater doors. I tug one of the doors open just as the music starts.

ACKNOWLEDGMENTS

In Deadly Company was fun to write, but, much like the story itself, this book took some twists and turns for it to come into fruition. I want to thank all three . . . yes, THREE editors who helped with this novel. I want to thank my former editor at Union Square & Co., Laura Schreiber, for enthusiastically endorsing the idea for *In Deadly Company* and having so much faith and confidence in me as a writer. I also want to thank Jaime Levine for stepping in with the wordsmith duties and making the book an even better mystery. (Your ideas made the big reveal more of a surprise and your thoughtful reflections gave the story even more depth.) And finally, I want to thank my new editor at Union Square & Co., Mika Kasuga, for tying up the narrative loose ends and doing the hard work of packaging and ushering the novel to bookshelves.

I also want to thank the publicity and marketing teams at Union Square & Co. and BookSparks for the work they do. Promotion isn't my strong point, so having people I can trust to make sure my book doesn't die a silent death in obscurity is an introverted author's Godsend.

I want to thank my family (Andrew, Bean, Mom, and Dad) for their love and support. Writing novels is important to me, but it is only one facet of my life that competes with many others. Thank you for giving me the space and time to do what I love and for not complaining too much when I disappear into my writing cave.

And finally, I want to thank all the readers out there. From those who posted videos on YouTube, Instagram, and TikTok that encouraged other readers to pick up a copy of my book, to those who posted reviews online, to those who simply bought my novel or checked it out of their local library and liked it—I appreciate all of you. I will always say: *you c*omplete the circle. *You* are what give these stories flight and take them out of the realm of just one woman's imagination. You make it all worthwhile.